Oliver Optic

Cross and Crescent

Or, Young America in Turkey and Greece

Oliver Optic

Cross and Crescent
Or, Young America in Turkey and Greece

ISBN/EAN: 9783337211639

Printed in Europe, USA, Canada, Australia, Japan

Cover: Foto ©Andreas Hilbeck / pixelio.de

More available books at **www.hansebooks.com**

CROSS AND CRESCENT;

OR,

YOUNG AMERICA IN TURKEY AND GREECE.

A STORY OF TRAVEL AND ADVENTURE.

BY

WILLIAM T. ADAMS

(OLIVER OPTIC),

AUTHOR OF ' OUTWARD BOUND," "SHAMROCK AND THISTLE," "RED CROSS,"
"DIKES AND DITCHES," "PALACE AND COTTAGE," "DOWN THE
RHINE," "UP THE BALTIC," "NORTHERN
LANDS," ETC.

BOSTON:
LEE AND SHEPARD, PUBLISHERS.
NEW YORK:
LEE, SHEPARD AND DILLINGHAM.
1875.

TO

MY EXCELLENT AND ENTERPRISING FRIEND,

CHARLES T. DILLINGHAM, Esq.,

OF NEW YORK,

This Volume

IS RESPECTFULLY DEDICATED.

YOUNG AMERICA ABROAD.

By OLIVER OPTIC.

A Library of Travel and Adventure in Foreign Lands. First and Second Series; six volumes in each Series. 16mo. Illustrated.

First Series.

I. *OUTWARD BOUND;* OR, YOUNG AMERICA AFLOAT.

II. *SHAMROCK AND THISTLE;* OR, YOUNG AMERICA IN IRELAND AND SCOTLAND.

III. *RED CROSS;* OR, YOUNG AMERICA IN ENGLAND AND WALES.

IV. *DIKES AND DITCHES;* OR, YOUNG AMERICA IN HOLLAND AND BELGIUM.

V. *PALACE AND COTTAGE;* OR, YOUNG AMERICA IN FRANCE AND SWITZERLAND.

VI. *DOWN THE RHINE;* OR, YOUNG AMERICA IN GERMANY.

Second Series.

I. *UP THE BALTIC;* OR, YOUNG AMERICA IN NORWAY, SWEDEN, AND DENMARK.

II. *NORTHERN LANDS;* OR, YOUNG AMERICA IN RUSSIA AND PRUSSIA.

III. *CROSS AND CRESCENT;* OR, YOUNG AMERICA IN TURKEY AND GREECE.

IV. *SUNNY SHORES;* OR, YOUNG AMERICA IN ITALY AND AUSTRIA. In preparation.

V. *VINE AND OLIVE;* OR, YOUNG AMERICA IN SPAIN AND PORTUGAL. In preparation.

VI. *ISLES OF THE SEA;* OR, YOUNG AMERICA HOMEWARD BOUND. In preparation.

PREFACE.

Cross and Crescent, the third volume of the second series of "Young America Abroad," contains the history of a portion of the Academy Squadron on the voyage from the Baltic to Constantinople, and the experience of the young travellers in Turkey and Greece. As in the preceding volumes, an outline of the history of each of these countries is given, with its form of government, something about its commerce, the manners and customs of its people, and descriptions of its principal cities, and its natural and artificial objects of interest. In the journey of certain runaways, the details of a trip down the Danube, through Turkey, a sail on the Black Sea, and through the Bosporus, are presented. Various boat excursions are made in the Bosporus, the Golden Horn, and the Sea of Marmora, as well as in the waters of Greece, and many of the wonders of these distant lands are brought out in familiar conversations. The statistics and other information are derived from the latest and best sources, including books and pictures obtained by the author in Constantinople.

The story occupies a larger proportion of this book than in some of its predecessors; but the writer hopes that his young friends will derive from it the lesson of temperance, manliness, and self-reliance in emergencies. Though it is sometimes difficult to determine in what direction the path of duty runs, high aims and high principles will always justify the life-voyager in the end, and his mistakes will be those of the head, and not the heart. This is the lesson which the experience of the young officers of the Tritonia teaches, and those who tried to be true to the requirements of duty, however they erred in judgment, were not held responsible, in a moral sense, for their short-comings; while those who covered up their palpable intention to do wrong, under an adherence to mere technical routine, were the only sufferers.

Cross and Crescent is the ninth volume of the "Young America Abroad" series, and the author gratefully finds occasion again to acknowledge the continued and increasing success of these books, and to thank his young friends for the favor they have so long and so heartily bestowed upon his efforts to please and to instruct them.

Harrison Square, Boston,
    November 18, 1872.

CONTENTS.

		PAGE
I.	A CASE OF DISCIPLINE.	11
II.	THE WAY OF THE TRANSGRESSOR.	29
III.	THE ROUTINE OF SHIP'S DUTY.	47
IV.	AN INCIDENT IN THE CABIN.	64
V.	THE VICE-PRINCIPAL'S DECISION.	81
VI.	THE COLLISION AND THE FOG.	98
VII.	DOWN THE DANUBE.	114
VIII.	THROUGH THE BOSPORUS.	130
IX.	A DISH OF TURKEY.	150
X.	THE TRITONIA AT SEA.	172
XI.	THE STREETS OF CONSTANTINOPLE.	190
XII.	THE VICE-PRINCIPAL'S WRITTEN ORDER.	207
XIII.	THE DANCING DERVISHES AND THE DOGS.	221
XIV.	MR. TOMPION AND HIS BOTTLES.	238
XV.	THE SULTAN'S FIRMAN AND THE BAZAAR.	255

XVI. THE EARTHQUAKE ON BOARD OF THE TRITONIA. 274

XVII. SCUTARI, THE WALLS, AND THE HOWLING-DERVISHES. 287

XVIII. FROM THE TAGUS TO THE GOLDEN HORN. . 298

XIX. ANCIENT AND MODERN GREECE. 311

XX. ATHENS AND ITS SURROUNDINGS. 330

CROSS AND CRESCENT;

OR,

YOUNG AMERICA IN TURKEY AND GREECE.

CHAPTER I.

A CASE OF DISCIPLINE.

"I HAVE had about enough of this voting business," said Morley, the second lieutenant of the Tritonia.

"So have I," replied Greenwood, the third lieutenant.

"We are all mixed up. Of the nine new officers of the vessel, only three were in her last year," continued Morley, shaking his head in the intensity of his wrath and disappointment. "Four of them came from the Young America, and two from the Josephine. I don't think it was fair of the principal to send four of the ship's officers to cut out the officers of the Tritonia, who have done their duty faithfully in her for a year. About half the seamen are from the ship, and quite a number are from the Josephine, so that we are out-voted, and shoved down."

"I don't think it is right," added Greenwood.

"Just look at it. There is Wainwright, who was only fourth master in the ship, captain of the Tritonia; elected over me, who was first lieutenant in her last month."

"Yes, and Scott, who was only the fourth midshipman, — the lowest cabin officer of the Young America, — first lieutenant of the Tritonia; put in over me, who was her third lieutenant last month," echoed Greenwood, indignantly.

"They don't know anything about a topsail schooner, either of them."

"Wainwright was in the Josephine during his first year."

"As a seaman!" sneered Morley. "What does he know about the handling of such a vessel? There's no such thing as a gaff-topsail in the ship, and I don't believe Wainwright or Scott could set one to save his life."

"I suppose we are lying at anchor in this hole to enable them to learn their duties before we get under way."

Morley and Greenwood were very much dissatisfied. The captain of the Tritonia, who had retained his rank for several months by his superior scholarship and seamanship, was to be graduated at the close of the year, and had sailed for home with the rest of his class in the Josephine. Morley had calculated upon stepping into his place, for he had been first lieutenant for several months, and was a popular officer in the Tritonia. But at the commencement of a new school year, officers and seamen had been transferred from the other vessels of the squadron, and among them

Scott, known as the joker, whose humor, good nature, and general love of fair play rendered him almost a universal favorite. Unfortunately for Morley, this advocate of fair play did not see that the old officers of the Tritonia had any especial claims to the best positions under the new order of things, which began with the incoming year; and he labored for the election of Wainwright from the ship to the captaincy of the vessel. He was unselfish in that he worked for his friend rather than for himself; or, rather, he would have been elected himself, if he had permitted the students to vote without any electioneering. He was elected first lieutenant of the consort, without any effort on his own part, and without much on the part of his friends, for the seamen from the ship, and not a few from the two schooners, gave their votes for him.

The Most Respectable Order of Bangwhangers, invented, founded, and put into operation by Scott, had afforded an immense amount of amusement to the students in the squadron, for there had lately been a lodge in each vessel. The principal officers of the lodges formed a kind of grand lodge, at the head of which was the joker himself, formidably and formally designated the " Most Respectable Grand Chief Bangwhanger." He was honored as the inventor of the order and its tremendous mysteries, and there was no limit to his popularity. The students who remained in the Tritonia, with the exception of the cabin officers, welcomed his transfer to her with the liveliest satisfaction. Scott had promised to add a third degree to the working of the order, and the expectant members in the schooner were assured by his coming that they would be the first to enjoy the fun of the new degree.

Morley and Greenwood over-estimated the strength of their own position, for many of their shipmates of the last year voted against them. It was Scott's popularity, and this alone, that defeated them. His adherents would have chosen Allyn, late third master of the ship, second lieutenant; but at this point the joker interfered in the interests of fair play, and labored for the election of Morley and Greenwood. Perhaps, after doing this, he thought he had done enough for them, and that they had no right to complain.

The Young America and the Tritonia, with the two yachts in which Paul Kendall and Robert Shuffles sailed, were still at Swinemünde. The Josephine had sailed on her homeward cruise to convey the graduates, and bring back the new students. All the transfers had been made between the different vessels; the officers had been elected and installed into their offices. They had taken possession of their cabins, and put on the uniform of their rank. The several vessels were all ready to sail on their long voyage to Constantinople; but the principal deemed it advisable to give the officers and seamen a little practice in their new stations. One drill had already taken place, and there was so much confusion in executing the various evolutions of seamanship, that the wisdom of requiring the practice was very evident. A considerable portion of the crew of the Tritonia had never been in a topsail schooner, and were not familiar with all their duty, especially in handling the fore-and-aft sails. There was no such thing as a gaff-topsail on the ship, and the setting and furling of this sail were entirely unsatisfactory to Mr. Tompion, the vice-principal in charge of her. But the fault was with the under officers and the seamen, and not with the first lieutenant, who, in the Josephine, had been stationed at the out-haul of the gaff-topsail, and knew all about the sail, and its running rigging.

Captain Wainwright and Scott had no suspicion of any dissatisfaction among the officers. They saw that Morley and Greenwood were very still and reserved, and kept very much by themselves; but they regarded their immediate subordinates as old friends between themselves, and not disposed to be in haste in making new acquaintances. Scott treated them both very kindly and courteously, and did not put on airs, or make himself offensive in any manner. But this conduct did not conciliate the second and third officers, for the latter concluded that their superiors were only endeavoring to "curry favor" with them, in order to make everything go smoothly in the cabin and on the quarter-deck.

The conversation between Morley and Greenwood took place in the waist, after all the work of the day was done. On the quarter-deck, the captain and the first lieutenant were walking back and forth, talking about the third degree of the Most Respectable Order of Bangwhangers. Scott seemed to be in his usual good humor, for the captain frequently rewarded his sallies with a generous laugh.

"We shall have to stay here two or three weeks to enable the first lieutenant to learn his duties," said Morley, contemptuously. "The hands at the gaff-topsail were all snarled up by his blunders this afternoon."

"I don't like the idea, for the longer we wait, the hotter it will be up the Mediterranean. Besides, I'm in a hurry to see the Turks," added Greenwood.

" We shall get there soon enough ; but I don't like to be shut up here all summer. I want to go to sea, and have a little excitement to wake us up. As everything is in the first lieutenant's hands, I shouldn't wonder if he wrecked the vessel. I don't know but we ought to do something about it."

" What can you do ? " asked the third lieutenant.

" I don't know ; we can get up a breeze, if nothing more."

" That won't do any good. Wainwright and Scott are very popular. If our own fellows had only voted for us, we should have gone in."

" Humph !   Scott is nothing but a buffoon," snarled Morley.   " It was mean for him to come here — "

" Hush ! " whispered Greenwood.

"If you did not intend that I should hear you, I suppose you would not have spoken so loud," said Scott, who happened to come within hearing of the third lieutenant as he spoke.

" Listeners never hear any good of themselves," replied Morley, stiffly.

" As you did not finish your remark, I did not hear any evil of myself," added Scott ; " unless it was, I am a buffoon, and I suppose I have no right to complain of that. You said it was not fair for me to come here ; but you did not finish the sentence."

" I did not know you were listening to me," muttered Morley.

" I was not listening to you ; but as you spoke loudly enough to be heard nearly the whole length of the vessel, I could not help hearing you," continued Scott, gently. " However, if you did not intend the remark for my ear, I will not ask you to finish it, though it indicates that you are in some manner dissatisfied with my conduct."

" I am," replied Morley, whose anger had got the better of his discretion.

" I should be glad to know the ground of any complaint you have against me, in order that I may do what I can to remove it. If I have done anything unfair, it is contrary to my nature, and I did not intend it. If I have set up for anything, it is as a champion of fair play."

" I don't see it," growled Morley, who was depending very much upon the joker's well-known good-nature. " But you are my superior officer, and I suppose I must keep still, whatever my opinion."

" We are both off duty now, and you may speak as freely as you please."

" Well, I don't think it was fair for you and the captain to come into the Tritonia, and take the best offices from the fellows who had held them before, and were in the line of promotion," continued Morley, with a desperate effort.

" O, that's it — is it? " laughed Scott.

" I'm not the only fellow that thinks so, either," said Morley, glancing at Greenwood. " I was first lieutenant before, and I had the right to be captain now."

" Doesn't the right depend upon the number of votes you get? "

"Yes; but you brought your own voters with you."

"Wasn't Captain Wainwright fairly elected?"

"I suppose he was, according to the rules. But you brought so many fellows with you from the ship, that our men were outnumbered."

"The captain was eligible, for he was a cabin officer before. So was I; and I don't see that there was any unfairness about it."

"I don't mean to say that the vote was unfair," growled Morley. "But do you think it was fair yourself to shove me down, when I had been first lieutenant for several months?"

"I don't see anything unfair about it. Were you not one of those who went for electing the officers, when I opposed it?"

"I was; but I have got enough of it, and I want the old way restored."

"Didn't you vote and work against Captain Wainwright and me?"

"Of course I did."

"You did your best, I suppose."

"Certainly I did."

"Then, under the present system, I have just as much cause of complaint against you as you have against me. Am I right, or wrong?"

"I don't think you had any right to come into the Tritonia and tip things over as you did."

"When we were transferred to her, had we not the same rights as the rest of the ship's company?"

"Of course you had."

"We had the right to vote, and we voted to suit ourselves. If the captain and I had not worked for you and Greenwood, both of you would have been lower than you are, for our fellows and some of yours were going to make Allyn second lieutenant."

"I don't know about that."

"I do; but I claim no merit for it," laughed Scott.

"I should think not, after you had shoved me out of my place."

" We could have given you the lowest cabin office, if we had chosen."

"I don't think so. I have some friends left," added Morley, shaking his head.

"Be that as it may, the thing is done, and I don't want any hard feeling about it."

"Of course you don't. After you have knocked me down, you can afford to be magnanimous."

"What can be done?" asked Scott, earnestly.

"I don't know that anything can be done."

"As nearly as I can make it out, you grant that the election was fairly conducted, but some of us are to blame for what we did. I am willing to go to the principal, and ask that the elections be held over again," added Scott. "If Wainwright ought not to be captain, I am sure he does not want the place."

"He isn't the right fellow for it," growled Morley.

"Isn't he, indeed!" exclaimed Scott. "And I suppose I am not the right fellow for first lieutenant."

Greenwood punched his friend gently in the ribs to indicate that he was saying too much; but the hint came too late to influence him.

"It isn't your fault that you are not," replied Morley, as tenderly as he could.

"But it is my misfortune; that's the idea — is it?" laughed Scott.

"I think, if you will take a fair view of the subject, you will agree with me."

"Agree with you that Wainwright is not qualified to be captain?"

"Of course I don't mean to say that he is not a good seaman, and a good navigator, for I don't know anything about it."

"Well, I do; and I know that he is both," retorted Scott, rather smartly for him, for the conversation was becoming rather exciting even to him. "There is no better in this vessel, or any other of the squadron."

"I don't dispute it, for I don't know anything about it," added Morley.

"But you take it upon yourself to say that he is not fit to be the captain of the Tritonia. I had a sort of prejudice that a good seaman and a good navigator is just the person to be in command."

"You persist in misunderstanding me. Wainwright has served most of his time in the ship. He has had little or no experience in vessels like the Tritonia," said Morley, pettishly.

"Then you think it is a bigger thing to handle this little tub of a topsail schooner than it is to handle a full-rigged ship."

"I don't say it is a bigger thing, but it is a different thing."

"According to the Geometry, the greater includes the less. I dare say it is my misfortune that I have been on duty in the ship during the past year."

"I don't see how you can be expected to know how to set the mainsail, and the gaff-topsail, when you haven't had an opportunity to learn," continued Morley, in rather patronizing tones.

"And you don't even pity our ignorance," chuckled Scott.

"It seemed to me absurd to put persons into the two highest places who had had no experience in a topsail schooner."

"You really think the captain and I are lamentably ignorant?"

"I don't say so. I was only speaking of a certain kind of experience. I was first lieutenant — executive officer — of the Tritonia several months.   I know the vessel in detail; I am accustomed to her rigging, and to her working. Greenwood has been second and third lieutenant, and understands about her as well as I do."

"What a wonderful fellow he must be!" exclaimed Scott, laughing, as he glanced at the third lieutenant.

"I think we ought to know something about a topsail schooner," added Greenwood, vexed at the laugh of the joker.

"Certainly you ought, and no one else has any right to know anything about a topsail schooner, which I begin to think is a great institution."

"But in spite of the fact, that we two were left here, and were willing to serve — "

"I don't know that there was any doubt about your willingness to serve," interposed Scott.

"In spite of the fact that we were here, you came from the ship and cleaned us out," continued Morley. "I don't think it was fair."

"Now, my dear Mr. Morley, whether it was fair or not, you have put it out of our reach to do anything about it," said Scott.

" What do you mean by that? "

" You have declared that the captain and I are not qualified for the positions to which we have been elected.   We must prove that we are qualified, for we cannot retire with a stigma upon us."

" I haven't said that you were not good seamen, and good officers."

".But you have said that it is our misfortune not to be able to handle a topsail schooner.   I will not make it any worse than it is.   Now, I think it is child's play to handle this vessel, compared with the ship; and any one who knows where he is on board of the ship will be perfectly at home on the deck of the Tritonia."

" I don't think so."

" I can't believe the principal would have allowed us to be chosen to our present positions if we had been so lamentably incompetent."

"You use stronger terms than I do; but I think you have proved all I said already," added Morley.

" When, and where? " demanded Scott.

" At the drill this afternoon."

" Perhaps we did; but I was not aware of it."

" Didn't you get snarled up when you gave the orders to set the gaff-topsail? "

" I didn't know what I did.   If I did, it was very singular, for whatever may be said of Captain Wainwright, I served as long in the Josephine as you have in the Tritonia.   One of my stations was at the out-haul of the gaff-topsail; and if there is any sail in a schooner that I think I know, that one is the gaff-topsail."

" The hands were all snarled up," muttered Morley.

" That is quite true; but some of them did not know an out-haul from a boot-jack.   If you can indicate any order that was not correctly given, I should say you had some ground of complaint; otherwise you have not."

" My station as second lieutenant was on the forecastle; and of course I couldn't tell about the orders in detail; but I know there was confusion in setting the gaff-topsail."

" So there was in setting the fore-topmast staysail."

"It wasn't my fault, for the down-haul was foul," growled Morley.

"It is part of an officer's duty to have the rigging overhauled.   But I think we have said enough about this business.   I am sorry you are dissatisfied, Morley, and still more sorry that you have put it out of my power to do anything about it."

" But don't you think yourself that it was rather rough in you fellows to come here and shove us down?"

" I think we have the same rights and privileges here that any one has.   Since our incompetence is the ground of complaint against us, we have nothing to say, and shall stand on our dignity," replied Scott, as he turned on his heel, and walked aft.

" You have made a mess of it now, Morley," said Greenwood, who had prudently kept silence during most of the conversation.

" I have told him just what I think," replied Morley, smartly.   " I have been shoved down, and I don't mean to submit to it without a protest.   I have said what I had to say, and Scott knows my opinion of him."

" He don't seem to be very badly damaged," suggested Greenwood, for Scott had walked away as good-natured as ever.

" He understands me now, at any rate."

" Of course he will tell the captain all about it."

" I hope he will; that is just what I wish him to do," answered Morley. " There's Sherman; let's talk with him about it."

Sherman was the first midshipman. Unfortunately, he too had a " sore head," for he had expected a higher place than the one he had obtained. He was quite ready to take counsel of his superiors, and the trio agreed that neither the captain nor the first lieutenant was qualified for the position to which he was elected. Their conference was very private, and they spoke hardly above a whisper. Doubtless they had the power to do a great deal of mischief, and to place their superiors in difficult and trying positions. By their want of zeal, or by a careless attention to the details of their duty, they could create confusion at almost any time; and perhaps they were considering how they could throw discredit upon the first lieutenant in this manner.

Scott was a prudent fellow. He was much annoyed by what he had just discovered, but he did not do what Morley professed to desire of him — he did not say a word to Captain Wainwright about the conversation. The commander had gone below, and did not observe the conference. Scott knew that the knowledge of any dissatisfaction would annoy and embarrass him, and he determined, for the present at least, not to mention it.

After breakfast the next morning, the principal ordered another drill. The exercises at first were in detail; that is, each sail was handled by itself by the seamen at their stations, in charge of an officer. When all hands are called, the second lieutenant is on the forecastle, the third in the waist, and the fourth on the quarter-deck. The first lieutenant, under the orders of the captain, directs all the manœuvres. The midshipmen were stationed in the same manner; but the fourth was required to carry orders from the executive officer when necessary. By this arrangement Greenwood was in the waist, and Morley forward. That troublesome gaff-topsail was the especial care of Allyn, who came from the ship, and really did not understand its working.

The foresail and the mainsail were set; then the gaff-topsail, and the head sails. Now, Allyn had been studying up his duty, and Scott kept one eye on the gaff-topsail all the time. The sail was set and furled several times, till it could be done without confusion or blundering. On the topsail-yards, at the sheets, halyards, clewlines and gaskets, all the seamen were perfectly at home, and they were required to practise only on the fore and mainsails. The latter worked very well under the charge of the fourth lieutenant; but it was observed that there was a great deal of confusion at the foresail.

"Try it again!" shouted Scott to Greenwood, who was in charge of it.

"Man the brails!" said the third lieutenant, in a lazy tone.

Some of the boys laughed.

"Stand by the out-haul!" added the officer.

The students laughed again.

"Let go! Haul out," continued Greenwood.

Some let go, and some pulled. A portion of them heaved on the out-haul, and a portion on the upper brail, so that the work became a contest to see which should outpull the other.

"Avast, there! What are you about?" shouted Greenwood.

"We are doing just what you told us," answered one of the seamen. "We manned the brails, and stood by the out-haul."

The operation was repeated, but with no better success than before. Morley was having no better luck in setting the fore-topmast staysail.

"What's the matter there?" asked Captain Wainwright, annoyed by the confusion.

"I don't know; they are making bad work of it, setting the foresail," replied Scott, as he walked forward.

The laughing of the boys assured him something was the matter, and he determined to observe the next trial himself.

"What is the matter, Mr. Greenwood?" he asked.

"Some of the hands don't know the brails from an out-haul," replied the third lieutenant.

"Set the sail, if you please," added Scott.

"Man the brails!" said Greenwood.

"Are you going to set the foresail, or take it in, Mr. Greenwood?" asked the executive officer, sternly, as he saw the seamen laughing again.

"My orders were to set it."

"And do you man the brails in the Tritonia, when you set the foresail."

"Stand by the brails, of course; that was what I said."

"You did not say so; but that would sound better, though it is not the first order. If you don't understand your duty, Mr. Greenwood, I will send an officer to take your place."

"Man the foresail out-haul!" shouted Greenwood, giving the correct order this time. "Stand by the brails."

"All ready, sir!" responded the second midshipman, who was on duty with the lieutenant.

"Let go the brails! Haul out! Overhaul the brails!"

The sail was promptly and satisfactorily hauled out.

"Slack the weather vang, and man the sheet!"

There were seamen enough to handle the sail easily, and the work was well done.

"Very well, Mr. Greenwood," said Scott. "Now furl it."

Scott went aft, and directed the foresail to be set and furled again; and it was done to his satisfaction. The same confusion prevailed among the head sails, and the executive officer went forward again. On the forecastle he heard Morley giving wild and contrary orders, while the seamen were laughing at the confusion.

"That will do, Mr. Morley," said Scott. "You will suspend all operations till further orders."

The first lieutenant walked to the quarter-deck, and reported the state of things forward to the captain.

" Suspend him at once," said Scott, in a whisper, but very earnestly.

" You will relieve Mr. Morley from further duty, and require him to report to the vice-principal," said the captain in a loud tone.

" Mr. Prescott, you will request Mr. Morley to report at the mainmast."

In a moment the second lieutenant appeared at the mainmast, his face pale, and with the display of much emotion.

" I am directed to report to you, Mr. Scott," he began.

" By order of the captain, you are suspended from further duty, and required to report to the vice-principal in his cabin," said Scott.

" What for ? "

" I have nothing to say about it."

Morley touched his cap, and went into the cabin. An impressive silence prevailed on the decks of the Tritonia.

CHAPTER II.

THE WAY OF THE TRANSGRESSOR.

SCOTT fully comprehended the situation on board of the Tritonia, which the conversation the night before with Morley enabled him to understand. The second and third lieutenants were evidently to bring the discipline of the vessel into contempt, and to prove that the captain and executive officer were incompetent to perform their duty. The seamen seemed to regard the conduct of the two delinquent officers in the light of a joke; but the sharp dealing of the captain assured them that there was trouble on the quarter-deck.

Captain Wainwright sent Greenwood to the forecastle, and Allyn, the fourth lieutenant, into the waist, while the four midshipmen were each advanced one grade. The practice was continued, and the foresail and head sails were set and furled several times. Mr. Marline, the adult boatswain of the Tritonia, took his station on the forecastle, and Greenwood, either afraid of this man, or dreading the discipline which had been extended to Morley, gave his orders correctly. The seamen, startled by the sharp conduct of the captain, had ceased to laugh and joke, and every one of them performed his duty intelligently and promptly. In a short time the hands learned their stations perfectly, and the entire manœuvre of getting under way was executed to the satisfaction of the captain and the executive officer.   At eight bells in the forenoon the drill was suspended.

" How's that? " said Scott, pointing to the signal for sailing, which was displayed on board the ship.

" We are to sail to-day," replied the captain.   " I suppose Mr. Lowington is satisfied that we can handle the Tritonia."

" I think we can, if we have fair play," added Scott.

" I did what you advised me to do, Scott; but I thought it was rather sharp discipline."

" It was the only way.   I hadn't any ill will against Morley ; but he has been trying to make trouble.   He wants to have it appear that you and I can't handle a topsail schooner.   I had a talk with him last night, and he put on airs and grumbled because we were elected over him."

The captain was deeply interested, and Scott related the substance of his conversation with Morley.

" Why didn't you tell me of all this before, Scott? " asked the captain.

" Because I didn't wish to prejudice you against any officer," answered Scott.   " I don't wonder that Morley feels badly about being put down, when he expected to be captain.   I was sorry for him ; but I thought he would get over it in a few days.   If he had only talked fair about it, I should have tried to do something ; but when he attempted to make it out that you and I don't know our duty, of course I couldn't do anything.   I didn't think he would resort to such a mean thing as making trouble in the drill."

" I understand you now, and I am glad I followed your advice in suspending him," said the captain.

" That was the only thing you could do.   He was disobeying orders."

At this moment Prescott, the fourth midshipman, touched his cap to the captain.

" The vice-principal wishes to see the captain and first lieutenant in the cabin," said he.

" Very well, Mr. Prescott," replied the captain.

" He is going to overhaul the matter," said Scott; and he followed the captain down into the cabin.

Mr. Tompion, the vice-principal, had been waiting for the conclusion of the drill to hear the case of the second lieutenant.   Morley was seated at the table, turning over the leaves of an illustrated paper, glancing at the pictures occasionally; but it was plain that he was not at all interested in them.

" Captain Wainwright, the second lieutenant informs me that he has been suspended from duty by you, and directed to report to me," said the vice-principal.

" Yes, sir," replied the captain.   " I suspended him, and directed him to report to you."

" He has done so.   Do you wish to proceed any farther with this business?"

" Any farther, sir?" repeated the captain, surprised at the question.

" Of course this is an unpleasant affair."

" I know it, sir."

" It will make your relations on board very disagreeable," added Mr. Tompion.

"I am not responsible for it, if it does, sir."

"If you have been impatient and hasty, the matter need proceed no farther."

Both the captain and Scott were astonished at the words of the vice-principal, who seemed to be intent only upon giving the commander an opportunity to retire from the position he had taken.

"I have not been impatient or hasty, sir," added Wainwright, with dignity. "The first lieutenant reported that Mr. Morley was disobeying orders, and creating confusion on the forecastle. I suspended him for it. I don't know that I could have done anything else."

"Then you wish to proceed with this business?"

"Yes, sir. If I am to command this vessel, the orders which I give must not be treated with contempt, as they were to-day."

Mr. Tompion bit his lip, and did not seem to be satisfied with the position taken by the captain.

"Are you aware that there is some feeling in the vessel about the last election of officers?" he asked.

"I was not aware of it till a few moments since."

"Both the second and third lieutenants are very much dissatisfied at the result of the election, and I suppose that is the cause of the present difficulty."

"I did not know it till after I had suspended Mr. Morley."

"I thought it probable you did not," added the vice-principal, speaking in a low tone, so that Morley, who was at the other end of the cabin, should not hear him.

"But if I had known it, I don't see that it would have made any difference," interposed the captain. "Mr. Scott reported Mr. Morley's disobedience of orders to me, and it was my duty, under the regulations, to suspend him."

" All regulations must be interpreted with judgment and discretion."

" But everything was in confusion in the waist and on the forecastle. Mr. Morley and Mr. Greenwood were purposely giving contradictory and improper orders. The seamen were laughing at them, and there was no discipline at all."

" Why was not Mr. Greenwood suspended."

" Because he was not reported to me."

" And why was he not reported?" asked the vice-principal, turning to Scott.

" Because he mended his ways, and did his duty properly," replied the executive officer.

" You reported Mr. Morley — did you, Mr. Scott?" inquired the vice-principal.

" I did, sir."

" Were you aware that he was dissatisfied with the late election?"

" I was; he told me so himself, and said that the captain and I did not know how to handle a topsail schooner."

" And for this reason you reported him?" added the vice-principal, with a significant smile.

" No, sir!" replied Scott, decidedly. " I reported him because he was not doing his duty; because he was giving contradictory orders, and creating confusion. He had put three hands at the jib down-haul, who were pulling against three more at the halyards."

" But, Mr. Scott, you can see that your zeal will be misconstrued."

" I can't help it, if it is, sir.   The second lieutenant has declared, and published it through the vessel, for aught I know, that Captain Wainwright and I can't handle a topsail schooner ; that we don't know how to set the foresail, the gaff-topsail, and other sails ; and in order to bring us into contempt he disobeys orders, and makes confusion on the forecastle.   It was plainly my duty to report him, and I did so."

" Did you give the captain any advice in regard to the matter ? " asked the vice-principal.

" I am willing to take the responsibility, and bear the blame for all I did," interposed the captain.

" Of course that must be ; but Mr. Scott can answer my question."

" I did," replied Scott, squarely.

" What advice did you give him ? "

" I advised him to suspend Morley," answered Scott.

" Precisely so," added Mr. Tompion, who seemed to be taking the part of the disobedient officer.   " Mr. Morley had expressed his dissatisfaction to you, and intimated that you did not know how to handle a top-sail schooner."

" If he had done his duty, or even tried to do it, I should have had no trouble with him," said Scott, who could not help feeling that he was on trial himself.

" I do not mean to intimate that either of you has not done his duty ; but it would have been better for the peace and harmony of the ship if Mr. Morley had not been suspended."

" I submit, Mr. Tompion, that I am not responsible for Mr. Morley's conduct," said the captain.

" Certainly not.   You have done your duty, technically, and according to the regulations, Captain Wainwright; so has Mr. Scott.   But it is a question whether this business had better proceed any farther.   You can drop your charge, and permit Mr. Morley to report for duty again."

" If Mr. Morley is ready to do his duty, I am entirely willing to drop all further proccedings."

" You mean that Mr. Morley must apologize, and promise to do his duty in the future? " added the vice-principal.

" I will not ask him to apologize; only to say that he will do his duty in the future."

" But if I hear the case, I must settle it.   You can drop the matter where it is."

" I am not willing to do that, for it is virtually saying that I am in the wrong myself."

" Very well; then we must proceed with the business.   Mr. Morley," said the vice-principal, calling the delinquent officer.

Morley went aft to the part of the cabin where Mr. Tompion was seated.

" Now, you may state your charge, Captain Wainwright," said the vice-principal.

" Mr. Morley was reported to me by the executive officer for disobedience of orders."

" Mr. Scott, you will state in detail the charge."

The first lieutenant gave a full and particular account of the proceedings in the waist and on the forecastle, and stated what the improper and contradictory orders were.

" Now, Mr. Morley, what have you to say? " added Mr. Tompion, when Scott had concluded.

The second lieutenant denied the charge in general, and declared that the seamen from the ship did not know their duty. It was possible that their blunders had confused him, and caused him to give some improper orders; but he intended to do his duty. He then added that the first lieutenant was prejudiced against him because he had spoken his mind rather freely the evening before, and had " picked him up " for what was not his fault.

While Morley was defending himself, Mr. Tompion took from his pocket the principal's written instructions for the government of the affairs of the consort. He looked them over carefully, till he came to one of them which fixed his attention.

" I find that the vice-principals are required to refer questions of this kind to the principal, when the squadron is in port," said Mr. Tompion. " I have never had a case of suspension before, and had quite forgotten this rule."

Morley's face suddenly changed its expression, and he began to look anxious. He evidently felt that Mr. Lowington, the principal, was a different person from Mr. Tompion, the vice-principal.

" I only desire to have the case fairly settled," added Captain Wainwright.

" Mr. Morley says he did not intend to give any improper orders," continued Mr. Tompion.

" Then I must say that he does not understand his duty," interposed Scott. " The same hands set and furled the jib several times after he came below, without any confusion whatever."

" They had learned their duty by that time," said

Morley, in a grumbling tone. "It is a hard case to be picked up so suddenly for the blunders of the seamen."

Scott did not like to push the charge, though he felt that Morley's conduct was far from square and manly. Mr. Tompion, who was only anxious to patch up a peace, sent the delinquent on deck, and then hinted that the charges had better be withdrawn.

" In my opinion Mr. Morley intended to make confusion, and to bring his superior officers into contempt," said Scott, decidedly.

" He says he did not," answered the vice-principal.

" I think I can prove, sir, either that he does not know his duty, or that he purposely gave improper orders."

" Do you wish to call on the seamen to testify against their officers? " asked Mr. Tompion, sharply.

" No, sir. I will call Mr. Rimmer, the carpenter; and I think Mr. Marline also understood what was going on."

The vice-principal went on deck, and had a talk with the boatswain and the carpenter; but when he returned to the cabin he did not quote their opinions.

" Captain Wainwright, you can withdraw or drop your charges, if you wish to do so; otherwise I must refer the case to the principal."

" If Mr. Morley will say that he will faithfully perform his duty, and obey the orders of the captain and executive officer, I will drop the charges," replied Captain Wainwright.

Morley was called again. Perhaps he felt that Mr. Tompion was fighting his battle for him, for he was stiff and rather surly. The vice-principal stated the captain's position to him.

"I have tried to do my duty," said he; "but of course I don't expect to succeed while Mr. Scott is prejudiced against me, and is trying to pick me up at every chance he can get."

"Are you quite sure, Mr. Morley, that you did your duty?" asked Mr. Tompion.

"I did the best I could; but I am not to blame for the blunders of the crew."

"The Young America has hoisted the signal for sailing, and we must settle this case at once," continued the vice-principal. "If you cannot satisfy the captain, we must go to the ship."

"I am ready to go," said Morley, stiffly; but he was not half so ready as he pretended to be.

The first cutter was lowered, and the vice-principal, with the captain and first and second lieutenants, was conveyed to the ship. Mr. Lowington was on the quarter-deck, and the vice-principal told him the whole story of the trouble on board of the Tritonia. He did not omit the statement that the difficulty had grown out of the result of the late election. The principal was annoyed as much by the one-sided view which Mr. Tompion seemed to take of the case as by the fact that a dissension existed.

Retiring to the main cabin, he sent for the captain and first lieutenant of the Tritonia, to whom he gave a patient hearing. Then Morley's defence was as patiently listened to. The boatswain and carpenter were sent for.

"Mr. Marline, were you on deck just before Mr. Morley was suspended?" asked the principal.

"I was, sir."

"Did you hear the order given to set the jib?"

"I did, sir."

"What were Mr. Morley's orders?"

"I was in the waist then, and didn't mind what they were; but everything was snarled up on the forecastle."

"Mr. Rimmer, did you hear the orders in detail?"

"I did, sir."

"What were they?"

"Man the down-haul, and stand by the jib-halyards."

"No, sir.   I —"

"Silence, Mr. Morley!" said the principal, sternly. "I have heard you once; but I will hear you again by and by, if you wish."

The testimony of the two forward officers was direct and to the point.   They were both old seamen, and knew what they were talking about.   It was clearly shown that improper and contradictory orders had been given.

"Now I will hear you, Mr. Morley," said the principal.

"The crew made so many blunders that I was confused," pleaded the delinquent.

"Your first orders were wrong.   Do you man the down-haul to hoist a jib?"

"No, sir."   -

"The blunders of the seamen could not have confused you in the beginning."

"Mr. Scott is prejudiced against me, and —"

"Mr. Scott has proved his charge," interposed Mr. Lowington, sternly.   "If he was prejudiced against you, it was no excuse for you to disobey his orders. It appears that after you were suspended there was no more confusion. I was observing the Tritonia at the time, and I was so well satisfied with the discipline of the crew that I ordered the signal for sailing to be set."

"If Mr. Scott hadn't picked me up so quick, I should have set the sail right in another minute," muttered Morley.

"I'm not so sure of that. The conduct of the captain and first lieutenant is fully approved," added Mr. Lowington. "In regard to the election, it was fairly conducted. It appears that a portion of the old crew of the Tritonia voted for the present captain and first lieutenant. If it had not been so, they could not have been elected. These officers have done their duty, but you have not. If Mr. Scott is prejudiced against you, as you say, you should have done your duty, and when he failed in his, it would have been time for you to complain. Duty must be performed without regard to private feelings and personal jealousies. If Mr. Scott had been elected to his present position by fraud, it would still be your duty to obey his orders. But the substance of this lesson has been so often repeated that it is useless to enlarge upon it."

"But it was rather a hard case to have two students transferred from the ship, where they had never even served as lieutenants, elected to the two highest places, over the heads of those who had stood next to the commander," suggested Mr. Tompion. "Mr. Morley was first lieutenant of the Tritonia for several months, and now, by the coming of Wainwright and Scott, he is reduced to second lieutenant."

"I see no hardship whatever in it," replied Mr. Lowington, with something like a frown on his face. "Wainwright and Scott were both cabin officers, and were both eligible to the highest places. Since the ship's company of the Tritonia elected them, they are rightly and properly in their present positions. Mr. Morley advocated the present system of electing the officers by ballot."

"I did, but I am heartily sick of it," replied the delinquent, in disgust.

"But the system is to teach you a needed lesson, one which every republican ought to learn. You must submit to the will of the majority, constitutionally expressed. Because you do not like the action of the majority, you get up a revolution, as they do in Mexico and some of the South American states. The Tritonia is not officered and manned simply to gratify even your reasonable ambition, Morley."

"I didn't suppose it was, sir," protested Morley.

"One would think you did, from your conduct. Because you are not chosen captain, you are determined to destroy the discipline of the vessel. I will not tolerate such conduct. There is no excuse whatever for it. I can understand that you were disappointed because you were not elected captain, or first lieutenant ; but that is no reason why you should disobey orders, or neglect your duty. The action of Captain Wainwright is confirmed, and you are suspended from your office. In other words, you are reduced to a seaman, and the crew of the Tritonia will elect your successor by ballot."

Morley turned pale, and actually trembled with

emotion, for he had not anticipated a sentence so severe. The thought of going into the steerage again was intolerable. Mr. Tompion seemed to be quite as much surprised as the subject of this sharp discipline. He wished to speak to the principal alone, and when the rest of the party went on deck, he remained in the cabin with Mr. Lowington.

"Morley has always been a very good officer," said he.

" He is not now," replied the principal. " I have no patience with an officer who disobeys orders because he has a personal grievance."

" But there was some trouble between Scott and Morley the night before."

" No matter if there was."

Mr. Tompion went over the ground again, and even stated his belief that Morley ought to be excused ; but the principal was inflexible.

" Morley does not even offer to apologize, or to make any reparation for his conduct," added Mr. Lowington.

" He has had no opportunity to do so, sir."

The principal did not like the action of Mr. Tompion in attempting to palliate the offence of Morley, and he expressed himself plainly on this subject. If a student was to be tolerated in bringing the discipline of the vessel into contempt whenever he was dissatisfied on personal grounds, it would not be safe to go to sea. Mr. Tompion offered no further objection, and followed Mr. Lowington on deck.

" You have done your worst now, and I hope you are satisfied, Scott," said Morley, bitterly, as they came out of the cabin.

"I did not do it. The captain offered to drop the charge if you would simply say you would do your duty in the future. He didn't even ask you to apologize," replied Scott, gently. "You refused to do it."

"I was a fool!" exclaimed Morley.

"I am sorry for you, and I had no idea it would come to this," added Scott. "What can we do?"

"I can't go into the steerage again. I will apologize; I will do anything," said Morley, impulsively.

Scott talked with Wainwright, and together they put in a petition to the principal for the remission of the heavy penalty.

"I will consider it," replied Mr. Lowington. "Such a request from you will have great weight with me. Return to the Tritonia, and I will visit her myself after dinner."

The first cutter returned to the consort. After dinner, at the request of Morley, all hands were called, and when they had assembled in the waist and on the quarter-deck, the second lieutenant, in a loud voice and in rather flippant tones, acknowledged his fault, and tendered his apology, with a promise to do his duty faithfully in the future.

"I don't know about that," said Scott, in a low tone, to the captain, who stood near him.

"He seems to be very jolly about it," added Wainwright.

"And the crew look as though they wanted to laugh at it."

"If he does not mean what he says, it will do no good."

"Here comes Mr. Lowington," said Scott. "Of

course he means it, though he was not willing to say anything until he had been reduced."

" Shall we let him up?" asked the captain.

" Yes; I don't want to have him sent into the steerage."

The principal came on deck, and all the officers touched their caps to him.

" Mr. Morley has apologized in the presence of the whole ship's company, sir," said the captain.

" Are you satisfied?" asked Mr. Lowington, as he glanced at the half-comical faces of the crew.

Wainwright hesitated, in spite of the advice of Scott.

" If you are not satisfied, you should say so," added the principal.

" I hope you will remit the sentence, sir," replied the captain.

"Mr. Morley," said Mr. Lowington, " am I to understand that you are really sorry for your conduct?"

" I am, sir," replied the delinquent, touching his cap, and looking very humble.

" I learn that you have apologized in the presence of the ship's company."

" I have, sir."

" Then, at the request of Captain Wainwright and Mr. Scott, you are restored to your rank, and will report to the first lieutenant for duty."

" Thank you, sir; and I will endeavor to do my duty faithfully," replied Morley.

Those who saw the sly wink of Morley as he turned away from the principal fully understood the value of his apology and his promise.   Mr. Lowington made a speech to the students upon the necessity of obeying orders without regard to personal feelings. He went over the whole of Morley's case, and explained its bearings upon the discipline of the vessel. He commended the magnanimity of the captain and executive officer in requesting the remission of the penalty, without which he could not have abated it.   He hoped that Morley would appreciate the action of his superiors by promptly and zealously performing his duty. As he finished, the students applauded, rather from the force of habit than because they approved the principles which had been enunciated.

" Captain Wainwright, we shall get under way at four o'clock," continued Mr. Lowington, as he went to the accommodation steps. " The wind is northwest, and we shall have to beat dead to windward. If we are separated in the night, you will anchor off Copenhagen till the ship comes up with you."

" Off Copenhagen, sir," replied the captain.

" The Tritonia will beat the ship going to windward," suggested Mr. Tompion.

" You will follow the Young America," said the principal ; " but fogs are frequent in the Baltic, and if you lose sight of the ship, make the best of your way to Copenhagen. Good afternoon, young gentlemen."

The principal seated himself in the boat, and it returned to the ship.

" I couldn't say I was satisfied with Morley's apology," said Captain Wainwright, when the principal had gone.

" He was decidedly airy about it," replied Scott.

"I don't think he meant it."

"Well, if he didn't, he will break out again in another place, and next time we shall understand him better."

"But he may get up a mutiny."

"I'll risk it," laughed Scott. "We can carry most of the ship's company in a game of that sort, and make it altogether too hot for him."

"It seems to me that Mr. Tompion takes his part."

"I should think he did!" exclaimed Scott. "Never mind; if we do our duty, we shall come out all right."

The two officers went into the cabin to study the charts in preparation for the voyage.

CHAPTER III.

THE ROUTINE OF SHIP'S DUTY.

NEARLY all the officers of the Tritonia were in the cabin, studying the charts, or engaged in other nautical occupations. Morley and Greenwood were on deck, discussing the exciting events of the day. Neither of them was any better satisfied than before; but they agreed that it would not be prudent for them to attempt to " mix things " again. Wainwright and Scott, placing but little dependence upon the second and third lieutenants, were careful to inform themselves fully in regard to the courses, bearings, and distances in this part of the Baltic, and before the hour for sailing arrived, both of them had written down everything they were required to know.

" It is quarter of four, captain," said Scott.

" Call all hands, Mr. Scott," replied Wainwright.

" All hands, up anchor! " piped the boatswain a moment later; and officers and men hastened to their stations.

The cable was heaved in to a short stay, which Morley reported to Scott.

" Stand by to set foresail and mainsail! " shouted the first lieutenant.

"All ready, sir," reported the officers at their stations.

"Top up the main boom!"

"Man the out-hauls. Stand by the brails!" said Scott.

Fourteen hands seized the out-hauls, while others stationed themselves at the brails.

"Let go the brails! Haul out," continued Scott; and all his orders were repeated by the officers at their several stations.

The fourteen seamen at each out-haul walked away with it, and the great sails began to shake and flutter in the breeze.

"Belay!" cried the executive officer, when the sails were hauled out. "Slack the port vangs!"

"The ship is off," said the captain.

"Her sails were loose before we began," replied Scott. "But we shall be up with her before she has made a mile. "Stand by to set the gaff-topsail!"

"All ready, sir," reported the fourth lientenant, when the hands had taken their stations.

"Man the halyard and out-haul! Stand by the tack! Hoist away! Haul out!"

Perhaps Morley was disappointed when he saw this sail go into its place with so little difficulty. As it was not set exactly as he had been in the habit of doing it, he maintained that it was not properly done.

"Man the bars! Ship and swifter them!" continued Scott.

"All ready, sir," reported Morley.

"Heave around!"

The hands walked around the capstan with a measured tramp on the deck, for it was easy work for so many of them.   The midshipman watched the position of the cable, and reported to the second lieutenant.

"Cable up and down, sir!" shouted Morley.

"Man the jib and flying-jib halyards," responded Scott. "Stand by the down-hauls!"

Morley repeated these orders, and the seamen, who were stationed at the ropes indicated, took their places.

"Avast heaving!" shouted the executive officer, as the head of the Tritonia began to swing the wrong way. "Hard a port the helm!"

"Hard a port," repeated the quarter-master at the helm.

In a moment the head of the vessel began to pay off.

"Heave around, lively!" shouted Scott.

"Anchor aweigh, sir," said Morley.

"Let go the down-hauls! Hoist the jib and flying-jib," added Scott. "Stand by the jib-sheets! Trim them down!"

The breeze caught the head sails, and the Tritonia went off beautifully on the port tack, to the disappointment of Morley, who had hoped to see her cast on the other tack, as her head swung around. But Scott knew what he was about, and everything worked exactly as he intended it should.

"Anchor at the bow, sir," reported Morley.

"Avast heaving! Pawl the capstan! Stopper the cable! Cat and fish the anchor!"

The vessel heeled over, and began to move at a lively rate through the water. The pilot, who spoke

English very well, took his station on the quarter-deck.

"Shall we set the topsails, Mr. Pilot?" asked the captain.

"Yes, if you please; but we tack abreast of that buoy," replied the pilot, pointing over the lee bow.

"Set the fore-topsail and fore-topgallant sail, Mr. Scott," added Captain Wainwright.

"Stations for loosing topsails!" shouted Scott. "Lay aloft, sail-loosers!"

The orders were repeated forward, and the seamen who were stationed on the yards ran nimbly up the fore rigging.

"Lay out, and loose," said the first lieutenant; and the hands went out on the foot-ropes, each in his proper place. "Man the topsail-sheets and halyards." And the seamen on deck, who belonged at these ropes, hastened to their stations.

The captain of the foretop reported that all was ready, which implied that the gaskets had been cast off.

"Let fall!"

The two sails dropped together at this order.

"Lay in, and lay down from aloft," added Scott; and all the hands, except two on the topsail-yard, and one on the topgallant-yard, who remained to light up and overhaul the running rigging, came down upon deck.

"Sheet home, and hoist away," continued the executive officer.

The seamen at the sheets, which are the ropes attached to the lower corners of the topsails, running through sheave holes in the ends of the yards below the sails, and leading to the deck, walked away with them. The lower corners of the sails were thus drawn down to the end of the yards below them. At the same time, the hands at the halyards, which are the ropes by which the yards are hoisted up on the masts, pulled down upon them; and in a few moments the topsail and topgallant-sails were hauled out flat.

" Man the lee braces ! Stand by the weather ! Brace up ! "

The yards were swung around so that the sails filled and bellied out. The Tritonia was now close-hauled, or braced sharp up, on the port tack. She heeled over still more, and instantly increased her speed. In a moment she was abreast of the buoy.

" Go about, if you please, captain," said the pilot.

" Ready about ! " added the captain.

" Ready about ! " shouted Scott.

All the officers repeated the order at their several stations, and every seaman, knowing his place, flew to discharge his proper duty in tacking. Some went to the braces, some to the jib-sheets, some to the foresail-sheets, and some to the mainsail-sheets. There was no need to tell any one what he was to do, for each had been drilled in his specific work in all the evolutions.

" Ready ! " shouted the first lieutenant, hardly an instant after his first order was given.

" All ready, sir," replied the officers, each of whom was required to superintend the handling of a particular sail, or set of sails.

" Put the helm down ! " continued Scott.

" Helm down, sir," replied the quarter-master, who was conning the helm, as he assisted the two hands in throwing over the wheel. "Helm's a lee, sir," he reported, when the order had been obeyed.

The head of the Tritonia came up into the wind with all her sails shaking. When she had swung around so that the wind began to catch the flying-jib on the other tack, —

"Ease off the jib-sheets," called Scott. "Let go and haul!"

At this order, the vessel being well around, so that she had the wind on her starboard side, the yards were braced up, and the sheets secured on the other tack.

"Right the helm," said the first lieutenant, as she came about, and as soon as her sails began to fill on the starboard tack.

"Right the helm! Meet her!" added the quarter-master; and this change prevented the vessel from falling off too far.

The Tritonia gathered headway on the new tack, heeling over and bowing gracefully as the puffs of wind struck her. She went but a short distance on this tack before the pilot requested the captain to go about again; and the manoeuvre described was repeated. After tacking twice more, the vessel was in the open sea, the pilot took his leave, and the starboard watch was piped below, leaving the port watch in charge of the deck. This consisted of four officers and eighteen seamen, a sufficient number to work the vessel, except in emergencies. Contrary to the practice in men-of-war, the first lieutenant kept a watch. All the lieutenants and masters whose rank was indicated by odd numbers, as the first and third, belonged in the starboard watch.   Every seaman was numbered each month, and all the odd numbers belonged in the same watch.   All the even numbers were in the port watch.   Scott and Greenwood were on duty in the starboard watch, and Morley and Allyn in the port, so that the two conspirators against the discipline of the vessel were not on duty at the same time.

By the ordinary rule on board of ships and other vessels, performing long voyages, one watch would be in charge of the deck, while the other was off duty. This would give the Tritonia four officers and eighteen seamen to work the vessel at all times, night and day. But she was very heavily manned, though her ship's company was composed of boys.   Yet they were from fourteen to eighteen years of age.   Some of them were able to do a full man's work in ship's duty, such as pulling and hauling, which required only strength, while the average was at least three fourths of a man.   But the greater part of the work did not require mere brute force, and in the matter of agility, of nimble fingers, the boys were superior to men.   At the topsail-sheets and buntlines, at the jib-sheets, halyards, and down-hauls, any of the boys were just as serviceable as so many men.   Eight or nine men would have been deemed a sufficient crew for a vessel of the Tritonia's tonnage in the merchant service, while her actual number was thirty-six, who were fully equal to twenty-seven men.   The system of quarter watches, used in the navy, but amplified in the Academy Squadron, had been introduced.   Each watch was divided into two parts, and the quarter watch consisted of two officers, a lieutenant and a midshipman, and nine hands, which was a sufficient force to handle the vessel under ordinary circumstances. Mr. Marline, the boatswain, was always on duty with the starboard watch, and Mr. Rimmer, the carpenter, with the port. It was watch and watch for them, or four hours on duty and four off alternately for each of them.

In good weather, this arrangement of the watches allowed every officer and seaman six hours of continuous sleep, and two hours more before or after his watch on deck. In the daytime, from eight in the morning till eight in the evening, six hours of study and recitation were required, which was just half the time; so that while the starboard watch was on deck, the port was at study or recitation, and *vice versa*. But, as only a quarter watch was required for actual duty on deck, the second part of the watch could read, sleep, play, or " loaf," three of the six hours not devoted to study in the steerage. Of course some of the more ambitious students used this time for study, or to improve themselves in seamanship and navigation; and such were permitted to join any of the classes of the other watch.

Tom Morgan is a seaman, and is one of the quartermasters. In order to give the reader a clearer idea of student and sailor life on board of a vessel of the Academy Squadron, we will follow Tom through the first day of his ship life on board of the Tritonia, commencing at eight o'clock in the evening, after she sailed from Swinemünde. He is a good sort of fellow, steady and reliable. His ship's number is twenty-three, and therefore he belongs in the starboard watch. No. 1, and every alternate odd number in the watch, belong to the first part, which places Tom Morgan in the second part. The first watch is from eight o'clock till twelve, during the first two hours of which the first part of the starboad watch is on duty. Tom has nothing to do till ten o'clock, and may lie down in his berth and sleep for a couple of hours, or amuse himself in any manner he pleases. If he stays in the steerage, he must not indulge in loud talking or " skylarking," or make a noise in any manner. Everywhere, between decks forward or aft, comparative stillness must prevail; for the port watch, which will go on duty the first part at twelve, and the second at two, are supposed to be asleep. Conversation in a low tone is permitted; but noise of any kind is strictly forbidden, and the rule is rigidly enforced. The steerage is well lighted till ten o'clock, after which time only a single lantern breaks the gloom. Tom may read here; he may walk the deck, or he may settle himself away under the bulwark, or alongside the skylight, with a friend, and talk over home, or the sights seen in foreign lands.

At half past eight, one bell is struck; at nine, two; at half past nine, three; at ten, four; and so on up to twelve, when eight are sounded. At four bells the second part of the starboard watch is called. The third midshipman on duty forward says, " All the second part of the starboard watch, on deck!" One of the seamen appointed for this purpose goes to the berths of all who are to come on deck, and calls them. The third midshipman goes to the cabin, and calls the third lieutenant and the first midshipman, who are required immediately to relieve the officers of the

watch. If the relieving officer is more than five minutes late, it is the duty of the one relieved to report
him, and he loses a mark. Those of the watch who
have not turned in are expected to hasten on deck,
without being called by name.

Tom Morgan appears in the waist the moment the
call for his part of the watch is sounded. The first
midshipman, when he comes on deck, calls the roll of
the officers and seamen of the quarter watch, and Tom
answers to his name.

"Relieve the helm, quarter-master," says Greenwood.

"Helm, sir," replies Morgan. "Tinkner, take the
wheel," he adds, indicating the one who is to have the
first trick, for he keeps a list of the quarter watch, and
sees that each takes his turn at this duty.

Morgan goes to the wheel, and the quarter-master
whom he relieves says, —

"North by east, half north," which is the course of
the vessel as given out by the sailing-master.

"North by east, half north," repeats Morgan, as he
looks into the binnacle, which contains the compass,
lighted by lamps.

"Helm relieved," says the other quarter-master, as
Tinkner takes the wheel; and he and the seaman
retire.

"Luff a little, Tinkner," adds Morgan. "You are
off the wind. Steady!"

Tom Morgan glances up at the sails, and then at the
compass, giving directions to the helmsman until the
Tritonia is exactly on her course, with all her canvas
drawing. She is following the ship, and therefore is

not lying up to the wind as near as she can go. Before night the captain had ordered the light sails to be furled, so as not to run ahead of the ship. The sails are not trimmed down very closely, and it is not a difficult matter to keep the schooner on her course. But Tom must watch the compass all the time, and not permit Tinkner to steer wild ; to shake the head sails, or to fall off from her course. The Tritonia carries a weather helm, and the puffs of wind have a tendency to throw her head up into the wind, and the helmsman must turn the wheel up a spoke or two to counteract this inclination. And so, when the breeze falls below its average force, she will keep off, and the wheel must be put down a spoke or two. Tom is therefore fully occupied, and must have his thoughts about him every moment of the time. Occasionally, if the puffs come strong, he takes hold of the wheel himself, and helps steer. Tinkner will have the helm only an hour ; but the quarter-master serves two hours. The wheel is continually in motion ; it is hardly ever still a moment at a time.

If Tinkner gets sleepy and neglects his duty, Tom must wake him up, and see that the vessel is steered properly. If Tom neglects his duty, he will hear from the officer of the deck, or the midshipman in the waist, for the compass which the quarter-master watches is not the only one on deck. Just abaft the mainmast there is one which Greenwood consults occasionally, as he walks up and down. Half way between the fore and the mainmast there is another, for the use of the midshipman of the watch, at which he glances on an average once a minute. If the vessel is off her course ever so little, one or both of these officers will discover the deviation, and will shout to the quartermaster to "luff," "mind your course."   In addition to these compasses on deck, there are tell-tales, which are inverted compasses, attached to the deck-beams overhead, in the main cabin, and in the cabin of the vice-principal and the captain.   Mr. Tompion and Captain Wainwright can lie in their berths, or sit in their cabins, and observe every deviation of the Tritonia from her course.   Tom Morgan knows that the two officers on duty are watching him, and possibly all those in the cabin.

On the top-gallant forecastle two of the seamen are on the lookout.   Sometimes one of these is sent aloft. The other five seamen of the quarter watch have nothing to do, unless the wind changes, which may require the sails to be trimmed, or it becomes necessary to tack ship.   Two of these will relieve the lookout at the end of an hour, and one of them the helm.   When it blows heavily, two hands will be needed at the wheel besides the quarter-master.

At five bells the midshipman of the watch, with the five hands unemployed, came aft to heave the log, and Tom took the thirty-second glass in his hand. The officer threw the chip overboard, one of the men holding the reel, and two others standing by to veer out the line.

" Turn," said Sherman, the midshipman, when the stray line had run out.

" Turn," repeated Tom, as he inverted the glass in his hand, and held it up to the lamp in the companion-way, the shade of which he had removed for the purpose.

The two hands pulled the line off the reel as fast as the chip would take it, until the sands in the glass had all run through.

"Up!" shouted Tom, sharply; and the two hands caught the line on the instant.

" Seven knots," said one of them; and the midshipman wrote it down on the log slate.

At twelve o'clock, midnight, Tom Morgan strikes eight strokes on the small bell at the wheel, which is repeated by the lookout on the large one forward. Besides watching the compass and the sails, Tom has to keep an eye on the clock, which hangs in the companion-way of the cabin, and is lighted by a shaded lamp. But the quarter-master is so familiar with his duty, that he knows the time pretty well without looking at the clock.

" All the first part of the port watch, on deck!" says Sherman, as he sends a hand into the steerage to call the seamen, and goes into the cabin himself to call the officers.

Within the five minutes allowed all the first part of the port watch appear, and the same formalities as before are gone through. Tom gives the course to the quarter-master who relieves him, goes below, turns in instantly, and is asleep in three minutes. The first part of the port watch are on duty from twelve till two; the second part from two till four. The first part of the starboard watch are on deck from four till six; and at six Tom Morgan is called again with the second part. He has charge of the helm until eight, when he breakfasts, and attends to his studies and recitations till twelve. From twelve till two he is off duty; and then he goes to the wheel again for another two hours. From four till six, except half an hour for supper, he attends to his studies; and this time includes the first dog watch. From six till seven he is off duty, and from seven till eight he is on duty with his quarter watch; and at this hour the day ends, and he turns in for his six hours' sleep, for dividing the watch from four till eight in the afternoon into two dog watches changes the hours of all hands every day. The next night he will be on deck from two till four, instead of during the two quarter watches from ten till twelve, and from six to eight in the morning.

The day's routine given is Tom Morgan's busiest one, for they are not all alike. The change made by the dog watches, in order to give the watches different hours, make the alternate days of unequal length so far as the actual ship's duty is concerned. On the day described, he was off duty, including the time for sleep, eleven hours; on duty, seven hours; and at study, six hours. But the next day he will be off duty thirteen hours; on duty, five; and at study, six. This arrangement makes an average of twelve hours off duty for sleep and recreation; six hours on duty in working ship; and six hours in study and recitation. The time for meals is taken from the study hours, and from the hours when he is off duty. In heavy weather, when it is necessary to keep the whole watch on duty on deck, the additional hours will be those during which he would otherwise have nothing to do. Then he will be on duty fourteen hours one day, and ten the next, which is the ordinary rule on board of merchant vessels in which the crew have watch and watch.

What is true of Tom's quarter watch is equally true of the other three.   All the officers, except the captain, are occupied the same number of hours, though there are some extra duties, such as writing up the log-book, working up the ship's position, keeping account of clothing and stores, which must be done in their own time.   Every day at half past eleven, all the officers must take their instruments to the deck, and look out for the meridian altitude, which is also taken by the vice-principal, who is the instructor in navigation.   Each officer must obtain the result himself, without consultation with any one.   Mr. Tompion examines them, and indicates whether they are correct or not.   Other observations for ascertaining latitude and longitude, or correcting them, and for determining the variation of the compass, are made during the day, and the results worked up.   This constant practice makes them very accurate.   Each officer, except the captain, keeps a log-book, which is examined daily by the instructor.   All the problems in navigation are practically worked, and the judgment of the officers is sharpened in making allowances for leeway, drift of currents, for a heavy sea in heaving the log, and other matters which cannot be mathematically determined.   Each of the young navigators is required to make these estimates, and enter them in his log, using the best information he can obtain from books, charts, nautical almanacs, and other sources, as the basis of his judgment.   As all these results are compared, every one is interested to be as nearly correct as possible.

The captain has no fixed hours except for study;

but he is responsible for the discipline, and for the working of the ship.   He turns in and turns out when he pleases.   He is on deck or in the cabin, as suits his fancy.   He has a large state-room, all to himself, fitted up with all the appliances of comfort, and even luxury.   It contains a berth hung with curtains, a case of drawers with a desk, a lounge, a marble washbowl, and every convenience to be found in a first-class hotel.   But he does not have so easy a time as might be supposed, for not a sail can be set or taken in without his order, by day or by night, except in the case of a squall or other sudden emergency.   The course cannot be changed unless by his order.   He is supposed to direct everything that is done on board, and if he has a reasonable degree of professional pride, he will keep the run of the ship's course, and of all that transpires on board.

The Tritonia sailed from Swinemünde at four o'clock in the afternoon.   Captain Wainwright remained on deck most of the time till dark.   When it was evident that the vessel was sailing faster than the Young America, he ordered the top-gallant sail to be furled. In the evening the wind was a little fresher, and the officer of the deck sent word to him below that she was gaining again, and the flying-jib was taken in. Still she gained, and the fore-topsail was furled.   Then she was losing, and the topsail was set with a single reef in it.   This made it an even thing with the two vessels.   The captain went on deck a dozen times during the evening, and turned in at ten o'clock.   At twelve the midshipman of the watch knocked at his door to inform him that a light was visible over the lee bow.   He knew that it was on the western extremity of the Island of Bornholm.   At two he was told that the ship had tacked, and he sent word to the officer of the deck to do the same when the light bore northeast from the vessel, and keep her west by north, half west.   He got out of his berth, and looked at his memoranda on the desk.   He knew just where the Tritonia was, and how far she had run from the port she had left.   He turned in and went to sleep. He was not again disturbed, though he was liable to be awakened to receive reports a dozen times in a night.

CHAPTER IV.

AN INCIDENT IN THE CABIN.

ON the morning after the Tritonia sailed, the wind was lighter, though it still came from the north-west. The vessel was making but four knots an hour; but after the sun rose, the breeze freshened a little, and increased the speed to five knots, and then to six. At seven bells in the forenoon, when the officers were called to look out for the meridian altitude, land was in sight, dead ahead. According to the dead reckoning on the log-slates, the vessel had run fifty-one nautical miles on her present tack since she came about off Bornholm. The land, therefore, ought to be the Island of Moen, belonging to Denmark. The shore was low, and could be barely discerned from the foretop, being about twenty miles distant.

" The longitude, young gentlemen," said Mr. Tompion, when the results of the observation had been worked up. " Mr. Scott? "

" 12°, 59′, 12″, east," replied Scott, reading his figures.

The other officers read their results, and they agreed to a second, with one exception.

" The latitude, Mr. Scott? " added the vice-principal.

" 54°, 58,' 59", north," answered Scott; and the others had it the same.

" Now examine the chart, and compare the ship's position with that obtained by the dead reckoning."

There was not half a mile difference between them, and it was demonstrated that the land ahead was the Island of Moen.

" The ship has tacked, sir," said the midshipman of the watch, reporting to the captain.

" Very well, Mr. Campbell," replied Captain Wainwright, as he went on deck.

When the Tritonia was as far to windward as the ship had gone, he gave the order to tack ship.

" North by east, half north," said he to Scott, who was the officer of the deck.

" North by east, half north," repeated Scott to the quarter-master at the wheel.

" North by east, half north," said the quarter-master.

An hour later land ahead was discovered at the mast-head. This was the south-western point of Sweden, and when the two vessels had approached it as near as it was prudent to go, they tacked, and stood off towards Denmark again. In the second dog watch she was again headed to the north. At half past ten in the evening the squadron was off Copenhagen, where the ship signaled her consort to come to anchor, for the wind had hauled more to the northward, and it was not prudent to beat through the sound in the night. The anchor watch of one officer and two seamen was selected by lot from the quarter watches that would have served if the squadron had continued on its course.

" I don't see but that we are nice little lambs," said

Greenwood, as he met Morley in the waist, after the Tritonia had come to anchor.

" What do you mean ? " asked the second lieutenant.

" We have behaved ourselves beautifully, obeyed orders, and made no blunders," laughed the third lieutenant. " Professor Primback, the chaplain, can pat us on the head, and say that we are good boys."

" There has been no chance to do anything."

" I don't see that anything can be done, unless we run away, or get up a mutiny. The captain has brought the vessel so far on her voyage, and Scott has made no mistakes."

" But I want you to understand, Greenwood, that I'm not going to submit to this sort of thing, even if I have to run away," added Morley, in a low tone. " If Wainwright and Scott had come into the Tritonia, and the fellows had voted for them of their own accord, it would have been different."

" The fellows were not obliged to vote for them."

" No ; but Scott electioneered for Wainwright, and Wainwright for Scott. It was ' you tickle me, and I'll tickle you.' "

" It was that secret society," said Greenwood.

" Of course it was ; and that society is a nuisance."

" We ought to have joined it."

" No, sir ! I believe in fair play, and I won't have anything to do with it, for one."

" The principal encourages the thing, and allows the members the use of the cabin one evening in a week ; but Tompion don't believe in it, I know."

" It is an unmitigated nuisance."

" But what are you going to do about it ? "

" I don't think it is right to compel me to obey officers elected by such machinery; and if we are separated from the ship, so that Lowington can't interfere, you can bet your life I'll do something, if I can get half a dozen fellows to stand by me."

" Don't be rash, my little lamb," said Greenwood.

" I don't mean to be; but we'll stir the thing up, and have a new deal."

" How can you do it? "

" Never mind now.   Don't let those flunkies see us talking together much.   I have the idea, and we will work it up in good time."

" But I want to know about it.   Nearly all the fellows have turned in.   There goes the captain," added Greenwood.

" The Whangbangers — "

" Bangwhangers, you mean."

" I don't care what they are called; they are a nuisance.   They have made all the mischief."

" But all that belong say they have not meddled with the elections since the first one, and that not a word is said about voting in the meetings," suggested Greenwood.

" Tell that to the marines! " sneered Morley.   " Do you believe it? "

" I don't believe all the members would lie about it, and I don't believe the principal would encourage the society if they did."

" It don't make any difference whether they talk about the elections in the meetings or not. Scott is the biggest toad in the puddle, and they all do whatever he tells them. If he says vote for Wainwright,

they do it. They are all banded together. It makes
me mad to think of it. But I'm going to rip the
thing up."

" Easier said than done." •

" Not many of the officers joined the secret society,
you know, and only those that came from the ship are
members. Wainwright, Scott, Allyn, and Campbell
are the only officers that belong. The other five don't
belong, and on them we must work."

" How do you know who belong and who don't?"
asked Greenwood.

" I know who went to their meeting the other
night."

" But they went into the cabin through the steerage."

" Our three fellows who were in the Tritonia last
year and the two from the Josephine were on deck.
The four from the Young America couldn't be found,
for I looked for them," said Morley, taking a paper
from his pocket. " If the two fellows from the Josephine will go with us, we shall be in the majority. I
have here the slate we made up before Scott came on
board."

" What slate?" asked Greenwood.

" Why, the list of candidates for the offices in the
Tritonia, as you and I talked them over."

" I don't remember about that," added the third
lieutenant, scratching his head to stimulate his
memory.

" You don't! I was to be captain, and you were
to be first lieutenant. Do you remember that?" demanded Morley, impatiently.

"Certainly; I know all about that part of the pro-gramme," laughed Greenwood.

"Well, I wrote down the name of Sherman for second lieutenant, and I spoke of him to you for that position."

"You did say something; but the question was, whether it should be Sherman or one of the fellows from the ship."

"But I was in favor of Sherman."

"So was I."

"Good! That's enough. Your recollection is a little too good sometimes, and you remember more than is necessary. Then I wrote down the names of Walker and Prescott, from the Josephine, for third and fourth lieutenants."

"Did you?"

"Certainly I did; if you don't believe it, here is the paper."

"Of course that proves it," added Greenwood, laughing.

"And don't you remember that I told you they were higher in rank last month than the four fellows from the ship?"

"My memory is at fault again."

"But I did."

"I don't deny it."

"And here is the paper."

"Well, allow that you did, what does it all amount to?"

"It amounts to this: Sherman, Walker, and Pres-cott would have been lieutenants instead of midship-men, as they are now, if Scott hadn't come on board with his Whangbangers, and upset all our calculations. Don't you see that they would?" said Morley, earnestly. .

"Possibly."

"Probably, Greenwood. You and I intended to work for them, because they were higher in rank before than the fellows from the ship."

".I certainly should have worked for them rather than for Wainwright and Scott and their friends," added Greenwood.

"Of course you would. It's as plain as the nose on a man's face. They are in the same boat with us. Sherman, Walker, and Prescott don't belong to the secret society, which has crowded them down from lieutenants to midshipmen. I think they will see it, and won't feel any better about it than we do. This is the card we are to play next. Sherman is in the quarter watch with you. Talk it into him when you are off duty. Prescott is in the quarter watch with me, and I will do the same with him. We will walk into Walker afterwards. When we have got them on our side, we shall be in the majority — five to four."

"And what then?" asked Greenwood.

"We must wait for our chances," replied Morley.

"But I tell you in the beginning that I don't want to take any stock in a mutiny, or anything of that sort," added the third lieutenant.

"I don't mean mutiny."

"What do you mean, then?"

"I mean to make it too hot for our tyrants. Tompion goes with us, you know. If the ship had not been near us, he would have decided in our favor.

Leave it all to me, and I will find the powder to load the gun with."

" But don't you fire it off till I know what's coming. Guns kick sometimes."

" You shall see your way through before you go in."

" If I don't, you needn't count me in. We didn't make much when we tried it on in port the other day."

" It was only because we were under the lee of the ship. This is the season of fogs on the coast, and we are sure to be separated from the Young America before we get to Constantinople. Keep your weather eye open for that time. But we must turn in now."

They descended to the cabin, and were soon asleep in their berths. Perhaps the officer of the anchor watch wondered what they were talking about so long, for he knew that they were discontented ; but the conspirators had spoken in a low tone, and not a word could be distinguished.

The next morning the wind was very light from the northward, too light for the Young America to beat through the Sound, and with hundreds of other vessels waiting for a fair wind, the little squadron remained at anchor during the forenoon. At the usual hour the recitations were commenced for all hands ; but after dinner the wind veered to the westward, and the signal for sailing was displayed by the ship. An order from the principal came to the Tritonia, requiring her to put into Cowes, in the Isle of Wight, if the two vessels were separated on the passage. With her port tacks aboard, the schooner followed the ship through the Sound, and at five o'clock in the afternoon she had passed the frowning battlements of Kronberg Castle, at Elsinore. The breeze was moderate from the west-south-west, and the two vessels laid their course for the northern point of Denmark. The third watch day of the voyage commenced at eight o'clock in the evening, and the routine of the first day was repeated. Scott had the deck with the first part of the starboard watch. The captain was on deck, observing the progress of the vessel, and studying the indications of the weather, which were not altogether satisfactory.

"Slack off the main sheet a little," said Scott to a couple of the watch he had called aft. "Ease off the lee braces; a small pull on the weather," he added.

"What is that for?" asked the captain.

"The wind is a little more to the southward," replied Scott.

"Do you see that bank down to the south-west?"

"Yes; it's fog, and is coming up this way. We shall be buried in it within an hour or so."

"I think so myself. How much are you making now?"

"Four knots and a half the last time we heaved the log."

"We are all right till daylight to-morrow morning," added the captain. "At this rate we shall be up with the light-ship off Anholt Island about five o'clock."

"We have plenty of sea-room for the present," said Scott, as he glanced at the compass.

In less than an hour the fog swept down upon the Tritonia. The lookout men were ordered to keep their eyes wide open, and a hand was stationed at the bell forward, and directed to strike it several times every two or three minutes. The strokes were continuous, to distinguish the fog signal on the port tack from the watch bells, which were struck by twos. Occasionally bells and fog-horns were heard in the distance. Captain Wainwright was anxious, for the Tritonia was in the track of vessels bound from the North Sea up the Baltic, and it was impossible for the lookout to see a ship's length ahead. He went to the forecastle, where Mr. Marline was stationed. When a bell or a fog-horn was heard, the lookout reported the direction from which the sound came. As soon as the signal was heard, the officers and the seamen busied themselves in " working it up."

" Bell on the lee bow ! " shouted the lookout.

" She is on the port tack," said Campbell, the midshipman of the watch.

As she was going the same way as the schooner, there was no immediate danger. The strokes of the bell were repeated on the lee bow at intervals, and every time with greater distinctness.

" It is the ship," said Captain Wainwright.

" No doubt of it," added Mr. Marline.

" We are overhauling her, and we must shorten sail," continued the captain ; and he gave the order to furl the top-gallant sail and take in the flying-jib.

" Fog-horn on the weather bow ! " called the lookout.

This announcement indicated that the vessel making the signal was on the starboard tack, and was, therefore, approaching the Tritonia.

" Strike the bell ! " shouted Scott.

Several sharp strokes were struck, and immediately the fog-horn responded. The signals were repeated several times.

" How does she bear ? " asked Scott.

" About two points off the weather bow," replied Campbell.

" Keep her away one point, quarter-master," said Scott.

" Keep her away one point," repeated the quarter-master.

" I see her ! " shouted one of the lookouts ; and immediately a bark emerged from the fog, passing to windward of the schooner.

" Starboard the helm ! "

" Starboard, sir."

" Lay her course again."

The quarter-master gave out the course which the vessel had been steering since she passed Kronberg.

Half an hour later the whistle of a steamer was heard, and the bell was struck more frequently. By observing the sounds for a time, a correct idea of the steamer's course and bearings was obtained. As she seemed to be nearly dead ahead, the Tritonia was kept away. Presently the steamer gave one sharp whistle, to indicate that she would go to starboard, and she passed without being seen, for Scott was inclined to give steamers a wide berth in a fog. The course was resumed ; but a vessel was passed about every half hour during the night.

" Has Mr. Tompion been on deck since we ran into the fog ? " asked Captain Wainwright, just before four bells.

" I haven't seen him," replied Scott.

" He don't trouble himself much about the vessel," added the captain.

"I suppose he has perfect confidence in the officers," laughed Scott.

"Mr. Lowington used to be on deck at such times as this, and I'll warrant he is planking the deck of the Young America at this time."

"No doubt of it. By the way, we haven't heard the ship's bell for some time."

"Perhaps she has been gaining on us since we shortened sail," suggested the captain. "But I would rather fall behind than run ahead of her. When the fog lifts, we will crack on again."

"Four bells," said Scott, as the quarter-master struck the bell. "Mr. Campbell, call the officers of the second part."

The watch was relieved, and Greenwood took the deck; but the captain did not go below. Scott, who was to be on duty again at four o'clock in the morning, turned in at once. All the officers appeared to have retired; but there was a light in the vice-principal's cabin. Morley and Greenwood had already commenced their mischievous work, and they were not much surprised to find that Sherman and Prescott had been greatly disappointed at the results of the election. As they were not members of Scott's secret society, they had no friendship for him, or for the captain. They were quite willing to believe that they had been "shoved down" by the unfairness of Scott and Wainwright, and their indignation was readily stimulated to fever heat. Prescott had discussed the subject with Walker, and he also was willing to believe that he had been cheated out of his proper rank.

"Here is our list of candidates, Prescott," said

Morley, producing his paper, which had been crumpled up in his pocket, and certainly looked like an original document. "You see you were to have been fourth lieutenant, instead of fourth midshipman, and you would have been if those fellows hadn't come from the ship. Wainwright was only fourth master in the Young America, which is the eighth officer in rank, and about equal to fourth midshipman in the Tritonia; and Scott was the lowest officer, and had only just crawled into the cabin when he was transferred."

"I think it was rascally mean for them to crowd down their betters. I was a lieutenant in the Josephine for four months," replied Prescott.

"Of course it was mean. They didn't even talk the matter over with the old officers of the Tritonia and the Josephine," added Morley.

The conspirators found it an easy matter to get up all the indignation they desired. In fact, Scott himself felt that the election had gone rather rough for Morley and Greenwood; and when he spoke to them, after hearing a portion of their conversation at Swinemünde, which he believed had been intended for his ear, he meant to propose a change, and was willing to petition the principal for a new election. But when Wainwright and himself were charged with incompetency, his self-respect would not permit him to do so. He had done nothing to procure his own election as first lieutenant, and had voted for Morley for this position. He did not expect to be chosen, yet could not decline after the election; but he had then done his best for Morley and Greenwood, and had secured their election to the next two offices.

The Tritonia's officers were now divided into two parties, with a majority of one against Scott and his friends. Morley was satisfied, and he sat in the cabin considering what he should do next. He did not heed the fog-signals, so often repeated, or notice that all the officers in the cabin had turned in. He was to take the deck at twelve, and he decided to remain up, because he was too much excited to sleep. He sat at the head of the table, near the door of the vice-principal's cabin. Presently this door opened, and Mr. Tompion appeared in his shirt-sleeves. Something in his looks and manner, as seen in the dim light of the single lantern which burned in the cabin after ten o'clock, attracted the attention of the second lieutenant.

"Mr. Morley," said the vice-principal.

The tones of his voice were very thick, and sounded strangely to the young officer.

"Sir," replied Morley.

"Where is the steward?" asked Mr. Tompion.

"Turned in, sir."

"Zo early?"

"Four bells struck nearly half an hour ago, sir."

"I didn't know it was so late," added the vice-principal, stepping out of his room, steadying himself with both hands at the sides of the door.

While Morley was wondering what ailed him, Mr. Tompion, releasing his hold of the door, stepped forward towards the table. As he did so, his legs seemed to give out beneath him, and he sank down upon the floor, bringing up on his stomach and face. The lieutenant sprang to his assistance, supposing he had a fit, or was very ill. He bent over him, and raised him up. As he did so, the nature of his illness was fully evident. His breath smelled of liquor. Was it possible that the vice-principal was intoxicated? No liquor, wine, or even beer was allowed on board of any vessel of the squadron, and Dr. Winstock, the surgeon, would not prescribe them in sickness, even for the adult forward officers. But it was unmistakably true that Mr. Tompion was intoxicated. He could not stand, and could hardly talk. Morley understood the case at once, for the fumes of the liquor were too potent to admit of an error.

He assisted the vice-principal to his state-room, where he seemed to be willing to go, for he still had sense enough to be conscious of his situation. Morley conducted him to the divan, upon which the sufferer seated himself, placing his hand to his head, as if he had a pain there.

"The ship rolls heavily to-night," said he, in his thick tones.

"Yes, sir, rather," replied Morley, though the roll was very easy and gentle, and would hardly have thrown a landsman out of his equilibrium. "Do you want the steward, sir?"

"I want a pitcher of ice-water, Mr. Morley," muttered the vice-principal.

"I will get it for you, sir."

"I — dzank you, Mr. Morley."

The officer procured the pitcher of ice-water, and his patient drank off a glass of it at a single gulp.

"I'm dzick, Mr. Morley," said he.

"I see you are, sir, and I'm sorry for it. What can I do for you?"

"Nozing, Mr. Morley, nozing. I'm better now. I shall be all zright in the morzing."

"I hope so."

"You needn't mention zat I'm dzick, Mr. Morley, if you please," said Mr. Tompion, suddenly looking up into the face of the young officer.

"Certainly not, sir, if you so desire."

"It's the effect of the medz'n, Mr. Morley."

"Indeed, sir?"

"You dzee, Mr. Morley, I was dzick. I had a pain in here," continued the sufferer, placing his hand upon his stomach. "I'm dzubject to it. The dzurgeon of the dzhip used to prescribe brandy for it. I dzook a glass of brandy to-night. I'm not used to dzaking brandy now, and it — it — it went into my head."

"I'm very sorry, sir," replied Morley, in sympathetic tones. "If you are sick now, we can hail the ship, and bring off Dr. Winstock."

"No, no!" exclaimed the vice-principal, very decidedly. "I don't want Dr. Winstock. He never does me any good when I'm dzick. I'm all zright now, or I zhall be in the morzing. I'll turn in now. I feel bezzer, dzank you, Mr. Morley. You needn't mention my case, if you please, Mr. Morley."

"O, no, sir! Certainly not, Mr. Tompion! Not for the world! You may rely upon me," protested Morley, warmly; and he could not help considering the bearing of this incident upon the plans he was maturing.

"Dzank you, Mr. Morley," added the vice-principal, as he rose, staggered to his berth, and, with the assistance of the young officer, crawled into it.

Morley arranged the bed-clothes about him, and made the patient as comfortable as an intoxicated man could be. On the wash-stand he saw a bottle. Half its contents had been consumed, and it was plain that he had drank more than one glass. In order that the momentous secret might rest with him alone, the lieutenant carefully corked the bottle, and put it away in one of the drawers, which he locked, placing the key on the desk. As he returned to the cabin, he heard six bells strike. Seating himself at the table, he began to think over his wrongs again. The vice-principal was now in his power, and he would not dare to decide against him, whether he was right or wrong. At eight bells Sherman called him and Prescott to take the deck.

CHAPTER V.

THE VICE-PRINCIPAL'S DECISION.

"HOW'S the weather?" asked Morley, as he took his overcoat from under his berth, when Sherman called him.

"Foggy and dark as a stack of black cats," replied Sherman, as he roused Prescott from his berth. "The captain has been on deck since dark."

"Humph!" sneered Morley. "What good does he suppose he does on deck? I don't want any one overseeing me when I'm on duty."

"That's just what he is doing," added Sherman. "It is a nasty night, and we are in the track of vessels bound up the Baltic."

"I think I know my duty as well as he does," replied Morley, as he went on deck, just soon enough to save himself from being reported.

The quarter watch on deck was relieved, and Morley took his place on the quarter-deck, while Prescott went to his station forward. Captain Wainwright was sleepy enough to turn in; but the fog was so dense, and so many vessels were in the track of the Tritonia, that he felt the weight of his responsibility resting heavily upon him. He could not help thinking that it was very strange Mr. Tompion had not been on deck during the evening. He had known Mr. Lowington to be up all night during a fog, and in heavy weather. It was true that, thus far, everything had gone well. The officers had faithfully discharged their duty, and the fog signals had been correctly interpreted. If he could be sure that the officers of the port watch would be as attentive and prudent as those of the starboard had been, he would have been entirely satisfied; but he had served with only one of them, and he desired to observe their conduct himself. His walk was on the weather side of the quarter-deck, abaft the station of Morley.

His relations with the second lieutenant had not been pleasant since the case of discipline. He was fully determined to forget and forgive, and he had been careful to treat Morley and Greenwood with even more consideration than he did the other cabin officers. But his courtesy and kindness were not appreciated by Morley, for he was stiff, reserved, and distant. The politeness which the discipline of the vessel required of him was laboriously extended. When he touched his cap to the captain, he did it with a jerk, and with a sneer on his lips. In his speech he was little less than insolent, and his tones were actually insulting. Wainwright was annoyed by this treatment, after he had requested the principal to reinstate the insubordinate officer. Under these circumstances, he refrained from all unnecessary intercourse with him. Morley took no notice of the captain when he came on deck, the darkness of the night affording him a sufficient excuse for not seeing him. He glanced at the compass, and then commenced a diagonal tramp from the binnacle to the weather rail by the mainmast.

" Prescott ! " he called, after a few minutes.

" On the quarter-deck, sir," replied the fourth midshipman.

" Come here."

Prescott left his station, and joined Morley on the quarter-deck, and they moved aft to the binnacle.

" The captain is watching us," chuckled Morley, in a low tone.

" We shall get into trouble," added Prescott.

" Don't you be alarmed. I am the officer of the deck, and I called you from your station."

" But you know the officers on duty are not allowed to converse except upon working the vessel."

" Precisely so. Is Mr. Rimmer on the forecastle ? "

" He is ? "

" Are the lookouts on the top-gallant forecastle ? "

" They are."

" There ! That's about working the ship — isn't it ? "

" Yes ; but hardly necessary."

Prescott wished to return to his station then ; but Morley detained him for nearly half an hour. This was plainly a breach of discipline, and Wainwright was very much annoyed by it. A fog-horn was reported on the weather bow, and the midshipman was permitted to go forward. The vessel was passed in safety, and the captain was debating with himself whether he should speak to Morley about his conduct, when he called the midshipman again. The conversation was resumed in a low tone, so that Wainwright

could not hear it; but he was confident it did not relate to ship's duty. He distinctly heard a bell about
four points off the beam, which the lookout reported.
The sound came fearfully near, and the lookout repeated the call with great energy. Then the bell was
heard close aboard, and almost on the beam.

"Hard a port the helm!" shouted Wainwright, at
the top of his lungs. "Ease off the sheets!"

His order was promptly obeyed; but at the same
instant the dark form of a small schooner appeared in
the fog. Her helm had been put hard a lee, and she
had come up into the wind, almost alongside of the Tritonia. If the captain had not interfered, a collision
must certainly have occurred, for the small vessel was
laying a course diagonally across that of the schooner, as
her direction and her bell signal clearly indicated; but
it was plain that she had not struck her bell till she
heard that of the Tritonia, or she would have been
made out before. As it was, if she had put helm up,
instead of down, the collision would have been inevitable. The Tritonia went off almost before the
wind, and the stranger disappeared in the fog, hardly
a glance of her having been obtained.

"Lay her course again, Mr. Morley," said the captain, struggling to keep down his emotion.

"Perhaps, as you have taken the vessel out of my
hands, you had better do it yourself," muttered the
officer of the watch, but in so low a tone that Wainwright did not understand him.

But he gave the necessary orders, and the Tritonia was
hauled up to her course again. The bell of the stranger
was presently heard astern, and the danger was passed.

The captain felt that he was too much excited to say anything to Morley, and he planked the deck in silence. Two bells, or one o'clock, struck, and then, to the intense indignation of Wainwright, Morley called Prescott again. The latter evidently did not like to leave his station, after the exciting event that had occurred less than half an hour before.

" Is Mr. Rimmer on the forecastle, Mr. Prescott? " asked Morley.

" He is, sir."

" Are the lookouts on the top-gallant forecastle? "

" They are, sir."

" Well, how are you now, old fellow? "

" First rate ; but there will be a row to-morrow," added Prescott, nervously.

" I hope so."

" We came pretty near having a smash-up."

" That's so, and all because the captain took the vessel out of my hands."

" I thought he prevented the smash."

" Nothing of the sort. I knew just where that little schooner was, and we should have gone by her if the captain hadn't interfered."

The second lieutenant was somewhat excited, and perhaps he spoke louder than he intended, and Wainwright heard a portion of the remark. Possibly Morley intended he should. The captain desired to avoid a collision with the refractory officer ; but he felt that his duty required him to interfere, and a crash into another vessel might soon admonish him that he had weakly neglected that duty. He stepped forward to the station of the officer of the deck.

"Mr. Morley, I am sorry to feel obliged to say that you are not performing your duty in a proper manner," said he, as mildly as he could speak. "Mr. Prescott, you will return to your station in the waist."

"Mr. Prescott is here by my order," replied Morley, angrily.

"He will go forward by my order."

Prescott touched his hat, and began to move off.

"Stop, Prescott!" shouted the lieutenant.

"He will obey my order," added the captain, struggling to keep calm.

The midshipman did obey it, for he saw that Wainwright was not to be trifled with; and the incident at Swinemünde was still fresh in his mind.

"Mr. Morley, you will not call an officer from his station, unless it is necessary to do so," said the captain, as he turned to go aft again.

"I shall call him when I think proper," muttered Morley. "I am to be my own judge of the necessity."

"You know your duty. I hope you will do it."

"I intend to do it; but I will not be snubbed when I have the deck," replied the lieutenant, angrily, as he walked forward.

The captain watched him, and saw him take his stand by the side of Prescott. He heard him use loud and angry words. As the officer of the watch, Morley had the right to leave his station, but not to be absent from it more than a few moments at a time. Wainwright waited a reasonable time, and then went forward.

"Mr. Morley, you will return to your station," said he.

"I have a perfect right to be here," growled Morley.

"No, you have not. I hope you will not make trouble."

"I shall stay where I please."

"Once more, I ask you to return to your station."

"I consider this an unreasonable interference on your part with my duty, Captain Wainwright," answered the lieutenant, trembling with rage. "You staid on deck on purpose to watch me, and find a chance to make a row with me."

"I have nothing to say until you obey my order," said the captain,

"I am here in the discharge of my duty, and I intend to stay here," added Morley.

"Then I suspend you from duty, and order you to report to the vice-principal," continued the captain, firmly.

"Shall I report to him to-night?" demanded Morley, in a sneering tone.

"As you please. But you will leave the deck at once," replied Wainwright, as he went aft, and took the station of the officer of the deck.

"I shall leave when I get ready," added Morley.

"There will be a tremendous row about this," said Prescott.

"That's just what I want."

"But you are suspended."

"No matter for that ; I shall be restored in the morning, as I was before."

"After an apology."

"No apology this time."

"But the vice-principal cannot restore you after what you have done."

"You see if he don't."

"I don't see how he can, if we are to have any discipline."

"Discipline! Do you think the captain ought to stay on deck all night to watch an officer against whom he has a grudge, to make a row with him?"

"He has a right to stay on deck all night if he chooses to do so."

"But not to watch me."

"Mr. Morley, I ordered you to leave the deck, and you remain here talking with an officer of the watch, and preventing him from doing his duty," said Wainwright, going forward again. "Do you intend to leave the deck, or not?"

"When I get ready, I do," replied Morley, in the most insolent tones.

"Mr. Rimmer!" called the captain, sharply.

"Here, sir!" replied the burly carpenter, hastening to the waist.

"Mr. Morley refuses to obey orders, and I have suspended him. He refuses to leave the deck at my order. You will commit him to the brig," said the captain.

"The brig!" gasped Morley, as he rushed towards the quarter-deck.

But the carpenter seized him before he had taken ten steps, and brought him back. He held his prisoner by the collar with a grip of iron. Mr. Rimmer understood the case perfectly, for he had seen everything that transpired since the quarter watch came on duty.

He knew that both the officers of the watch had grossly neglected their duty, and he was entirely willing to obey the orders of the captain ; and being a strict disciplinarian himself, he was inclined to shake the culprit till his bones rattled in his skin.

" Do as I told you, Mr. Rimmer," added the captain. " Lock the door, and give the key to Mr. Marline when he comes on deck."

Morley began to feel that he had gone a little too far. The idea of being committed to the brig — which is the ship's prison, — had never occurred to him. He was decidedly unwilling to have the seamen in the steerage looking at him through the bars of his cage in the morning.

" I will go below, Captain Wainwright, if you will let me," said he, in an altered tone.

" Though I should be fully justified in committing you, after your mutinous conduct, I will be no harsher than the occasion requires," replied the captain. " Release him, Mr. Rimmer, but see that he goes below."

The carpenter followed him to the companionway, and waited till he had disappeared in the cabin. Morley went to the door of Mr. Tompion's cabin. He opened it, and heard the heavy snoring of the drunken man, as he slept off the fumes of the liquor. It was of no use to report to him while he was in that situation, and Morley seated himself at the table to think it over. He was confident that the vice-principal would restore him to his rank as soon as he reported to him; for how could he do otherwise?

" That's an uncommon bad officer," said the carpenter, as he paused by the captain.

"I hope you have noticed particularly all that has occurred in this watch, Mr. Rimmer."

" O, I have ! And I think you have been uncommon tender with him.   Both the officers neglected their duty."

" I only want the truth to come out," added Wainwright.

" All the young gentlemen must see that you have done just right," said the carpenter, as he returned to his station on the forecastle.

Wainwright sacrificed his dignity as captain of the Tritonia, and took the place of the refractory officer until four bells, when the watch was changed, and Allyn and Walker had the deck.   The former was very much surprised to find the captain at the compass, but no explanations were made till morning.   Wainwright was very tired and sleepy, for it was now two o'clock ; but he decided to observe in what manner the officers did their duty before he went below.   Before he could settle this question, the fog lifted, and it was plain sailing again.   He went below then, turned in, and was soon sound asleep.

At four o'clock, the midshipman of the watch, who had come below to call the relieving officers, knocked at his door.

" Come in," replied the captain, who, weary as he was, heard the knock at his door.

" Land on the weather bow, with a light ship near it, sir," reported Walker.

" It is the light-ship south-east of Anholt Island," added the captain.   " How does it bear ?"

" About one point on the weather bow."

" Have you called Mr. Scott?"

" Yes, sir."

" Send him to me."

The midshipman retired, and Scott presented himself in a moment. The captain told him to keep the light-ship on the port bow, and give it a berth of about a mile. The first lieutenant went on deck, and Wainwright, satisfied that the duty on deck would be faithfully performed, turned over and went to sleep again. The island was passed, and the Tritonia still held on her course, with a steady wind from the westward, making about five knots an hour.

Neither the captain nor the vice-principal had appeared at seven bells, which was breakfast time in the cabin. Both were called by the steward, in accordance with a standing order. Wainwright was the first to appear. Morley was eating his breakfast, apparently in the best of spirits. The captain seated himself at the head of the table, and presently Mr. Tompion came out of his state-room, and took the place at the opposite end. He looked pale and haggard, and evidently had no appetite for the morning meal, for he only drank a cup of coffee. As he rose from his seat, Morley rose also, and approached him.

" I was suspended from duty during my watch this morning, and ordered to report to you, Mr. Tompion," said the refractory officer, saluting the vice-principal with the utmost deference.

" Again?" exclaimed Mr. Tompion, with a start of astonishment, the effect of which was heightened by his unsteady nerves after his debauch.

" Yes, sir."

" State the circumstances."

" It was foggy last night, as you are aware, sir." The vice-principal was not aware of it, for everything that occurred after nine o'clock the evening before was an utter blank to him. " The captain remained on deck all night, on purpose to find fault with me, as I have reason to believe. I went forward to speak to the midshipman on duty with me, and for this I was suspended."

" You will report to the captain for duty," said Mr. Tompion, without asking any more questions.

" Thank you, sir," added Morley, as the vice-principal hastened into his state-room, perhaps afraid that some one might observe his shaking hands, and other evidences of his tippling.

Wainwright had left the cabin and gone on deck. It wanted but a few minutes of eight o'clock when the quarter watch, in charge of Morley, would take the deck. As the second lieutenant was under suspension, he was thinking who should be appointed as his substitute, for it was not practicable to change the officers of the watch. He had decided to place Prescott in Morley's place, and appoint the petty officer highest in rank in Prescott's position. He was about to issue an order to this effect to the executive officer, when Morley presented himself, with a rather extravagant salute.

" I reported to the vice-principal that I had been suspended, and am directed by him to report to you for duty," said the refractory lieutenant, with something like a chuckle accompanying his words.

" Very well, Mr. Morley; you will report to the

first lieutenant for duty," replied Captain Wainwright, promptly.

Morley touched his cap, and with another of his exaggerated bows, walked over to Scott, to whom he reported in the same manner. The first lieutenant simply ordered him to take his watch when it was called.

Wainwright was astonished and confounded at the action of the vice-principal, whose authority in the absence of the principal was absolute. He yielded without a protest to the power above him; but he was confounded and indignant none the less. By this time the fact that Morley had been suspended, and that he had even been ordered to be committed to the brig, was known to all the officers. The exciting events of the mid watch had been considered and debated by the partisans on each side. The quartermaster at the wheel struck eight bells, and to the astonishment of the seamen, Morley took his place as the officer of the deck. Wainwright immediately went below, and entered his state-room. He wanted to consult with Scott; but all the starboard watch had gone to the steerage to attend to their studies. After the excitement of the moment had subsided, he went to the vice-principal's door, and knocked.

" Come in," replied Mr. Tompion.

Wainwright entered the room. The vice-principal was lying in his berth, with his clothes on. He glanced at the captain, and then partially covered his face with his handkerchief.

" Captain Wainwright," said he.

" Yes, sir. Did Mr. Morley report to you that he had been suspended?"

"He did. I inquired into the case, and directed him to report for duty."

"I thought there must be some mistake, sir," added the captain, puzzled at the prompt but strange answer of the vice-principal. "I expected to be called upon to state the circumstances."

"Mr. Morley did that. It is very evident, Captain Wainwright, that you have a grudge against the second lieutenant. You staid on deck all night to watch him, and when he left his station to speak to the midshipman, you suspended him."

If Wainwright was confounded before, he was overwhelmed now.

"I did not suspend Mr. Morley for going forward, but for gross neglect of duty," said he, hardly able to control his indignation. "I did not stay on deck to watch him, but to see that the vessel was properly handled in the fog. I have no grudge against Mr. Morley, but he has a grudge against me. If I had not been on deck, and taken command, there would have been a collision, for he not only left his station for an unreasonably long time, but he was talking with the midshipman of the watch, so that neither officer was giving any attention to the vessel. More than this, he was insolent and mutinous. He refused to obey my order."

"Possibly I have decided the matter too hastily; but I am sick, very sick, this morning," replied Mr. Tompion, in a whining and impatient tone. "You are too stiff and overbearing. It is not courteous to take the vessel out of the hands of the officer of the deck. You make a great thing out of mere technical neglect of forms. I have sailed with Mr. Morley several months, and know him to be a good officer, and I insist that you cease to quarrel with him. But I am too ill to talk about the matter any more. I have settled it, and it must rest as it is. You will please inform Professor Primback that I shall be unable to attend to the classes in navigation to-day."

Mr. Tompion turned over in his berth, and evidently intended that nothing more should be said on the subject. Wainwright withdrew, therefore, with the feeling that discipline in the Tritonia had suddenly come to an end. He went into the steerage, and delivered the vice-principal's message. The class in navigation was excused till nine o'clock, and Scott was therefore relieved till that time from his studies. The captain invited him to his state-room, where they had a long and serious conference. Wainwright minutely detailed the events which had led to the suspension of Morley.

"It's a plain case," said Scott; "and I'm sorry you reversed your order to commit him to the brig."

" If I had committed him I should have been obliged to report the fact immediately to the vice-principal," added the captain.

" It would have brought the matter to a head at once, and you might have got in the evidence of the carpenter."

" Mr. Tompion decided against me without any hearing from me, and of course Morley did not state all the facts."

" No, nor half of them."

" I think I did no more than my duty."

" Certainly not ; and if Mr. Lowington had settled

the case, he would at least have degraded Morley from his rank."

"What can I do about it?" asked Wainwright, anxiously.

"Nothing at all, till we get to Cowes, where you can appeal to the principal."

"I don't like to do that. I have no doubt Morley will insult me the first chance he gets. I didn't say a word this morning till we were almost in collision with that schooner; then I ordered the helmsman to keep away. But after this Morley went forward again; and then the row came."

"I can't understand the action of Mr. Tompion."

"I could, prove all I said to him by the carpenter and others on deck at the time; but he told me I was too stiff and overbearing. It is plain enough that Morley is a favorite of the vice-principal, or he would not have decided against me without hearing a word on my side."

"He would have decided in the same way before," added Scott. "It is clear enough that we are not to have fair play in the Tritonia."

"I'm afraid not; and I wish I was out of her," continued the captain. "I have nothing against Morley, and am willing to treat him as well as I know how, though he has tried to injure me. If he will simply do his duty, he will have no trouble with me."

The interview closed when it was time for Scott to attend to his school duties in the steerage. Wainwright went on deck. The ship was not in sight, and had not been seen since the fog lifted.

"Mr. Morley, you will furl the top-gallant sail, and the gaff-topsail," said the captain.

" The top-gallant sail and the gaff-topsail," repeated Morley, touching his cap.

His manner was respectful, and the order was promptly obeyed. Perhaps Morley was satisfied with the victory he had won, and he behaved himself tolerably well for the next week.

The captain had shortened sail in the belief that the Tritonia had gained on the ship; but as she did not appear when the Skaw, which is the northern point of Denmark, was doubled, he concluded that she had outsailed him, and the course for the Strait of Dover was laid. The weather was foggy and variable, and five days from the Skaw, the Tritonia arrived at Cowes; but the ship was not there, and did not put in an appearance for the next thirty hours.

7

CHAPTER VI.

THE COLLISION AND THE FOG.

"DON'T give up the ship " is one of the watch-words of the navy ; and while we treat in whole or in part of nautical subjects, we desire to follow the traditions which gain favor on shipboard.   In other words, we do not mean to give up the Young America. . The Tritonia followed her till she was lost sight of in the dense fog.   She was well officered and well manned, and her crew worked well together. Captain Cantwell was the highest juvenile dignitary on board, — if we may be allowed to call a young gentleman of seventeen, as tall and manly as he, who held his head high, and wore unexceptionable eye-glasses, — if we may be allowed to call such a one a juvenile.   He was now quite popular on board, but some of his fellow-students could not entirely forget the conceited and disagreeable traits he had formerly manifested, though he had now entirely changed his manner.   He was affable and gentlemanly, for he had been taught to realize his dependence upon others.

The ship ran into the dense fog, as the Tritonia had done.   Extra lookout men had been stationed on the fore-yard, and the great bell on the forecastle was frequently sounded. The captain was as anxious and troubled as Wainwright was in the schooner. Though Mr. Lowington, the principal, was on deck, closely watching the discipline of the vessel, he said nothing, and did not interfere, even with a suggestion. It was not necessary for him to do so, for the routine of precautions for such an occasion was so thoroughly understood that every officer performed his duty almost without prompting. But the ship was not so fortunate as the Tritonia had been, in spite of the efforts to avoid collision.

"Fog-horn, dead ahead!" shouted the lookout.

The cry was repeated by the officers at their stations. The principal suddenly halted in his walk, ready on the instant to interpose if any mistake was made.

"Port the helm!" said Captain Cantwell, instantly.

"Port, sir!" repeated the quarter-master at the wheel.

The ship stood off in prompt obedience to her helm; but in an instant more the dark form of a schooner appeared in the thick gloom. It was evident then that the stranger had not observed the "rule of the road," and kept her course, being on the starboard tack, but had put her helm to starboard when the sound of the ship's bell was heard.

"There she is, dead ahead!" yelled the lookout on the top-gallant forecastle.

"Hard a starboard the helm!" shouted Captain Cantwell.

"Hard a starboard!" repeated the quarter-master.

But it was too late, and the next instant there was the snapping of one or more spars, and a hard bump.

The ship came up into the wind, with everything aback, and the schooner slid off to windward of her.

" Port the helm," added the captain, as the schooner went clear of the ship.

The Young America had not entirely lost her steerage way, and filled away again in obëdience to her helm.   The stranger had also come up into the wind when the ship was discovered ; but as she did so, her jib-boom came against the cutwater of the larger vessel, and was carried away.   Then followed the bump, as the sea threw the port bow of the schooner against the ship.   As both vessels came up into the wind, the sails of the smaller flapped amidships, and she did not foul the rigging of the larger.

" Mr. Brown," called the captain to the third lieutenant, who happened to be on deck, though it was not his watch.

" Here, sir."

" You will direct the carpenter to sound the well ; take hands, and visit the hold, to ascertain if the ship has sustained any damage in her hull."

" Yes, sir. — Pass the word for Mr. Bitts," replied the third lieutenant ; and calling three hands from the idlers on deck, — for most of the crew had come up from the steerage during the commotion, — he hastened below.

In the mean time fearful yells came from the schooner, which had now disappeared in the dense fog.

" Call all hands, Mr. Sheridan," said the captain.

" Boatswain, call all hands," added the first lieutenant ; and in a moment every officer and seaman was in his place.

"First cutters clear away their boat," continued the captain, and the executive officer gave the order to the boatswain.

The well-trained crew of the first cutter sprang to their duty, excited by the prospect of an adventure. The coxswain was directed to light up the boat compass, and in a moment the cutter was ready to be lowered into the sea.

"Haul up the courses!" said the captain. "Put the helm down, and brace aback the main-topsail."

The ship came up into the wind, and her main-topsail went back against the mast, which immediately checked her headway.

"Mr. Murray, you will go in the first cutter, and give the schooner whatever assistance she may require," added Captain Cantwell. "Take a lantern with you, and mind your courses. The schooner is about south-west of us."

"Let Mr. Peaks go in the boat also," said the principal; and the adult boatswain took his place in the stern-sheets with Murray, who was the second lieutenant.

"Lower away!" shouted Sheridan, when the headway of the ship was sufficiently checked to render it safe to lower the cutter.

When it touched the water, the coxswain and bowman cast off the falls.

"Up oars! Shove off! Let fall! Give way together," called the coxswain in the darkness; and the cutter sped off into the gloom and the fog.

"You have done very well, Captain Cantwell. I entirely approve all your action," said the principal, by whose side Cantwell stood.

"Thank you, sir," replied the captain, touching his cap, and perhaps blushing under the compliment.

One of the chapters in the text-book on seamanship was "Emergencies;" and all sorts of impending disasters and calamities had been considered by the students. The very problem of two vessels approaching each other in a fog, with the wind on the beam of both, had been given out, adding to it the contingency of the stranger putting her helm the wrong way. The principal had "laid down the law" for such a case, and it had been considered in all possible ways. The judgment of the young officers had therefore been fully exercised, and they were prepared to meet just such emergencies as the one which had been presented on this occasion. The brains of all of them had been racked over ships in peril on a lee shore, in sudden squalls, in heavy gales with high seas, and in every kind of danger to which a vessel may be subjected. Cantwell was a diligent student, and he had faithfully considered all the problems of this kind suggested by the instructor in navigation, or to be obtained from books. His study bore its legitimate fruits, and the hearty approval of the principal was an all-sufficient reward for the thought and investigation he had bestowed upon the subject.

The first cutter was absent more than an hour, and Captain Cantwell feared the boat was unable to find the ship, though the fog signals were continually repeated on board. The two brass twelve-pounders, used only on the Fourth of July and for signaling purposes, when the ordinary means were not available, were prepared for use; but the boat appeared before they were fired. Murray ran up the accommodation ladder, while the cutter drew off to keep from chafing against the ship's side.

"On board, sir," reported Murray, touching his cap to Cantwell.

"What is the condition of the schooner?" asked the captain, the principal standing at his side.

"She carried away her jib-boom and stove her bulwarks; otherwise she is not much injured; but we have lost two of our boat's crew, sir," added Murray, whose tones betrayed his emotion.

"Lost them?" exclaimed Mr. Lowington.

"I don't mean that any harm has come to them," answered Murray, thus removing the heavy burden from the mind of the principal and the captain.

"What do you mean, then?" demanded Mr. Lowington.

"The people on board the schooner were frightened, and thought she was going to the bottom. We could not understand them; but we examined the bows of the vessel. Her bulwarks were stove, but she was sound below the plank-shear. The jib-boom was dragging overboard, and the crew were getting the boat into the water, intending to abandon her. We boarded her, and, with Mr. Peaks, cleared away the wreck forward. One of the men spoke a little English, and we told him the vessel was all right. We went below with the captain, and convinced him that she was not stove. She was loaded with dressed stone, and the man said they were afraid she would go down before they could get out of her. The captain was more than half drunk."

"That explains his stupidity in putting his helm to starboard. But you don't tell us how you lost your two hands," said the principal.

"I was coming to that, sir. After we had cleared away the wreck of the jib-boom and the bulwarks, Mr. Peaks took the helm, and filled her away, to convince the captain that she was all right. He laughed, offered us some brandy, and then wanted to take the tiller himself. Mr. Peaks threw her up into the wind, and we piped into our boat again. The captain filled away before we could cast off our painter; but the man who spoke English did so for us. Then we found that two of our crew were missing."

"Who were they?" asked Mr. Lowington.

"De Forrest and Beckwith."

"That explains it all," added the principal, for these were the two degraded officers, who had run away once before, and had attempted to do so again.

"Before we could get under way, the schooner disappeared in the fog. We pulled in the direction we supposed she was headed, but were unable to overhaul her, though Mr. Peaks and the coxswain pulled the two spare oars, and I steered the boat. I don't know whether the vessel changed her course or outsailed us."

"It makes little difference," added the principal. "You have done all you could."

"Mr. Peaks said, if we went any farther, we should lose the ship; and then we returned."

"Nothing can be done in this fog, Captain Cantwell," said the principal. "I have no doubt the runaways are safe, and that is the principal thing."

The captain gave the order for the cutter's crew to

come on board, and for the boat to be hoisted up to the davits. Peaks was satisfied that De Forrest and Beckwith had concealed themselves in the hold or cabin of the schooner, for he was sure they were not on deck when the crew returned to the boat. Mr. Lowington directed that the ship should continue on her course, and she immediately filled away again.

The carpenter had reported that there was not water enough in the well to indicate a leak, and not a plank was started in the bow or sides of the ship. The delay caused by the accident had occasioned the parting of the Young America and the Tritonia ; for the latter, unable to see the ship, had outsailed her before the collision. Then Mr. Lowington decided to run into the harbor of Gottenburg, which was thirty miles off her course. The ship arrived there the next morning, and the principal telegraphed to his banker in Copenhagen, requesting him to procure the arrest of the runaways, or, failing in this, to employ a suitable person to follow and capture them, and to write to him the result at Cowes. When this business was done, the ship went to sea again. In the fog and the variable weather of the North Sea, she made a long passage to Cowes ; and thirty hours after the arrival of the Tritonia, she had not been seen or heard from, as we have before related.

Our readers may think that Beckwith and De Forrest were " smart ; " and so they were in a very unworthy sense, if this peculiarly American adjective ever has any other sense. As detailed in a former volume, these young gentlemen, the victims of disappointed ambition, were utterly dissatisfied with their situation on board of the ship. Their application for a transfer to the Tritonia had been refused for obvious reasons, and the special duty of watching them had been assigned to Peaks. The old " sea dog " had faithfully discharged this duty, and under ordinary circumstances the scheme of running away was hopeless. But the discontented seamen were continually on the lookout for their opportunity. Beckwith had a considerable sum of money, and De Forrest, besides his funds, was provided with a letter of credit. Both of them kept their sinews of travel as well as of war always upon their persons, in order to be ready at all times to take advantage of any event which might favor their escape.

Under the new organization of the ship, they belonged to the crew of the first cutter. They were politic enough to be active and zealous in the discharge of their ship's duty, and on board of the damaged schooner they had been among the foremost to render assistance. With several others, they had followed Peaks into the hold to ascertain if the bow was stove in.

" Now's our time," whispered De Forrest, as the big boatswain and the rest of the crew returned to the deck.

" Right; I'm with you," replied Beckwith.

" Follow me," added De Forrest; and they crawled upon the top of the blocks of stone which lay in the bottom of the hold as far as they could get from the hatchway.

Then each for himself wormed his body into some apertures between the stones, and finally into the spaces under the blocks, and between the skids on which they were laid. The boatswain would be as likely to suppose that they had fallen overboard, as that they had hidden in such narrow spaces. Possibly he would have found the runaways, if the drunken captain had not prevented the crew from going into their boat in ship-shape order, by filling away before they had cast off the painter. Peaks was mortified when he discovered who were missing, and had done all it was prudent to do to recover his charge.

The schooner heeled over, and the runaways heard the noise of the dashing waters at the side of the vessel. The stones above them caused the vessel and the dunnage to creak and groan, and their situation was very uncomfortable. The hatches were on, and there was a terrible odor of bilge-water in the hold. Miserable as they were, not only from the actual discomfort of their confined position, but from the fear that the stone would shift and crush them, they did not move for half an hour. Then De Forrest crawled out, not without much difficulty.

"We are safe enough now, Beck; the boat has gone back to the ship by this time," said he.

"I can't get out," groaned Beckwith.

"What's the reason you can't?"

"I'm wedged in so tight I can't move."

"Well, work yourself out, as I did."

"I can't," answered Beckwith, in tones which indicated that he was in actual pain.

"Where are you?"

"Here," replied the sufferer.

The gloom was as deep and dense as that of Erebus itself; but De Forrest groped his way to the assistance of his friend, guided by the sound of his voice, which, however, seemed to come from the solid blocks of stone beneath him. He felt for an opening, but found none, near the spot from which the sound came. Farther along towards the leeward side of the vessel, he discovered an open space. Reaching down into the interstice, he placed his hand upon one foot of his companion, who was lying on his stomach between the skids. He tried to pull him out by sheer force, but could not.

"I shall die in here," cried Beckwith.

"Don't be alarmed," answered De Forrest, though he was frightened himself.

"Call the crew, and get me out. I am suffocating."

Just at that moment the hoarse bray of the fog-horn was heard, followed by sharp shouting on deck. The vessel suddenly came up to an even keel, as though the helm had been put down to throw her head up into the wind. De Forrest heard a struggle beneath him, and in another instant Beckwith had extricated himself from his uncomfortable and dangerous position. He stood up, and seized hold of his friend, panting with terror and from the effects of the pressure upon his body.

"What's the matter?" asked De Forrest.

It was some time before the sufferer could find breath to answer; and while he was trying to do so, the schooner filled away again, heeling over as before.

"How could you get into a space so tight as to crush you?" said De Forrest.

"I don't know," gasped Beckwith; "but the moment the vessel heeled over, the stones above me began to bear heavily upon my back, and I thought they would crush the breath out of me. The moment she righted, the pressure was removed, and I crawled out quick."

"I see how it was: when the vessel heeled over, it threw more weight on the lee side, which pressed the skids down on the boards below. This is an old tub, and her timbers and skin are probably rickety. Do you feel better?"

"Much better now. I wouldn't try that over again for a thousand dollars; or a hundred thousand, for that matter."

"Why didn't you sing out?"

"I did — a dozen times."

"I didn't hear you till I crawled out myself. Well, you are out of the scrape now."

"I am, but I wished myself back in the ship fifty times, while I lay there crushed under the rocks."

"Never mind it. We are both out of trouble now, and out of the ship. I don't mean to be caught again."

"You didn't mean to be caught before," suggested Beckwith.

"We were careless then."

"We were! You mean that you were; for I was not in favor of wearing our uniform, and tagging after that girl who fascinated you. I wasn't smitten, and I didn't believe in venturing into the lion's den. The amount of it is, De Forrest, you want to be a leader always, and never a follower. I have an opinion sometimes, as I had in that scrape, but you overruled me."

"Well, I think I found the brains for that enterprise," said De Forrest, complacently.

"I know you did, and we were captured by the police on the Volga, and by the principal of the Academy Squadron in Prussia. It was a disastrous enterprise."

"But we had a good time."

"You did, for you were smitten with Miss Gurney. I did not, and I felt all the time that we were running into hot water," protested Beckwith. "I want you to understand, in the beginning, that I mean to have something to say about our future movements."

"Of course I am willing to hear all you have to say," added De Forrest.

"Something more than that, for I don't mean to be dragged where I don't want to go, this time."

"All right, Beck; we shall not quarrel about this matter." But whatever De Forrest said, his vanity led him to believe that he was born for a leader, and he expected to control the will of his friend.

"I don't think the case looks entirely hopeful yet," continued Beckwith. "Here we are shut up in the hold of this vessel, and we don't even know where she is bound."

"I have no doubt she is going to Copenhagen; but I don't know that I care where she is bound."

"But what shall we do?"

"O, I'll manage it all right."

"Perhaps you will; but I would rather know beforehand what you intend to do."

"I think we had better stay where we are till morning. We can sleep for the rest of the night on the soft side of one of these rocks. In the morning we will make peace with the captain of the vessel, and ask him to land us at some place in Denmark or Sweden."

Beckwith, happy in the comfort of his present condition as compared with his situation under the stone, did not object to this course, and the runaways passed away the rest of the night in the hold, though neither of them obtained much sleep.   The hours hung heavily upon them, but at last the schooner came to anchor in still water.   De Forrest groped his way to the hatches, guided by a single gleam of light.   He could not open them, though he and his companion exerted their utmost strength.   But there was another ray of light forward, which might come through the fore-scuttle, and they felt their way to this part of the hold.   The supposition proved to be correct, and the scuttle was not fastened.   De Forrest easily raised it, and leaped upon the deck, followed by his friend.

It was daylight, but the sky was clouded over.   De Forrest looked at his watch, and found it was half past five o'clock.   None of the crew of the vessel were on deck, and the quarters of all hands were in the cabin. The runaways seated themselves on the heel of the bowsprit to consider the situation.   The schooner had anchored off the Castle of Elsinore, the wind being light and contrary.   There was no sign of life on board, and the runaways concluded that the captain and crew had turned in and gone to sleep.   The dip of a pair of oars attracted their attention, and they saw a boat, containing a single man, rowing towards the shore. They beckoned to him, and he promptly came alongside.   De Forrest spoke to the boatman in English, but the latter shook his head.   He then pointed to the shore, and exhibited a silver coin.   The man understood this language, especially the idea conveyed by the silver, and the runaways stepped into his boat. The noble Dane pulled for the shore, to which De Forrest pointed and they left the stone vessel, without a suspicion on the part of her captain and crew that she had brought two passengers about forty miles of her voyage.

When the boatman landed his fare, De Forrest gave him a German half thaler piece, which the man evidently regarded as a magnificent reward, for he was profuse in his bows and acknowledgments.

"Now let us go to a hotel and get some breakfast," said De Forrest.

"No, sir!" replied Beckwith, decidedly. "I don't go to any hotel till I get rid of this uniform. Let us walk off on the beach, and keep out of sight."

Beckwith walked in the direction indicated by himself, and his companion followed him. They soon reached a lonely place, where they endeavored to clean the dirt from their clothes, for after their experience in the hold of the stone vessel they were in a sorry plight. With grass and water, they removed the worst of the dirt from their garments, and were in a more presentable condition. They had been in Elsinore before, and knew its localities well enough to find the way to the railroad station, to which they directed their steps. The train left for Copenhagen at seven, and they were just in season for it. The money of both the boys was napoleons, which are current in every part of Europe. Taking third-class tickets, they received Danish money for change, each buying his own ticket, in order to obtain more of it. At nine o'clock they reached their destination, and hastened to a clothing store, where each purchased a new suit, without much regard to the fit or the style of the garments. The shop-keeper spoke English fluently, and cared for nothing but to sell his goods. He went with them, as interpreter, to a neighboring store, where the runaways purchased hats, and their rig was complete.

De Forrest requested the man to do up their sea-clothes in one bundle, and to keep them till they called or sent for them. The name of "John Walker" was inscribed on the package, and the customers departed, satisfied with themselves and with the merchant. Returning to the railroad station, they had half an hour to wait for the train to Korsœr, which they improved by appeasing the pangs of hunger at the restaurant. At noon they departed in the train.

In the mean time, the police and other agents of Mr. Lowington's banker were overhauling every vessel that arrived, in search of the runaways. But the principal's telegraphic despatch did not reach Copenhagen till after the arrival of the fugitives, and the search was confined to vessels from the north.

8

CHAPTER VII.

DOWN THE DANUBE.

THE usual route from Copenhagen to Hamburg, where De Forrest and Beckwith intended to go, is to Korsœr by rail, then to Kiel by steamer in seven hours, and thence by rail the rest of the way. But the war between France and Germany had closed this important route, for it was understood that the French were fitting out a naval expedition to operate in the Baltic, and the Germans, fearing that Kiel was one of the intended points of attack, had closed the harbor by sinking hulks at its entrance. The other routes opened during the war were by steamer direct to Lübec, or by railroad all the way, except the passage of the Great and Little Belt, by steamer. The latter was the route chosen by De Forrest, but no connections were made between railroad and steamers, or even between the trains in Denmark and Schleswig, and it was two days before they reached their destination.

In Hamburg they breathed more freely, for no pursuit appeared to have been undertaken. The Denmarkers to whom Mr. Lowington had intrusted this duty moved slowly, and accomplished nothing. The police discovered that two young sailors had come into

Copenhagen on the train from Elsinore, but they failed to ascertain when or how they left the city. The change of dress made by the fugitives threw the detectives and other agents entirely off the track, and the banker was obliged to write to the principal, at Cowes, that he could obtain no intelligence of the runaways after their arrival.

"I think we are out of the woods now," said the confident De Forrest, as they seated themselves in their room at Streit's Hotel, in Hamburg.

"I think so myself," replied Beckwith, by far the more prudent of the two. "If we are careful, we shall get along very well."

"We are in no danger whatever now."

"Not if we mind what we are about.   Of course we mustn't say anything about the Academy Ship ; and if you see any girl that knows you, keep out of her sight."

"You needn't keep flinging that at me, Beck," replied De Forrest, pettishly. "It wasn't my fault that we were caught."

"I think it was.   Didn't you insist upon going after that girl?"

"What difference did it make which way we went?"

"A great deal. If we hadn't gone to Königsberg, we shouldn't have been caught.   Then you insisted on wearing the uniforms. You know I was opposed to both things."

"It's no use to talk about them now."

"If we are not wiser and smarter now than we were then, we shall be caught again."

"We have thrown away our uniforms now ; and I don't intend to go near where the ship comes into port," added De Forrest. "If you think you can manage this better than I can, go ahead. We must make up our minds at once what we are going to do."

"There is no hurry. We are as safe here as we shall be anywhere."

"I don't think so. Suppose the Young America should take a notion to come to Hamburg?"

"She can't get in if she does, for they are sinking vessels across the river."

"But they leave a passage through for the steamers."

"No matter if they do. I think we shall be better off away from the sea-coast."

"Well, where shall we go?"

"I don't know. I don't want to manage the affair alone. Two heads are better than one, if mine is a sheep's head," laughed Beckwith. "We will talk over the matter, and do only what we can both agree upon."

"That's sensible," replied De Forrest. "What shall we do, and where shall we go?"

"I think our plans must depend upon the state of our finances. How much money have you, De Forrest?"

"I have my letter of credit for one hundred pounds. I haven't drawn anything on that yet."

Both of them pulled out their purses, and counted the napoleons left in them.

"I have seven napoleons left," said De Forrest.

"I have seventeen," added Beckwith; "and that is all I have. It won't last me over ten days if we travel, and then I shall come to the end of my rope."

"But you wrote to your father to send you a letter of credit — didn't you?"

"I did ; but I asked him to send it to the bankers in Constantinople, and I must go there in order to get it."

"That will be the same thing as going to Königsberg."

"Not at all, for we shall get there long before the ship can arrive. It will take her twenty or thirty days to make the voyage. But I haven't money enough to pay my fare to Constantinople, to say nothing of expenses on the way," replied Beckwith in desponding tones.

"How much will it cost?" asked De Forrest.

"I don't know, but it must be a pile."

"Let's find a Bradshaw and figure it up."

A copy of this valuable work was found in the coffee-room of the hotel, and it was anxiously studied by the young travellers. They ascertained that the fare, second-class, by the cheapest route, would be about three hundred francs. The time occupied by the journey would be five or six days, and the expense of living could not be less than fifty more.

"Three hundred and fifty francs!" exclaimed Beckwith. "That's more than I have."

"That isn't much."

"But it is more than I have ; so it's no use talking."

"I will lend you ten pounds — two hundred and fifty francs," suggested De Forrest.

"I may not be able to pay it again. If my governor don't send me the letter of credit, I shall have to surrender to the principal at discretion."

"Never mind ; I will run my own risk. We will be off for Vienna to-morrow."

"There will be no fun in travelling night and day.

You have money enough ; why should I punish you by dragging you through the country at railroad speed."

"When we come to any place where we wish to stay a day or two, we can do so."

"All right, if you will lend me the money, for I shall be busted by the time we get to Vienna."

"When I say a thing, I always do it, you know, Beck.   Here's my hand ; and as long as I have a franc, you shall have half of it — if you won't say anything more about Königsberg and that girl."

"Not a word," replied Beckwith, heartily, as he took his companion's offered hand.

"I think we understand each other first rate now."

"That's so."

"By the way, Beck, how long is it since you wrote to your father for the letter of credit?" asked De Forrest.

"About a month."

"Where did you write?"

"At Passau."

"Twenty-six days," mused De Forrest. "It is hardly time yet for the letter to be in Constantinople, unless your governor sent the credit by telegraph."

"By telegraph?"

"Certainly ; he could telegraph to Bowles Brothers, London, to give you a credit for a hundred pounds, and direct them to send the letter to you in Constantinople."

"I wrote my father to send it as soon as possible."

"He is a business man, and perhaps he has sent it in this way.   "If he has, the letter is waiting for you. While we were at Passau, the principal sent a telegraphic despatch to Constantinople ; and I heard him say it cost seven francs for ten words to any part of Germany.   If you think it will pay, you can telegraph for your letter to be sent to Vienna.   Then you will be in funds when we reach that place."

" That would be first rate, if I only knew my father had sent the order for a letter of credit by the cable. I wrote him that the ship would not be there till about the first of August," added Beckwith.

" If you wrote him that, it is not worth while to throw away seven francs on a despatch.   I will lend you the ten pounds, and we shall be all right."

" But there will be an end to your hundred pounds, De Forrest.   It is only twenty-five hundred francs."

" I need not use the letter till I get to Vienna.   I know of men who have travelled for six months in Europe on a hundred pounds.   But my father has money enough, and will send me another hundred pounds when I write to him, for I don't believe he has heard yet that I have fallen from grace," laughed De Forrest.   " When I became an officer of the ship, and then went up to third lieutenant, he thought I was cured ; in fact, I thought so myself."

" You were the last fellow in the ship whom I should have expected would ever run away," added Beckwith.

" Things went wrong, you know."

" You made them go wrong, for it was you who suggested the electing of the officers."

" I think we had better change the subject of con-versation," said De Forrest, shrugging his shoulders like a Frenchman.   " By the way, Beck, we haven't any baggage, and it isn't respectable to travel without a bag or a valise."

"What do we want of a bag or valise?   We have nothing to put in it."

"We have our pea-jackets."

They had worn these garments in the boat, and when they left Copenhagen they had carried them on their arms.   Each had purchased a woollen shirt, and now wore it, instead of the one with a broad collar, which formed part of the uniform of the ship.

" Better have a valise, just for the looks of the thing ; and perhaps we had better have one or two boiled shirts, in case any of these kings or dukes should ask us to dine with them.   Besides, we don't look like young American gentlemen, travelling for pleasure. I'm afraid the bankers will look at me twice before they will pay anything on my letter."

"We will take a walk, anyhow, for I want to see something of Hamburg."

They left the hotel, and wandered through the Jung-fernstieg and some of the other principal streets of the city.   They made a short excursion in one of the little steamers that ply on the Alster, and walked over to the Elbe.   On their return to the hotel they pur-chased a couple of cheap travelling bags, and a pair of white shirts each.   By this time they were tired out, for wandering aimlessly about a foreign city is the most fatiguing work one can do.   They slept soundly that night, for it was the first time they had been in a bed since they left the ship.   The next day, when they were ready to depart for Berlin, the bill was called for. It amounted to fourteen *marks* and ten *schillings*, a mark, of sixteen schillings, being about twenty-eight cents.

"That's about two dollars a day," said Beckwith. "I think we can live cheaper than that."

"It is only half what it costs to live in a first-class hotel in New York."

"That may be, but we haven't much money to spare."

"Shall we ride or walk to the station?"

"Walk, of course. I shall not throw away any money on hackmen," said Beckwith, decidedly.

"You talk as though you were as poor as a church mouse, when your father has his pile."

"My father may have his pile, but I haven't it here. We must keep an eye to windward, for we might as well be without heads as without money. Do you know the way to the railroad station?"

"I can find it."

They left the hotel; but as the streets of Hamburg are something like the threads of a cobweb in their arrangement, it was not so easy to find the station. But both of the students had a smattering of German, and if they could not understand the complicated directions given them by their informants, they could go the way pointed out to them. None too soon, they arrived at the station, and bought second-class tickets. This was an ordinary train, requiring three hours and ten minutes longer to make the journey of one hundred and seventy-five miles than the *Courier Zug*, or express; but the fare was ninety cents less. The railroad from Hamburg to Berlin is one of the best in Europe, and even the fast trains move with very little jar or reeling. The carriages are very comfortable, those of the second-class being quite as good as any reasonable American could desire. Near Hamburg the road passes through a region not unlike some portions of Holland, where the low lands are pumped out by windmills.

It was after nine o'clock in the evening when the travellers arrived at Berlin. The great city, and indeed most of the country through which they had journeyed, was alive with the military preparations for the great war with France. Thousands of freight cars stood at the stations, each of which bore a printed label, indicating the number of soldiers or horses to be carried in it, as, "36 *Mann oder* 6 *Pferde.*" As they walked from the station, following the crowd along the Thier-Garten to the Brandenburg Gate, and then through *Unter den Linden*, half the people they met were soldiers. Battalions and companies were marching from every direction towards the Potsdam Gate, near which is the railroad station, from which trains were started almost every hour for the seat of war. Everybody was whistling, singing, and the bands were playing, "*Die Wacht am Rhein.*" There was a tremendous enthusiasm among the people, from König Wilhelm down to the boot-blacks. The runaways enjoyed it, for it was decidedly exciting. They found what looked like a second-class hotel, which proved to be such in every sense of the word. As they had been prisoners on board of the ship while the rest of the students made their tour through Germany, they had not seen Berlin before. The excitement just suited them, and De Forrest even suggested that they should join the Prussian army, and "see the fun;" but Beckwith was cooler, and declared that, if he fought on either side, it would be for the French. He was content to see the show, without risking his head in a battle, or his comfort in a camp. Probably sausage and black bread would not have suited the taste of De Forrest any more than the fashion of the Prussian officers of keeping their men " steady " till all of them were shot down, unless the order sooner came to move.

The runaways remained three days in Berlin, and then left for Leipsig and Dresden, where they staid long enough to see these places, and then went to Vienna. By this time De Forrest had exhausted his funds; but Beckwith had two hundred francs left, or nearly one hundred florins in Austrian money. The former was an ambitious youth, and when his exchequer was exhausted, his self-respect was all gone. He felt like a nobody, and was troubled with a suspicion that the banker would not pay his draft, or that the principal had written to the various bankers, requesting them not to pay him. He hinted his fears to his companion.

" We shall be in a fix if the banker won't pay you," replied Beckwith, appalled at the suggestion. " What money I have won't last us a week, and we can't get out of the country without means. Does Lowington know that you have a letter of credit? "

" I don't think he does, but he may. He knows a great many things he ought not to know."

" That's so. He must understand that we can't get along without money. But then he will never suspect that we have come as far as Vienna. We will go to the banker's, and try it on, at any rate. Who is he? "

" Anglo-Oesterreichische Bank."

" Where is that ? "

" I haven't the least idea."

The porter of the Hotel National, where they lodged, gave them the location of the bank, and advised them to take an omnibus. After much inquiry, they found the bank, and De Forrest presented his letter of credit. He labored to look unconcerned, and to seem entirely at home, though he feared every moment that he might be captured by some Austrian police officer.

" How much do you want ? " asked the clerk, hardly glancing at the applicant.

" Twenty pounds," replied De Forrest, promptly.

" In paper or gold ? "

" Paper," added the applicant.

The letter of credit was carried into another room by the clerk, who presently returned with it, bringing the " *bordereau*," which is a memorandum of the rate of exchange, commissions, and the amount to be paid the drawer. He had also a draft on London, which De Forrest was required to sign. The money was paid to him, and the sum indorsed upon his letter. No officer appeared, and no one seemed to take any particular notice of him.

" That's all right," said De Forrest, exultingly, as he put the money in his pocket.

" I didn't expect any trouble here," added Beckwith.

They returned to the hotel entirely satisfied with the result, and proceeded to make their financial calculations for the voyage down the Danube.

" Now I have two hundred and forty-eight florins

and seventy-five kreutzers for my twenty pounds," said De Forrest, as he examined the *bordereau*, and counted the money.

"And I have a hundred florins."

"With what change I had left, we have three hundred and fifty florins.   Now let us go and get our tickets for Constantinople."

Directed by the porter again, — and the situation of this functionary is not a sinecure in foreign hotels, — the boys found the office of Danube steamers, in the *Hoher Markt*.   The agent did not speak English, but he answered De Forrest in French; and as Beckwith spoke this language better than his companion, he did the talking in the beginning, though De Forrest varied it with German.   The man handed them a couple of circulars in French, and pointed out the price of passage from Vienna to Constantinople.   It was one hundred and twenty-one florins, eight kreutzers, first class, and eighty-five florins and fifty kreutzers, second class.

"We must go first class in the steamers," said De Forrest.

"I don't think so; there is thirty-six florins difference between the first and the second class," replied Beckwith.

"But we shall be shoved into the forecastle with all sorts of people."

They argued the matter for some time, and the agent doubtless wondered what they were talking about, for he occasionally volunteered a remark, in French or German, which was quite irrelevant.   At last Beckwith yielded the point.

"*Deux billets, premiere classe*," said Beckwith. "*Combien pour les deux?*"

The man figured for a moment, and then replied, —
"*Trois-cent-sept florins, et vingt-quatre kreutzers.*"
"*Wie viel?*" asked De Forrest.

"*Drei hundert und sieben gulden, vier und zwanzig kreutzer,*" repeated the agent, at the same time writing the number on the paper — *f* 307.24.

"*Nein; das ist zu viel*" (no; that is too much), protested De Forrest, as he pointed to the tariff in the circular. "*Zwei plätze*" (two places).

"*In silber,*" explained the man, pointing to a line in the circular. "*Ces prix s'entendent en florins d'Autriche en argent*" (these prices are understood to be in Austrian florins, in silver.)

"It is all right; but this takes nearly sixty-four florins more out of us. Silver is about twenty per cent. premium," added Beckwith. "Don't you think we had better go second class?"

"No, I don't. I won't mix up with dirty Turks and other heathen."

The price was paid, and the tickets obtained. It included meals on the steamers of the Danube and the Black Sea, and the traveller had the option of going by rail or boat as far as Basiasch, a distance of four hundred and nineteen miles. The steamers left Vienna on Sunday and Wednesday mornings at half past six, and their passengers arrived in Constantinople at noon on the fourth day after. Those who leave by train on Saturday afternoon, at two o'clock, reach their destination on Tuesday at noon.

On Saturday evening our travellers left the hotel in a droschky, and rode to the river, which is several miles distant, rather than be turned out so early in the morning. Small steamers leave the Weissgärber, one of the quays of the Danube Canal, and convey passengers to the large boats on the river at Kaisermühlen. The boys found the steamer on the river to be an entirely different affair from what they had expected. She had a dining-saloon on deck; but the cabin below had no berths, only sofas to sleep upon, with no covering, though the night was quite chilly. They passed a cold and cheerless evening. Their only fellow-passenger was a Greek professor, who spoke French, but no other language save his own. He was cold and lonely, and therefore insisted upon talking. Poor Beckwith struggled, and labored, and blundered in his efforts to be sociable; but the professor was as polite as he was lonely, and refused to be disgusted with the lingual deficiencies of his fellow-voyager.

Early in the morning the steamer left the wharf, ran a short distance up the river, and made fast to a tree on an island. The current of the Danube is very swift, running from five to seven miles an hour. By this time there were some signs of life in the after part of the boat, which had appeared to be deserted by everybody except the three passengers. A couple of waiters brought coffee and little biscuits into the cabin, of which the lonely passengers partook. The professor paid for his coffee, and the waiter politely hinted to De Forrest that a similar proceeding on his part would be agreeable, but our travellers produced their tickets; whereat the " kellner " opened his eyes very wide, bowed very low, and his whole manner, being interpreted, seemed to say, " Is it possible that a young fellow like you is going all the way to Constantinople? "

From that moment the waiters were all attention, and it was evidently a big thing to be a " through passenger " on that line.

About seven o'clock the little steamer from the city arrived, crowded with people, who hurried on board, very much like Americans, as though they feared to be cheated out of some comfort or advantage by being an instant too late. The little steamer attracted the attention of our sailors, for she was a long, narrow thing, utterly unlike any other craft that ever floated. She was low in the water, with her cabins all on deck. She looked more like a plaything than a serviceable craft, as doubtless she was. The fasts were cast off, and the larger steamer — not very large at that — started on her voyage down the river. The Danube near Vienna is full of islands, so that the course was through narrow channels, between sand-bars and low bluffs covered with willows. There is nothing picturesque in the scenery. The water runs so swiftly that it is always discolored by the soil. It certainly is not the " blue Danube " below Vienna, whatever it may be above.

The runaways were not intelligent travellers, and they identified only Presburg and Komorn of the numerous towns on the banks of the river, and were more interested in the bridges of boats at these places than in the historic legends connected with these localities. There was no attraction in the river's banks below Presburg, for the country is flat, and subject to inundations. At half past ten a waiter called our travellers from the hurricane deck, and bowed them into the saloon, where their breakfast was served in several courses, with two bottles of Hungarian wine, of which they partook to such an extent that things around them were rather confused for a time. Dinner was served in the same style; and the wine made them so sleepy that they took to their couches in the lower cabin, and knew nothing more till the steamer arrived at Pesth, at eight o'clock in the evening. At this city the through passengers are transferred to a larger steamer; and De Forrest and Beckwith were conducted by an attentive waiter to their new quarters; but they were too sleepy and stupid to notice the contrast between her and the boat they had just left. In the cabin the beds were large, and made up with the whitest of linen. They were placed "athwartships," the upper ones slung by a strap from the deck beams. The space between every four — two above and two below — was enclosed by a curtain. The boys took possession of two of these berths on one side, and turned in. Berths were not assigned to passengers, but every one took his choice — "first come, first served;" and the last were not served at all. One of the other berths in the space was taken by a gentleman who had kept one eye on our enterprising travellers from the moment the steamer made her landing at Pesth.

9

CHAPTER VIII.

THROUGH THE BOSPORUS.

"THIS is something like a steamer," said De Forrest, the next morning, as they went on deck, having slept off the effects of the Hungarian wine, which is altogether too strong for boys.

" That's a fact," replied Beckwith. " This looks more like home than anything I have seen in Europe."

" She's a very fine steamer," interposed the gentleman who had occupied a berth opposite their own, and who had followed them on deck. " I dare say you have nothing finer than this in America."

" I'll bet we have; as much finer than this as this one is finer than the one in which we came from Vienna," replied De Forrest, rather pleased to hear the English language, and especially to be able to correct any wrong impression of things in America. " We have them three times as large, four times as comfortable, and five times as handsome."

" Is it possible !" exclaimed the gentleman, who was plainly an Englishman.

" It's a fact, sir ; " and De Forrest proceeded to describe the Bristol, the Providence, and some of the Hudson River steamers. " Why, sir, they are actually four stories high, and have three hundred and fifty state-rooms on board, besides four or five hundred berths."

" Can it be possible ! " added the amazed Briton.

" They carry between two and three thousand passengers, and they are not crowded, either.   They have a concert on board every night, and sometimes a ball. The grand saloon is about twenty feet high, with galleries around the sides, from which the upper story of state-rooms open.   They are lighted with gas, and are fitted up as elegantly as any palace in Europe."

" You quite surprise me ! "

" Still, this is a very fine little boat," added De Forrest, patronizingly.

" And they say she is built after the American fashion."

" Not much ! She is more like our boats than your English steamers ; and that's all you can say."

The name of the Danube steamer was the Orient. On her main deck, aft, was the saloon for first-class passengers, and forward was that for the second class. The sleeping accommodations for both were below. Her main deck was housed in from the stern to the bow, making a vast hurricane deck above, on which was no " house " of any kind.

" By the way, what are those rooms below, marked ' kabine ' ? " asked Beckwith, alluding to several mysterious apartments forward and aft the paddle-boxes, and in other parts of the main deck.

" I don't know," replied De Forrest.

" Those are private cabins. I dare say they are what you call state-rooms," said the English gentleman.

" I remember seeing the word in the circular,"
added De Forrest, as he took the paper from his pocket. " Cabines, eighty-one florins. How big are they?"

" They are quite small — seven or eight feet square,
with a sofa on each side, on which the bed is made at
night."

" Eighty-one florins in silver extra for one of these!"
exclaimed De Forrest. " That's a first-class fraud!
Why, it's twenty-seven florins a day, about fourteen
dollars! Seven dollars a day for each person!"

" Pray, how much do you pay in America?"

" One or two dollars for a night; and each room
has two berths. It's a swindle!"

" But these cabins are engaged for two or three
weeks before the journey; and they would be if the
price was twice as high."

" In America we should have a saloon on this hurricane deck, extending the whole length of the vessel,
with state-rooms, or *cabines*, on each side. There
would be fifty or sixty of them up here. On our
western rivers nothing extra is charged for them."

" But the boat must be top-heavy."

" Not a bit. One was never known to upset; and
on a river like this they are perfectly safe."

De Forrest's argument was undoubtedly correct;
and it is to be hoped that real American boats will be
placed upon the Rhine, Danube, Volga, and other
large rivers of Europe.

" You are going down the river, young gentlemen?"
said the Englishman.

" Yes, sir; to Constantinople."

" Ah, indeed! I am happy to hear it. We shall

be fellow-passengers. Allow me to introduce myself — Mr. Englefield."

" Glad to know you, Mr. Englefield. My name is De Forrest, and my friend is Mr. Beckwith."

Mr. Englefield bowed politely. He was alone, and lonely, and was always glad to know American travellers. They were always intelligent and agreeable. He was a commercial traveller, had been in every part of Europe, and hoped he could be of service to his young friends. The runaways voted that he was a good fellow, and received him with open arms, as they would not have voted and received him if they had known more about him.

Before seven o'clock the passengers, most of whom had arrived from Vienna by railroad the day or the night before, came on board. A few of them wore the fez; and all the nations of Eastern Europe seemed to be represented among them. A considerable number were Wallachians, wealthy wheat-growers, with families, coming from the large cities and the watering-places, not a few of them driven by the war from Paris, Baden-Baden, and Homburg. Our travellers had the idea — perhaps obtained from the school geographies — that Wallachia was a wild region, inhabited by a semi-barbarous people; but the representatives of these provinces on board of the Orient were in no way to be distinguished from other intelligent and refined ladies and gentlemen. All of them spoke French, even the children, with fluency and ease. They were very wealthy, and occupied most of the " *kabine*." The common people of the provinces, as in Russia, are in tremendous contrast with the higher class.

For four hundred miles below Pesth the country is flat and uninteresting. There was little to entertain our travellers outside of the steamer, except the current-mills, which are moored in the river. Each of these consists of a large flat boat, covered by a house containing the grist-mill, and a smaller boat near it. A large wheel, perhaps twenty feet in diameter, with floats, so that the current turns it, extends between the two boats, the axle reaching into the grist-mill, where it turns the stones. Half a dozen of these mills are often moored near each other, in diagonal lines from the shore, extending out nearly to the middle of the river. There are thousands of them on the Danube, whose swift current furnishes a sufficient power to turn their wheels.

Breakfast and dinner occupied a considerable portion of the day, for it required about an hour and a half to serve all the courses in each meal. The first meal was at half past ten, the last at five; but tea, coffee, and chocolate were supplied in the morning at call, and in the evening to the few who desired them. There were seven or eight courses to each full meal, and the food, both in its quality and in the preparation of it, was equal to that of the very best hotels in Europe, and much superior to a vast majority of them. The courses were soup, fish, two made dishes, a roast joint, poultry and a salad, " sweets," fruit, and coffee. Between every two plates was a quart bottle of Hungarian wine, of excellent quality, alternately red and white. Everything was very " nice " — perhaps the best steamboat fare to be found in any country.

The next morning the steamer was at Basiasch,

which is only a railroad station.   Peterwardein, a rock-built fortress, Semlin, and Belgrade were passed in the night.   More passengers came on board at the railroad station, and the Orient continued her voyage.   In a couple of hours the river began to contract its banks, as it passes through the Carpathian Mountains.   The shores were now high and rocky, and the scenery was grand and picturesque.   For a few miles it compares with, if it does not surpass, that of the Rhine below Bingen.   The rapids of the Danube at this point are very mild, and do not justify the extravagant description in Murray.   There are several lines of ripples, and some smart dashes of water; but any one who has passed through the rapids of the Ohio or the St. Lawrence would not regard them as worthy of mention.

On one side of the river the Austrian government has built an excellent road, which is sometimes hewn from the solid rock.   On the other are seen a great many square holes in the stone, where Trajan's road was constructed, which was the wonder of his age. There are many Roman remains in this region, including a tablet in honor of Trajan, set in a wall, and farther down the remains of the bridge built by him across the river.

At three o'clock the Orient arrived at Orsova, where the passengers were transferred to a smaller and inferior steamer, called the Sophie.   Warned by their English friend, the runaways rushed on board of her, and secured berths before the crowd had taken them all.   They placed their pea-jackets and travelling-bags upon them, and these were enough to secure their possession.   Orsova is the last town of the Austrian empire on the Danube, and the river now flowed through the Turkish provinces.   On the left was Wallachia, and on the right was Servia, as it had been from Belgrade.   The boys went on deck to see the sights, and were rewarded by observing a few Turks, or Bulgarians, in full costume.   They were rather amused to see one of them carry a fat woman, closely veiled, on his back to his boat, in which were several children. Boats loaded with vegetables, coming up the river, were overhauled by the custom-house officers, who are stationed at this point.

The Sophie soon started, and our voyagers kept both eyes wide open in search of things Turkish ; but not a crescent was yet to be seen.   Below Orsova they saw the ruins of a Turkish fortress, which was in the keeping of a live pacha, though he had no garrison, and the few Turks there were wretchedly poor.   Farther on the steamer entered the Iron Gate, which is nothing more than some rapids, rather more formidable than those above, but not very savage to an American traveller.   It is not a narrow pass in the mountains, as the name would suggest, but only an inclined plane of slate rock, down which the water rushes at a lively rate.   It is full of eddies and whirlpools.   The name, in Turkish, is *Demir Kapi* (Iron Gate), which is, metaphorically, difficult to pass through.   Tugboats, drag-boats, and barges are drawn up the rapids —a service which is rendered, on the Servian shore, by teams of ten or a dozen yoke of oxen.   This is the last difficulty in the navigation of the Danube.   This region is rich in Roman relics, and all the passengers gazed with wonder upon the remains of Trajan's Bridge, which would be a great undertaking at the present time. Thirteen of the twenty piers are visible, which have stood for sixteen hundred years.

"There you are!" exclaimed De Forrest, as they went on the hurricane deck after dinner, which was at a later hour than usual.

"What?" asked Beckwith.

"The crescent! There are a score of them on those churches."

"Mosques, you mean," suggested Mr. Englefield.

"Mosques, then; see those fine steeples! They look like needles in the distance."

"Those are minarets; and if you should go on shore, you would hear the Muezzin calling the faithful to prayers from little galleries far above the ground."

"This is a big fort," added De Forrest.

"It is indeed, for it has two hundred and eighty guns. This country is the province of Bulgaria, and this place is Widdin, one of the largest Turkish towns on the Danube. There is a Greek archbishop here."

"Then they have both the cross and the crescent?"

"Yes; but more crescent than cross. You are fairly in Turkey now."

The river now flows through a pleasant country, diversified with hills and plains. The stream is full of islands and sand-bars, which render the navigation difficult. But the night came on, and the passengers retired early.

The next morning, when they went on deck, the scenery was about the same. Turkish towns and villages, with mosques and minarets, were to be seen on the right. At noon the Sophie arrived at Giurgevo, on the north bank of the river. Three miles from the shore is the town, of eighteen thousand inhabitants, who live generally in mud huts. This place is the port of Bucharest, forty-four miles distant, which is the capital and chief city of Wallachia. This is a great grain-growing country, and hundreds of schooners were loading with wheat at the port. When the steamer had landed her passengers, she steamed across the wide river to Roustzouk, where our travellers were to take the train for Varna, on the Black Sea, a distance of one hundred and forty miles.

Taking their bags and pea-jackets, they climbed up the steep bank of the river to the railroad station, satisfied that they were really on Turkish soil. They saw a train of cars, and walked towards them; but an old Turk, with a long knife and a pair of enormous pistols in his belt, intercepted them and others, as one would check the advance of a flock of sheep. He was shouting and swinging his arms.

" How are you, Turkey? " said De Forrest, as they halted before him.

" Sho, sho ! " exclaimed the Turk.

" ' Shoo, fly ; don't bother me ' ! " hummed Beckwith. " He must be a turkey-buzzard."

" What does he mean ? "

" You must go up, and have your baggage examined," said Mr. Englefield, coming up at this time.

The porters were bringing up the trunks from the steamer, and several custom-house officers, in fez and great bagging trousers, were putting leaden seals upon them, for they were not opened till they arrived at

Constantinople.   The boys walked up to one of these officials, who made a sign to them to open their bags. The Turk looked very wise and solemn, and pulled out everything the bags contained.   Perhaps he was astonished at the meagreness of the Christians' wardrobe.   They unrolled the shirts, and then opened a paper in one, which contained some candy.   Evidently there was nothing in these bags which threatened the peace and dignity of the Turkish empire, or was likely to defraud it of any of the revenue, of which it stood so much in need.   The officers jammed the shirts in the bags again, to the peril of the starching, and then muttered in a low tone, —

" *Paras.*"

" Who ? " demanded De Forrest.

" *Paras.*"

" Who's he ? "

" *Paras.*"

" Don't know him. — What does he mean, Beck ? "

" I don't know."

" Ask Mr. Englefield.   Some of these fellows with the daggers and big pistols will murder us if we go wrong."

" Paras means small money.   Give him a few kreutzers, if you happen to have them ; if not, it makes no difference," replied the Englishman.

De Forrest held out a twenty-kreutzer nickel piece ; the man took it without a word, and in the most solemn manner, as though it were a perfectly regular transaction.

" These Turks are a nation of vagabonds," said Mr. Englefield ; " and it would be a blessing to Christianity and the world in general if they could all be sunk in the depth of the sea."

"You are rather rough on the Turkeys," laughed De Forrest, as they walked towards the train in which they were to proceed to the Black Sea.

The cars were of English construction, inferior, but tolerably comfortable. They took places in a compartment at one end of which were two gentlemen, one evidently a German, and the other with a very dark complexion and of doubtful nationality, but very genial and polite, for he saluted the new comers as they took their seats, according to the custom in many parts of Europe. He opened a conversation with Beckwith, who sat next to him, in French, upon indifferent topics — the steamer, the train, the Turks, and the custom-house. Beckwith struggled with the difficulties of the language for a considerable time, wishing that some happy circumstance would relieve him of the heavy labor.

"What the dickens does he say?" asked De Forrest.

"O, you speak English!" exclaimed the dark gentleman.

"We do, sir," replied Beckwith, the heavy pressure suddenly removed from him.

"But you are not English people?"

"No, we are Americans."

"Ah! I thought you were a Frenchman."

"I!" ejaculated Beckwith, suspecting that the gentleman was making game of him. "You certainly could not have supposed I was a Frenchman."

"I did suppose so."

"Impossible! My French would not permit you to

think so. You speak French very well — better than I do; and English quite as well. But I thought it probable that you were a Frenchman."

"No; I am an Armenian. I have lived in Constantinople many years. Do you go there?"

"Yes, sir."

They talked about Constantinople and America till the train started. The boys were desirous of seeing Turkey, and they looked out at the windows for a time, but there was little or nothing to see. Hardly a town or a village was passed on the entire journey. Two or three were seen in the distance, which appeared to be carefully avoided by the railroad. The people live in hamlets, and not a single detached dwelling was observed. This is true in Russia, Spain, Italy, and other countries of Europe. The inhabitants build their houses in villages, not because they are more social than other people, but because in the past, if not at present, it was necessary to concentrate the population in spots for purposes of defence against robbers and brigands, as well as the national enemies.

Most of the country through which the train passed was waste land grown over with bushes, with an occasional field of grain or Indian corn. Turkey exports eighteen million dollars' worth of grain, of which sixteen millions is Indian corn. The station-houses on the road were of stone, with large store-houses near them for the storage of grain, which is carried by rail in bulk to Varna for exportation. At these stations wagons drawn by oxen and buffaloes — as Mr. Englefield called them — were constantly arriving with the produce of the country. Their Bulgarian drivers stared at the Europeans with apparent wonder, and regarded the locomotive with a kind of awe, as though they had never seen anything of the sort before.

Half way to Varna there is a *buffet*, and as our travellers had not dined, they were disposed to test the quality of the viands. The restaurant was kept by a German, and everything about it was in the most primitive style. Soup and roast chicken, with red wine, constituted the bill of fare, and the meal was as deficient in quantity as it was in variety, so that the travellers departed almost as hungry as they came. At ten o'clock the train arrived at Varna; but it was too dark to see anything except the interior of the station and the Turkish policemen, whose belts were loaded with long knives and horse pistols half the size of a musket. The train proceeded down a long pier, and the runaways obtained their first view of the Black Sea. The pier was more ornamental than useful, for the steamers do not come up to it, but anchor at some distance from the shore. Two large boats were in readiness to take them off, and in a short time the party were on board.

The steamer was the America, one of the Austrian Lloyds, a comfortable vessel, with an engine from the Allaire Works in New York. She was not elegant in any sense. Her waiters all spoke Italian, which is the most serviceable language in Constantinople, and one or two of them French. One of them assigned state-rooms to the passengers, two in each, as they came on board. As our Americans were progressive and enterprising, they were among the first to enter the saloon on deck, and were quartered in one of the rooms leading from it.   Many who came later were obliged to take rooms below, which were hot and close.   As soon as the passengers were berthed, the bell rang for dinner, though it was half past eleven at night. The meal consisted of several courses, one of which was boiled beef and cabbage.   As the train was about three hours late, the food was rather over-cooked and unpalatable ; but it was just as effectual in producing the nightmare as if it had been more toothsome.

The America sailed while the passengers were at dinner, and De Forrest and Beckwith turned in as soon as they had eaten all they could, for they were very hungry.   They slept, but their slumbers were troubled, and the Turkish policemen they had seen at Varna danced hornpipes on their stomachs, brandishing fiercely their enormous weapons.   At seven in the morning De Forrest woke heavy and unrefreshed.   Beckwith was dreaming that Mr. Lowington stood over him armed with eleven long knives and nineteen horse pistols, which he had taken from the Ottoman police, ordering him to leap to the shore a dozen miles distant.   The rain was pouring down in torrents upon the deck above them, and the steamer was pitching and rolling heavily in a Black Sea tempest.   Looking out at the window, the sea was black enough to justify its name, though the waves were covered with white caps.   From the ladies' cabin came forth sounds which indicated that Neptune was extorting his dues from the inexperienced in the ways of the sea.   Everything looked disagreeable and gloomy, and the young seaman turned in again and went to sleep.   At nine both of the runaways turned out, and after partaking of the coffee and bread in the lower cabin, made a survey of the vessel and the surroundings.   The shores of Turkey were to be seen on the starboard, over a long reach of stormy sea.   The seasick Turks on the quarter and elsewhere on the deck of the steamer were a disagreeable spectacle.   Civilized Christians, when seasick, are repulsive enough, but Moslems are infinitely more so ; and our travellers were satisfied with a single glance at their woful condition.

At eleven o'clock in the forenoon, the land was seen ahead ; but there seemed to be no opening among the hills on the shore, and the location of the Bosporus became an interesting conundrum to the voyagers. In due time the passage appeared, and the steamer entered the strait.   It was the renowned Bosporus, which the young Americans had all their school lives spelled wrong, and longed to see.   More had been said about it on board of the ship than any other locality in Europe.   Doubtless the boys had read Eastern romances till their imaginations were inflamed by the barbaric splendors described, and such palaces, kiosks, mosques were located on the Bosporus.   De Forrest and Beckwith were on the hurricane deck, expecting to behold something like the last scene of a theatrical spectacle.   The rain had ceased, and the sun shone brightly to light up the golden domes and the shadowy minarets.

The steamer entered the strait.   There were strong forts on each side.   Some irregular-shaped rocks rose from the water near the European shore.   The hills were steep and brown, and the ground was as red as a New Jersey peach orchard.   For two hours the steamer continued on her course, and the young voyagers gazed upon the celebrated scenery; but in less than half an hour they insisted that " the whole thing was a humbug."   It was not the last scene of the spectacle, or anything like it; but the fault was more in their imaginations than in the Bosporus.   The hills were too brown, and the palaces were very commonplace buildings.   Yet the scenery is very beautiful. Nearer to Constantinople the palaces were more elegant. The Armenian gentleman pointed out the objects of interest, such as the palaces of the sultan, and of various pachas.   Though the boys were disappointed, the shores were full of interest, for the kiosks, the buildings, the boats, were different from anything they had seen before.   The new palace of the sultan is a magnificent edifice.

The first full view of the city of Constantinople was entirely satisfactory.   Seen from a distance, it is, perhaps, the most beautiful city in the world; but the illusion utterly fails when one enters its streets.   The steamer anchored in the Golden Horn, and was immediately surrounded by a crowd of boats.   Runners from the hotels came on board, and took violent possession of the passengers.   Mr. Englefield was going to the Hotel d'Angleterre, oftener called Misserie's, and the runaways decided to accompany him.   They landed at Galata, where the custom-house officials examined the bags of the travellers, and then walked up the steep hill to the Grand Rue de Pera, where the hotel is situated. The street was narrow and extremely filthy, but the people, especially the women, were enough to engage the attention of the boys. Everything was novel, and utterly strange.

The runaways obtained a room at the hotel, which is kept on the English plan, the wife of the landlord being an English woman. The *chambermaids* are men — Turks or Arabs. The boys wandered about the narrow streets the rest of the day, observing the strange sights to be seen in every direction. Beckwith was very anxious about his letter of credit, and the next morning he hastened to the banker's. There was a pile of letters for him and De Forrest. In one of them was the coveted credit for one hundred pounds, which made him very happy, and relieved him from many uncomfortable doubts.

"I should like twenty pounds," said Beckwith; which was promptly paid, without a question.

"You are all hunky dory now," added De Forrest. "What's the next move?"

"We will see what we can of this place, and then get out of the way before we are caught."

"How shall we get out, and where shall we go? I don't want to go by the way we came."

"Nor I."

"Here is Mr. Englefield. He can tell us all about it."

The polite Englishman saluted them as he entered the office of the banker.

"There are half a dozen ways to get out of Constantinople," he replied, in answer to De Forrest's question. "You can go by the Black Sea and the Volga to St. Petersburg; you can take the Danube route; you may go by Smyrna and Syria to Alexandria, and then to Gibraltar or England by steamer; you can go by the Austrian Lloyds to Trieste, or by the French steamer to the Piræus, Messina, and Marseilles."

"The last is the one we want," said De Forrest; and Beckwith coincided with him.

"But you are not going for several weeks, I suppose," added Mr. Englefield, indifferently.

"O, yes; we shall go in a few days, just as soon as we have seen a little more of Constantinople," replied Beckwith.

"But there is no steamer for a week."

"Well, we can stand it for a week here; but we had better engage our passage at once."

"I wouldn't," laughed Mr. Englefield.

"Why not?" asked Beckwith.

"Because you will not be ready to go in a week; in fact, not for a month."

"We shall be ready in three days."

"I think not; you will wish to wait till your ship arrives."

"What ship?" demanded De Forrest, aghast.

"The Academy Ship — the America, or the Young America."

"I don't know anything about her," replied Beckwith.

"I am sorry that a young gentleman, otherwise so well informed, should suddenly become so ignorant."

"I really don't understand you, sir," added De Forrest.

"Indeed you do; you are far too clever to be

ignorant. Let us be candid, Mr. De Forrest. You have a comfortable room at Misserie's, and money enough now to pay your way till the ship arrives. The prisons are not comfortable here; the Turks don't manage those things well; and on the whole I think you had better remain at your hotel."

"What do you mean, sir?"

"Simply this: if you attempt to leave Constantinople before your ship arrives, which may not be for four weeks, I shall be obliged to cause your arrest," replied Mr. Englefield, blandly.

"Who are you, sir?"

"John Englefield, at your service; a London detective sent out by Mr. Lowington to find you and take care of you. I have followed rogues to Constantinople several times before."

Beckwith looked at De Forrest, and De Forrest looked at Beckwith, and the look of either was enough to tell the whole story.

"I don't see how you found us," added De Forrest.

"Very easily; the moment Mr. Lowington had told me the story, I knew very well you would go to Hamburg."

"How did you know it?" asked Beckwith.

"You had just come from the north, and I was satisfied you would go where you had not been; and all travellers from Copenhagen go to Hamburg. Well, you didn't even change your names, and I got on your track at Streit's. I was ten days behind you. You told the people at the hotel you were going to Berlin. I lost a day in finding your hotel there. Then I went to Leipsig, to Dresden, and to Vienna, where I learned that you had just gone on board of the steamer for Pesth, with tickets in your pockets for Constantinople. I went by train to Pesth the next morning, and arrived before you. I met you when you came, took a berth near you, and, I hope, made myself agreeable to you on the passage."

" This is a pretty kettle of fish," muttered De Forrest, utterly disgusted with the situation.

" Capital kettle of fish," laughed the detective ; " but don't kick it over, for the next time it may be filled with bad meat. I trust you will be happy, and see the sights of this strange city before the ship comes, for I am afraid you will have no opportunity afterwards."

De Forrest was not satisfied with the situation, but he hoped to change it for the better.

CHAPTER IX.

A DISH OF TURKEY.

THE Young America arrived at Cowes after a long passage, as we have before stated. The principal was very much surprised at not finding the Tritonia in port, and still more surprised, not to say indignant, when he learned that she had anchored there two days before, and departed after a stay of only thirty hours. This information was obtained from the pilot, who had also taken the Tritonia into port.

"Was there anything wrong on board of her?" asked Mr. Lowington of the pilot.

"Nothing at all, sir, that I could discover," was the reply. "The young gentlemen seemed to be in most excellent discipline, and I never saw a ship worked better or more promptly."

"And you say she was in port only thirty hours?"

"Not more than that, sir."

"Did the people go on shore?"

"Many of them did. The gentleman in charge of the vessel was on shore, and stores and provisions were brought on board."

"The understanding was, that the vessel which

arrived here first should wait for the other," continued the principal.

"I dare say there was a misunderstanding, sir, for everything appeared to be quite regular on board of the Tritonia. Doubtless when you arrive at Constantinople, you will find her there," added the pilot.

Mr. Lowington, without any suspicion of the exciting events which had already transpired on board of the Tritonia, was very much annoyed. It did not seem possible that his directions had been misunderstood. He was not alarmed about the safety of the vessel or her crew; but he concluded that Mr. Tompion must have had some good reason for his conduct. He began to think that the tendency to run away had exhibited itself in the Tritonia, and that the vice-principal had gone to sea to check the career of any who intended to leave. If this was the case, he thought it probable that Mr. Tompion would lie off and on in the Channel, and wait for the ship, though, if he had taken this course, he would have been likely to hail him as he came into port.

The principal went on shore, and hastened to his bankers for his letters, hoping to find one from the vice-principal explaining his action; but there was nothing from him, and the mystery deepened. But there were two letters from the Copenhagen banker, containing as many reports of the search for the runaways. These letters were a new source of vexation to him, and he was determined, at any cost, to capture De Forrest and Beckwith, if it were possible. He ran up to London, which is only three hours and a half from Southampton, where he employed the detective who followed the runaways to Constantinople, whither also he had been directed to convey them, if he succeeded in capturing them.

After waiting a day at Cowes, to give the Tritonia an opportunity to run in and join her consort, if she was anywhere in the vicinity, Mr. Lowington ordered the ship to be got under way again. We do not purpose to narrate the incidents of her voyage; but it was the last day of August when she anchored in the Golden Horn. On the passage the principal had directed a sharp lookout to be kept for the missing consort, but nothing was seen of her. He was certain of finding her at Constantinople; but he was still further confounded when he ascertained that she had not yet arrived. He began to fear that another runaway cruise had been planned, and successfully executed. At the banker's he found files of London papers, and he carefully examined the shipping news in all of them. He found the Tritonia reported at Lisbon, and immediately telegraphed to his banker there for information. A reply was promptly returned: " Tritonia sailed. Tompion left behind. Particulars by mail."

This despatch was more confounding than anything which had yet been learned in regard to the missing vessel. The vice-principal had been left behind ! This intelligence could only mean that there was a mutiny, and that the students had run away with the vessel. Mr. Lowington suffered the most intense anxiety; but he could only wait for the banker's letter containing the desired details. At the office of the Spanish consul he obtained a crumb of comfort. At Tarifa, on the Strait of Gibraltar, there is a signal station, where vessels passing through hoist their numbers, or signal their names. In a Spanish newspaper the Tritonia was reported as passing, bound up the Mediterranean. As this was a week after her departure from Lisbon, the event was slightly hopeful, though it might only mean that the runaways intended to cruise in the Mediterranean, instead of in the Atlantic.

While the principal was worrying about the Tritonia, and holding long and anxious consultations with Peaks, the boatswain, the students were attending to the usual routine of duty. Cantwell had proved to be a model captain, and the crew were never in a better state of order and discipline. As soon as the anchor was down, they climbed into the rigging to behold the wonders of Constantinople. They gazed at the domes and minarets of the mosques, at the hundreds of caiques darting around the ship, and at the Turkish fleet of iron-clads moored opposite the city. But while they were observing the strange things around, the boatswain piped the call for all hands to attend lecture. Mr. Mapps, the instructor in geography and history, had hung up several maps on the foremast and bulk-heads, where he could refer to them as he proceeded with his remarks.

"Where are we now, young gentlemen?" asked the professor, with an amiable smile, as though he were conscious that he had many good things to say, and was disposed to make the lesson as pleasant as possible.

"In a horn," replied one of the students.

"Quite right.   What horn?"

"The Golden Horn."

" Why so called ? "

The instructor " had them there," for no one could answer his question, even with a joke.

" The Golden Horn is an inlet of the Bosporus, about five miles in length.   Several small streams flow into it from the Valley of the Sweet Waters, and it receives its name from its curving outline, which is somewhat in the shape of a horn; and Gibbon says of it, ' The epithet of *Golden* was expressive of the riches which every wind wafted from the most distant countries into the secure and capacious port of Constantinople.'   It is properly the port, or harbor, of the city, for tremendous storms sometimes rake through the Bosporus, and this is the only shelter for vessels. It is crossed by two floating bridges, which connect the two parts of the city — Pera and Galata on one side, and Stamboul, or Constantinople proper, on the other.   But what is the title of the country in whose waters our ship is moored? "

" Turkey."

" Hardly ; and I doubt whether this word is known to the average Turk, any more than the name *Danube* is known to the average German, or *Florence* to the Italian. The *Turkish*, or *Ottoman*, empire is the proper title in English.   In Turkish it is *Osmanli Valaieti*. The Turks are a people who came from Turkestan, in Asia, and the name *Turkey* comes from them ; but *Osmanli*, or, in English, *Ottoman*, comes from *Othman*, who founded the empire.   Now we will have our dish of Turkey.

" The Turkish empire consists of three divisions — Turkey in Europe, in Asia, and in Africa, though much the larger portion of it is merely tributary to the Ottoman government. Roumania, with a population of nearly four millions, includes the two principalities of Moldavia and Wallachia, which are united under one government, practically independent, though it pays an annual tribute to the sultan of nearly two hundred thousand dollars. Servia, with about one million people, also pays the Turkish government about one hundred thousand dollars a year for the privilege of being independent so far as making its own laws is concerned.

" Turkey in Europe, without these provinces, contains two hundred and seven thousand square miles, or thirty thousand miles less than Texas. The population is about fifteen millions. This is the highest estimate, for no census is taken in Turkey, and the lowest places it below ten millions. Turkey in Asia contains three times as much territory, with an estimated population of from twelve to fifteen millions. This division includes Asia Minor, which is the peninsula between the Black and Mediterranean Seas, with Armenia, Mesopotamia, Syria, the Island of Cyprus, Arabia, and other provinces. As you are aware, this region is the scene of some of the most noted events in sacred and profane history. In Africa, Egypt, Tunis, and Tripoli are nominally subject to Turkey, but only Egypt pays tribute in money, which amounts to nearly three and a half millions of dollars a year.

" The mountains of Turkey in Europe are the Eastern Carpathians, which are on the west of Moldavia and on the north of Wallachia, the Balkan extending east and west through the centre, and the

Hellenic branch of the Alps in the western part. There are peaks in Turkey from seven to nine thousand feet high. Mount Ararat, in Asia Minor, is over seventeen thousand feet high, and there are many other high peaks in Turkey in Asia. The principal rivers are the Danube, the Save, the Pruth, and the Sereth. The Danube and its tributaries are of vast importance to the commercial interests of the country. The Euphrates and Tigris are the most noted in Turkey and Asia. The Garden of Eden is supposed to have been located between these two streams. In Europe the country is undulating, and often mountainous, and a considerable portion of it is sandy and barren ; but the greater part is fertile, and, with good husbandry, would yield abundant returns. Agriculture is the chief industry, but is carried on with the rudest implements, and in the most primitive manner. Grain, rice, cotton, and tobacco are cultivated, and large crops are obtained. The olive, grape, fig, date, orange, and citron thrive here, and yield profitable returns, in spite of the discouraging policy of the government. The most luscious grapes to be found in the whole world will soon be in season in Constantinople. Of the manufactures of Turkey not much can be said, for they are very miscellaneous ; but the most important of them are wax, raisins, dried figs — "

" Raisins ! " exclaimed a student. " I thought they grew."

" They are grapes, manufactured into raisins. Dried figs are also manufactured, and most of them are shipped from Smyrna. From the olive, oil is made. When you visit the Bazaar, you will see more of the manufactures of the Turks, as silks, red cloth, various kinds of leather, saddles, swords, copper ware, carpets, shawls, shoes, prune brandy, otto of roses, &c. Some of these articles are exported to a considerable extent; but grain, cotton, and tobacco are the heaviest productions sent out of the country. The total imports are about ninety millions of dollars a year, consisting mostly of manufactured goods, while the exports are not more than fifty millions, leaving a balance of forty millions against the country to be paid for in money. Roads, such as we should dignify by this name, are hardly known in Turkey. A plan for an extensive network of railroads was long ago adopted by the government, but less than two hundred miles have been built.

" The money of Turkey is generally reckoned in piastres and paras, and one piastre, worth five cents of our money, is equal to forty paras. At the hotels and foreign stores, prices will be given you in French money. A napoleon, or twenty francs, is equal to eighty-eight piastres. At the Hotel d'Angleterre the price of board is eighteen francs a day for an ordinary room, rather small and poor at that, and breakfast and dinner; lunch, extra.

" The government is an absolute monarchy; but, as in Russia, the power of the sovereign is not unlimited. He must conform to the truths of the Mohammedan religion. A code of laws, called the ' Multeka,' embracing the opinions of the prophet, and the decisions of some of his successors, is binding upon the sultan, being regarded as of divine origin. Another code, framed by Solyman the Magnificent, though not of the same authority as the first, is respected and obeyed by the sovereign. In 1856 the sultan granted a charter of liberties to his people, which included the freedom of worship to all sects in religion. No person can be compelled to change his creed; and all Turkish subjects, of whatever race, religion, or language, are to be regarded as equal before the law. Foreigners may own real estate while they obey the laws and pay the taxes. But this charter, in some respects, exists only on paper, for all its provisions are not yet executed.

" The supreme authority vests in the sultan; but it is exercised by two high dignitaries appointed by him, with the concurrence of a council composed of priests and law officers. The first of these is the grand vizier, who is the head of the government, the vicegerent of the sovereign, and the president of the divan, or council of ministers. The other is the Sheik-ul-Islam, who is the head of the church. In Turkey the ministers of religion are under the control of the civil officers; but both have the same education and training, for law, as well as religion, is derived from the Koran. A magistrate may perform all the duties of a priest, in the mosque or elsewhere. The civil officers and the clergy form a kind of aristocracy, called the ' Ulema,' under the government of the Sheik-ul-Islam. They pay no taxes, and their property is held more securely than that of other classes. Their persons are sacred; and imprisonment and exile are the only punishments that can be legally inflicted upon them. The Koran, and other sacred writings, encourage education; and there are public schools in all the large towns, though the instruction is rather limited. The pupils are taught to read and write, the Koran and commentaries upon it being the only text-books. In the colleges and higher schools a little history and geography, with philosophy, logic, rhetoric, law, and theology, complete the course.

" Of the population of Turkey in Europe about four millions are Mohammedans, eight millions are Greek and Armenians, and there are about a million Catholics, Jews, and other sects. In Asia three fourths of the people are Mohammedans.

" In the Turkish army the soldier serves six years in active service, six in the reserve, and is liable to be called into the field for eight more in case of war. In these three classes the government has an available force of seven hundred thousand men. Only Mohammedans are liable to do military duty, but all others have to pay an exemption tax. The navy of Turkey consists of eighteen iron-clad vessels and seventy-five wooden steamers. The quality of the former you have seen from the deck of this ship; but most of them were built on the Clyde, in Scotland. This navy is manned by thirty thousand seamen and four thousand marines.

" Now let us turn to the history of Turkey, and here we have the famous sick man. Early in the last century historians began to look up the reasons why the Ottoman empire had already begun to decay, and Russian statesmen have long persisted in believing that it was ready to crumble at the first shock. In 1844 the Emperor Nicholas thought the sick man's hour of dissolution was actually at hand, for he said to the British *chargé d'affaires*, ' We have on our hands a sick man, a very sick man. It would be a great misfortune, I tell you frankly, if, one of these days, he should happen to die before the necessary arrangements were made.' The sick man is still alive, thanks to the protecting care of England, France, and Sardinia, who saved him by the war of 1853. But he has been spared, not because his neighbors have any great love for him, but because they cannot agree upon the division of his real estate. Who is to have Constantinople is the troublesome question, for the situation of this city is incomparable. It is admirably located for purposes of defence, while its situation on the Bosporus and Golden Horn naturally fit it to become the first commercial city of the world. The ancients saw some of these advantages of situation. The old Greeks, when they intended to found a city, used to consult an oracle to ascertain where to locate it. When a body of them, purposing to build a city, applied to the oracle of the Pythian Apollo to guide them in the location, they were advised to ' seek a site opposite the habitations of the blind.' These Greeks took time to consider this reply, for the oracle did not always give answers and furnish the brains to understand them. The response was villanously indefinite; but finally they selected a site, and Byzantium, now Constantinople, was built. It was that portion of the present city on our port hand, or west of the Golden Horn. The founders concluded that they had correctly interpreted the enigma of the oracle; for, on the opposite side of the Bosporus, a couple of miles below Scutari, Chalcedon had been built some years before; and the Chalcedonians must have been the ' blind,' because if they had had good eyes, they would certainly have seen the superior advantages of a location on the other shore.

"The Emperor Constantine (A. D., 306–337) saw that Byzantium was the true centre of the Roman world; and he made it his capital, changing the name to Constantinople — the city of Constantine. Peter the Great thought that this city would be the best capital for a Universal Empire; and he declared that, when his successors could reign there, they would be the real sovereigns of the world. Napoleon I. was of the same opinion in regard to the value of this capital in the hands of the Russians. And so it has been the feeling of European statesmen that Constantinople must not come into the hands of any one of the great powers. The Turks may hold it because they are weak.

"The fame of the Turkish empire does not belong to the capital alone, for the land of the Ottoman was famous centuries before it was trodden by the Turk. Many of the great nations of antiquity, and a few of modern time, have acted their parts on the territory which is now the property of the sick man. Egypt, Chaldæa, Babylonia, Assyria; the kingdom of Solomon and David; Tyre, Sidon, and the other Phœnician states; the empire of Crœsus; the Grecian states; Macedonia; nearly the whole of the empire of the Medo-Persians — of Cyrus and Darius; much the larger part of the empire of Alexander the Great; the Roman Empire of the East; and all the more valuable portion of the empire of Mohammed's successors, were included within the limits of the Ottoman

Empire as it was fifty years ago; and if we except a portion of ancient Greece, which became independent in 1830, we may say within the limits of the Ottoman Empire of to-day.

"The Roman Empire, which 'filled the world,' was divided into the Eastern and Western Empires in the year 364. At that time the eastern portion had substantially the same boundaries as the Ottoman Empire of the present time; comprising, in Europe, the Macedonian Empire of Alexander the Great. In 476 the Western Empire fell, but the Eastern continued to exist under various names till the middle of the fifteenth century; but its territory became less, till, some time before the fall of Constantinople, the Emperor of the East 'could view all his possessions' from the terraces of his palace.

"As the history of the Turkish Empire does not commence with the Turks, so the history of the Turks does not commence with Turkey. They obtained the country by conquest, and remain in it as the dominant people, though many other races contribute to make up the thirty millions of people who are the subjects of the empire. The Turks are a very ancient race, and their origin may be traced back several centuries before the Christian era. No other people have made conquests so extensive. They subdued China before the Mongols; they formed a considerable portion of the armies of Genghis Khan, who overran Asia and invaded Russia, and of Tamerlane, or Timour, who also conquered the larger portion of Asia; and even now the Ottomans form but a small part of the whole race.

" The Ottoman is the third Turkish empire known to Europeans. The Turks were first recognized by this name in Europe in the middle of the sixth century. They were then the rulers of a large part of Central Asia. The second was the empire of the Seljuk Turks in the eleventh century. Seljuk, its founder, whose name is applied to a dynasty, made the celebrated city of Bokhara his capital, and before the close of the century his successors had extended their sway from the frontier of China to the Hellespont. Hardly had this vast region been brought under the sway of one sovereign when the new empire fell in pieces, and several smaller ones took its place. One of these comprised nearly the whole of Asia Minor. Just before this time, another tribe of Turks, driven by the tide of Mongol invasion from the north-east, fled westward to the mountains ·of Armenia. Ertogrul, a Turkish chief, at the head of about four hundred families, received, for some service, the grant of a small territory in Phrygia, from the sultan of Iconium. Ertogrul's son Othman (1299–1326), extended this small inheritance; and before his death was in possession of a great portion of Asia Minor. Othman, or Osman, was the first emperor of the present Turkish line, and gave his name to his people, who still call themselves Osmanlis, or sons of Osman. Though bred to war, this sovereign left˙ so great a reputation for gentleness to his people and generosity to his enemies, that the surname of ' the kind-hearted ' has been bestowed upon him by the Turks; and on the coronation of each new sultan, the people pray aloud that he may have the gentleness of Othman. All the tribute he levied he distributed among his followers, and at his death his wealth was found to consist of a wooden spoon, a salt-cellar, an embroidered vest, a linen turban, a few yoke of oxen for the plough, some flocks of sheep, and several Arabian coursers.

" His son Orchan (1326-1360) was the first of the sultans who coined money, placed his name in the public prayers, and promulgated laws ; and it is sometimes said that the Ottoman empire really dates from his accession. Orchan was a warrior, like his father, and was one of the greatest legislators of modern times. The institutions which raised a small band of emigrants into the founders of one of the great empires of the earth, before three generations had elapsed, were the work of this emperor. Up to this time every Turk was a soldier, and the army was the tribe on the march. In the frequent incursions made by the Turks upon the European continent and islands, multitudes of children torn from the families of Greek Christians were taken into the camp. These young Greeks were brought up in the Mohammedan faith, which was now the religion of the conquerors, and, as is proverbial with converts, they became the most inexorable enemies of Christianity. After the manner of the Egyptians and Persians, who made soldiers of captive foreigners, these young Greeks were organized in a military body, and became the pride and the strength of the new Turkish empire. They were the famous Janizaries, which means new soldiers. Their number was afterwards increased by forced levies of youths from the conquered Christians, and the corps became the keystone of the political and military power of the nation.   The tribute of Christian children was abolished in 1685, when the Janizaries became a kind of national guard, and were often more dangerous to the sultans than their enemies.

"Orchan made some conquests on the European side of the Hellespont, which, you know, is the Strait of Dardanelles.   Mourad I. (1360–1389) continued the Turkish conquest in Europe, and made Adrianople his capital.   Bajazet, or the Thunderbolt, extended the empire both in Europe and in Asia.   Thrace and Macedonia acknowledged his sway.   In the great battle of Nicopolis, he defeated the Christian army of one hundred thousand men, the greater part of whom were slain or driven into the Danube.   While his armies were thus triumphant in Europe, he learned that Tamerlane was ravaging his dominions in the East.   He hastened into Asia Minor, and encountered the army of the Mongol chief near Angora, where Bajazet was defeated and taken prisoner ; and a little later he died in captivity.   This defeat seemed to threaten the Ottoman empire with destruction ; but Tamerlane died two years after the event, and the Turks followed up their conquests in Europe, under the lead of the sons and grandsons of Bajazet, till his great-grandson, Mohammed II. (1451–1481) ascended the throne.   He was one of the greatest of the Ottoman sovereigns, both as a warrior and a statesman, and possessed considerable literary and scientific knowledge.   In Astrology, which was the fashionable science of the time, he had made great progress.   He was fond of reading, and spoke the Turkish, Arabic, Persian, Greek, Latin, and Sclavonic languages fluently.   In

1453 he captured Constantinople, which made an end of the Empire of the East; and in the course of fifteen years he had extended his sovereignty over the whole of Asia west of the Taurus Mountains; over all the provinces which had formerly belonged to the Eastern Empire; had carried his arms into Italy, sacked Otranto, and sent terror throughout Christendom. Selim I., his grandson, conquered Egypt, Syria, Tripoli, and defeated the Persians. The son of Selim I., Solymon the Magnificent (1520–1566), reduced Belgrade, which the Christians regarded as their chief barrier against the Turks, and annexed Hungary to his domain.

" During the reign of his son, Selim II., the Ottoman empire reached its highest degree of prosperity. Its wars were generally successful, and commerce, literature, arts and sciences flourished. But this golden age was of brief duration. In this reign occurred the famous naval battle of Lepanto, fought between the Turkish fleet and that of the allied Christians, under the command of Don John of Austria. The battle lasted nearly eight hours, and resulted in the utter ruin of the Ottoman navy. Thirty thousand Turkish sailors were killed or drowned, thirty-four hundred were taken prisoners, and fifteen thousand Christian captives were delivered from slavery. In this battle Cervantes, the author of *Don Quixote*, lent a hand, and lost one, or, rather, the use of one. For a century the Turks were at war on all sides — with Venice, Austria, Persia, Hungary, Poland, Russia, or Germany, sometimes with two or three of these nations at the same time, as I have told you in former lectures.

" In 1683, the Ottomans were defeated with terrible

slaughter by the famous John Sobieski, King of Poland, and the Duke of Lorraine, thus raising the siege of Vienna.   The Turks were commanded by the Grand Vizier Kara Mustapha, whose head is preserved in the Imperial Arsenal at Vienna.   They also lost, thirty years later, the great battle of Zentha, in Hungary, in which thirty thousand Turks were slain and drowned.   In these wars, Austria, Prussia, Poland, and the Venetians acquired territory from the waning Ottoman.   Russia obtained a foothold in the Crimea, and soon acquired all the territory.   At first the Turks had but little respect for the armies of the czar; but during the last two centuries Russia has wrested from Turkey in Europe a territory equal in extent to that of Prussia before 1866, exclusive of the Rhenish provinces; and in Asia, an area equal to Turkey in Europe, Greece, Italy, and Spain.

" The Ottoman government took little part in the wars which grew out of the French revolution, till Napoleon conquered Egypt.   The French were expelled by the English and Turks, and peace restored in 1802.

" An attempt was made in the reign of Selim III. (1788–1807) to introduce European discipline and tactics into the Turkish armies, though the effort failed, and resulted in the deposing of the sultan; but in 1826 the reform was made by Mahmoud II. (1808–1839), a more vigorous ruler than his immediate predecessors. It was effected then only by the complete destruction of the Janizaries, who were really the masters of the empire, had murdered or deposed not less than nine of the sovereigns of Turkey, and would have served Mahmoud II. in the same way, if he had not assumed the aggressive. He was obliged to pardon them, on coming to the throne, for the murder of Selim and Mustapha, but he formed the plan to exterminate them. He won over to his side the priesthood and some of the officers of the Janizaries, and disposed of the regular army and sailors from the fleet in a way to defend his throne. Having made all his preparations, he issued a decree directing a portion of the Janizaries from each regiment to be formed into regularly disciplined troops. As was expected, this led to a revolt, and the Janizaries committed their usual excesses. But the people, influenced by the priests, joined the regular troops. The rebels, according to their custom when in revolt, assembled around their reversed soup kettles. The guns, which had long been in position for the emergency, opened upon them; the regular troops poured in volleys of musketry; and the Janizaries fled to their barracks, which Mahmoud ordered to be set on fire. The gates of the city were closed, and the rebels were massacred wherever found. They made a desperate defence, but the whole corps were annihilated. Twenty-five thousand of them were killed, and the band was never reorganized.

" In 1821, the Greeks, who had failed in previous attempts to establish their independence, rose in revolt. For eight years they struggled alone; but finally England, France, and Russia came to their aid, and nearly the whole of the Turkish navy was destroyed in the celebrated battle of Navarino. In 1830 the Sublime Porte acknowledged the independence of Greece. Lord Byron assisted the Greeks in this war, contributed sixty thousand dollars to the cause, and organized a band of soldiers, though, as a commander, he was not a success.

"The Pacha of Egypt, perhaps stimulated by the example of Greece, revolted in 1831, and for several years carried on a successful war against the sultan. He was in a fair way, not only to establish the independence of Egypt, but to overrun Turkey, when the Allied powers interfered, and in 1841 settled the difficulty. The hereditary government of the country was vested in the family of Mehemet Ali, the pacha who had before been the viceroy of the sultan, but was now called Khedive, or King, of Egypt. Except in the payment of an annual tribute, the country is independent, and has its own separate government.

"Mahmoud II. made some reforms in his government, and his son, Abdul Medjid (1839–1861), introduced many improvements. Christians were allowed to hold office; and, of the thirty members of the council of state at the present time, nine are of this sect. The present sultan is Abdul Aziz, who is the second son of Mahmoud II. and the thirty-third male descendant of Othman. The law of succession differs from that in Christian monarchies, for the crown is inherited by the oldest male descendant of Othman, sprung from the Imperial Harem. The present sultan has four sons, the oldest of whom, *Yussuf Izzeddin* Effendi, is thirteen years old; but if his father should die to-day, he would not be succeeded by this son, but by *Mohammed Murad* Effendi, a son of the previous sultan, who is twenty years old. It used to be the fashion for the sultans, on coming to power, to strangle their brothers, and dispose of any children who might be in the way; but this custom hasg one out of use.

"The Imperial Harem is regarded as a permanent state institution, and all children born in it, whether their mothers be slave or free, are of equal rank, and are entitled to the same privileges. The female children of the Harem are princesses, but their rank ends with themselves. The sons must remain unmarried, or give up their rank. The sultans do not marry. The ladies of the Harem enter it of their own accord, or are purchased as slaves, mostly from Circassia. This institution is watched over by the Guard of Eunuchs, the commander of which is of the same rank as the grand vizier.

"Abdul Aziz is disposed to introduce European improvements into his empire, but whether òr not Turkey is actually progressing, is an open question. Its enemies declare that it is ready to fall, while its friends confidently assert that it is making sustantial progress. Changes have certainly been made for the better. All religions are tolerated, and it is proposed to establish a code of civil laws, to be used instead of the Koran, which is still to be authority in religion. The finances of the country may have been improved, but they are still in a desperate situation, the expenditures exceeding the revenue annually by about twenty million dollars. The government has been far behind the age in levying its revenues. The taxes have been let for a certain sum to men who, in Europe, are called 'farmers-general of the public revenue.' These men appoint their own officers, who are not responsible to the government for their action. Of course it is a speculation by which the 'farmer' profits, and by which the government loses. For example, the tax on tobacco in Turkey amounts to thirty million dollars a year, and the sultan sells the right to collect this tax to the ' farmer ' for twenty-four millions. If it costs the farmer three millions to collect it, he makes three millions by the operation, and the government loses this sum. But this method of collecting the taxes has been abolished, and they are now collected by government officials.

" I will not detain you longer now, young gentlemen, though I have much more to say to you."

The professor bowed, and the ship's company were dismissed. On the quarter-deck, waiting to see the principal, was Mr. Englefield; but the runaways were not with him.

CHAPTER X.

THE TRITONIA AT SEA.

WE left the Tritonia at anchor in the harbor of Cowes. Hardly were the sails furled, and the crew dismissed from muster, before Mr. Tompion, the vice-principal, ordered a boat to convey him to the shore. He took with him a valise, as though he intended to be absent a considerable time, though he did not intimate to the captain, or to any other person, that he should not return at night.

"Where is he going?" asked Greenwood, as the boat shoved off.

"I don't know," replied Morley. "He didn't say anything to me."

"Probably he did not to the captain, either," laughed Greenwood. "They don't appear to be as familiar with each other as the commander and the vice-principal should be. But you seem to be quite thick with Mr. Tompion."

"Well, I don't know; he don't say much to me, or to anybody, for that matter. He stays in his own cabin nearly all the time."

"Don't you expect some trouble when the ship arrives, Morley?"

"Trouble?"

"Don't you expect the captain will appeal from the decision of the vice-principal?"

"Certainly not. I had not thought of such a thing."

"In my opinion you had better be thinking of it. Wainwright won't let the matter stand as it is, you may depend upon it. He suspended you, and Mr. Tompion, without even hearing what the captain had to say about it, restored you."

"Precisely so; because the captain had no right to suspend me. That's a plain case."

"But the vice-principal did not even hear the captain."

"I told him all about the matter myself, and he knew very well that the captain was on the lookout for a chance to pick me up. Do you really think he will appeal?"

"I do; if I were in his place, I should," said Greenwood, decidedly.

"I didn't think you would go back on me, Greenwood," added Morley, with a reproachful glance at his fellow-conspirator.

"I don't go back on you. I am talking to you, and not to Wainwright. I don't say a word to him."

"You say you should appeal, if you were in his place."

"Certainly I should. He was snubbed by Mr. Tompion, and not even allowed to give his reasons for the step he had taken."

"I don't want the matter overhauled by Mr. Lowington," continued Morley, thoughtfully.

"He will reverse the decision of Mr. Tompion, in my opinion."

"I don't see how he can do that. If he does, the vice-principal's reputation is ruined on board of this vessel."

"That may be ; but you will acknowledge that he ought to have heard what the captain had to say."

"It would have made no difference if he had."

"Perhaps not ; but it would have looked more like fair play."

The appearance of the captain and first lieutenant on the quarter-deck terminated the conversation. Morley was troubled, and dreaded the arrival of the Young America. For several days the captain had been observed to be very busy in his state-room, spending a great portion of his leisure time at his desk. The officers who had occasion to report to him said that he was writing a long paper, which did not appear to be a school exercise ; and the second lieutenant now surmised that it was a history of the difficulty between himself and the captain ; perhaps a formal appeal from the decision of the vice-principal. Later in the day, Greenwood, who had been in the captain's room, informed him that a large envelope lay on the desk, directed to Mr. Lowington. This fact was ominous of the intention of Wainwright, and Morley feared that the appeal would result in his own disgrace.

Greenwood was not mistaken in regard to the captain's intentions. The envelope on the desk of the latter contained his appeal from the decision of the vice-principal, with a full record of everything which had transpired on board of the Tritonia since she sailed from Copenhagen, with the names of the witnesses by which each statement could be proved. Its tone was moderate, and entirely respectful towards Mr. Tompion.

"The vice-principal has gone on shore with his valise," said Scott.

"So I have been told. I wonder if he intends to stay all night," replied the captain.

"I don't know. He has acted very strangely lately," added Scott, in a very low tone.

"I don't know about that. We have hardly seen him for a week, to judge how he does act."

"That's what I mean. He spends about all his time in his cabin, and his recitations in navigation have been omitted, with only two exceptions, since we left the Baltic. Then he hardly speaks to you, though you are captain, and he restored Morley without even asking you to state your case."

"His conduct in regard to Morley was certainly very strange, and I had not thought about the rest before."

"I hope the ship will arrive to-day, for this suspense isn't comfortable. I feel like a fish out of the water, or a monkey in the water," laughed Scott. "I want to call a meeting of the Bangwhangers, and put the fellows through the third degree; but I don't like to ask the vice-principal for the use of the cabin."

"I wouldn't call any meeting at present. Morley and Greenwood have a great deal to say about the order, and accuse us of getting our places by its aid."

While they were talking, the boat which had conveyed Mr. Tompion to the shore returned, and the officer in charge of it reported to the first lieutenant that the vice-principal desired to come on board at sunset. No one was allowed to leave the vessel, for Mr. Tompion was the only one who could give permission to do so, and he was absent. The recitations proceeded with their usual order, except in the class in navigation, which was taken by Mr. Marline, the boatswain, who gave the lessons in seamanship. Morley failed in his studies that day, for his mind was not upon them. He was thinking of something else. The day wore away, and the ship did not appear.

At sunset the second cutter went to the shore for Mr. Tompion, and did not return until it was quite dark. The coxswain, who brought the vice-principal's valise on deck, said it was very heavy, and that something in it rattled like glass ware. The owner of it directed one of the stewards to carry it to his cabin, to which he presently retired himself, and was not seen again that night. Early in the evening Morley knocked at his door, and was admitted. He remained with Mr. Tompion about an hour — a circumstance which was noticed by all the officers, and was the subject of a conference between Wainwright and Scott.

The next morning Mr. Salter, the head steward, was directed to procure his fresh provisions and other supplies for the voyage. The water tanks were filled, and before noon the ice, fresh meats, vegetables, and fruit were in the store-rooms. Immediately after dinner Mr. Tompion appeared on the quarter-deck, and approached the captain. He looked pale, paler than usual, and his manner was strange, so much so that Wainwright wondered what ailed him. His speech was rather thick, and, though he stiffened his frame by an effort of will, his movements were slightly unsteady.

"Captain Wainwright, you will make ready to get under way," said he.

"Under way, sir!" exclaimed the captain.   "Are we to sail before the ship arrives?"

"We are to sail at once.   Call all hands."

Wainwright gave the necessary orders; but he was utterly confounded by this proceeding on the part of the vice-principal, which was contrary to all the established precedents by which the squadron had been governed.   Each vessel had always been required, if separated on a voyage from the others, to await the arrival of her consorts at the first port.   One had never before been known to sail without the others, for each was required to insure the safety of her companions.   But the orders of the vice-principal were imperative, and in the absence of the principal there was no appeal.   A pilot was obtained, while the crew were loosing the sails and heaving up the anchor, and thirty hours after her arrival at Cowes the Tritonia was at sea again, standing down the Solent towards the English Channel.

"I don't understand it," said Captain Wainwright, as soon as the crew had been dismissed from muster, and the watch stationed.

"Nor I," replied Scott; "but I begin to see a hole in the millstone."

"What do you mean?" asked the captain, anxiously.

"Haven't you an idea yet?"

"Perhaps I have."

"Don't you smell a rat?"

"No; but I smelt something else," answered the captain, with a smile of intelligence.

"And that something else was the vice-principal's breath," added Scott.

"Did you notice it?"

"I didn't smell the breath, but I noticed his manner. He had to stiffen up in order to keep from reeling, and his tongue was badly swelled, or some of his teeth were knocked out, for he did not speak in his natural tones."

"Have you ever seen anything of the kind before, Scott?"

"Never; never had the least suspicion that he crooked his elbow."

"Nor I, and I am utterly confounded by it. Why, Mr. Lowington never would allow a drop of liquor, wine, or beer on board, unless it was in the medicine chest, and I doubt whether there was any there. I never knew or heard of one of the adult officers taking anything to drink before."

"That's so; but I was sure Mr. Tompion had been imbibing, for he acted just as I felt after I drank that *finkel* in Sweden."

"I don't suppose there can be any doubt of the fact; but I think neither of us had better mention it," said the prudent captain.

"Not at present, at least; but things are going wrong in this vessel, and we must keep our weather eyes open, or we shall soon be sailing in hot water."

"It isn't a pleasant prospect that lies before us. I am just beginning to understand the events of the past."

"Since we have found the hole in the millstone, I think we had better look through it," added Scott.

"Morley spent an hour in the vice's cabin last night, and the cabin of the vice now is almost as bad as the tents of wickedness."

"Had that anything to do with our sailing to-day?" asked the captain.

"I don't know; but it is as clear as dish-water to me that Morley has some hold upon the vice-principal."

"Perhaps he has found him drunk in his cabin, or on shore. Certainly he would not have decided against me, when I suspended Morley, without hearing my reasons for doing so, if he had not been biassed in some way."

"I have no doubt of it; and if Morley owns the vice, there will be a row before we reach Constantinople. By the way, have you any idea of the contents of that valise which Mr. Tompion brought from the shore last night?" laughed Scott.

"It was reported to be heavy, with a suspicion that it contained glass ware."

"In a word — bottles!"

"And one of them has since been opened," added the captain.

"The vice must have emptied one by this time, for he didn't show himself last evening, and he was pretty well set up at noon to-day."

"I can hardly believe that Mr. Tompion was drunk, and I should not, if I had not the evidence of my own eyes," continued Wainwright.

"Do you mean to say that the vice-principal was intoxicated?" demanded Morley, stepping up from behind the mainmast, where he had evidently been standing during a part or the whole of this conversation.

Morley was the officer of the deck, and he ought to have been on the weather side of the quarter-deck, out of hearing of the speakers.

"I was not addressing my remarks to you, Mr. Morley," replied the captain, with dignity. "You will take your place on the weather side, where you belong."

"But you make a charge which is a disgrace to any officer of this vessel," added Morley. "You used my name also."

"You will return to your duty, Mr. Morley," repeated the captain.

"You have made charges against Mr. Tompion and me which it is my duty to resent."

"This is not the time, nor the place to bring charges, or to try them. If you do not obey my order, I will suspend you, and commit you to the brig."

Morley suddenly turned upon his heel, and walked aft. Probably he thought he had been a little too fast, and both the boatswain and the carpenter were in the waist, always ready to obey the orders of the captain.

"We are in for it now," said Scott.

"Sooner than I expected. I didn't suppose that fellow was within hearing distance of me. Come down into my room, and we will look over the situation, for I have put my foot into it now, beyond the possibility of a reasonable doubt."

"So have I; we are both in the same boat."

The captain and first lieutenant retired to the state-room of the former, where there was no possibility of interruption.

"Morley clearly does duty as vice-principal in the

Tritonia, besides being second lieutenant," said Scott. "He would not have dared to say what he did if he had not been the proprietor of Mr. Tompion."

"There is something or other that hasn't come out yet," added the captain.

"But it has come out that the vice tipples, and is unfit to do his duty. Morley has a charge to make against both of us, and when the vice is sober enough to hear it, we shall be suspended."

"I hardly think that," mused Wainwright. "I am not quite willing to be suspended by the vice-principal in his present condition."

"He is the power on board, and we must obey. He may commit us both to the brig."

"I am not afraid of that."

"I am not afraid of it; for, having done my duty, it would not vex me very much to spend a week, or even a month, in the brig, for I know that Mr. Lowington would set me right in the end."

"But there is a limit to the vice-principal's power. Suppose he should order the Tritonia to the East Indies without the principal's knowledge or approval; must we go to the East Indies?"

"Certainly not; but it is rather a nice point to take the power out of his hands."

"I don't propose to take the power out of his hands; neither am I quite ready to have it taken out of my hands. The matter is becoming serious, Scott, and we must make up our minds what to do."

"In my opinion, we shall very soon have nothing to do, for both of us will be suspended."

"Very well; let us look that question full in the

face.   Mr. Tompion is at this moment intoxicated, and unfit to do his duty.   Shall we obey his orders?"

" Query — shall we?"

" Though I am captain, and you are executive officer, of the Tritonia, we are both boys."

" I beg your pardon, captain, I am as old as Charles XII. was when he came to power."

" Never mind your joke, Scott.   This is a serious business.   If you are not a boy, you are young; and I think we had better take the advice of some of the old ones on board.   Let us talk over the situation with Professor Primback and Dr. Crimple."

" Right ; that's a good idea," replied Scott.   Let us do it at once ; and it wouldn't be a bad idea to ring in the boatswain and carpenter, for they are seamen, as the professors are not.   Besides, Mr. Rimmer was on deck when you suspended Morley, and understands the merits of the case."

" I think we had better talk with the professors first."

Scott assented, and they went to the double state-room, occupied by the two instructors, both of whom were there, correcting compositions.   They knocked, and were admitted.

" Ah, Captain Wainwright ! Good afternoon. It is an unexpected honor to receive both the captain and the first lieutenant at the same time," said Mr. Primback.

" We come on serious business, sir," added Wainwright ; and he proceeded to describe the situation on board of the vessel.

" Intoxicated !   It cannot be possible !" exclaimed Mr. Primback.   " I have never seen anything of it."

"Nor I, until to-day, sir."

"I think you must be mistaken, Captain Wainwright," added Dr. Crimple. "Mr. Tompion has complained of being unwell, and stays in his state-room a great deal."

"The truth may be easily determined by either of you gentlemen," suggested Scott. "It would be quite proper for Dr. Crimple to visit the vice-principal in his room."

"I will do so," added the doctor, who was a physician, though he was employed on board only as an instructor.

He was absent some time.

"Did you see him?" asked Professor Primback.

"I did; I knocked at his door several times, but obtaining no answer, I entered. Mr. Tompion is certainly intoxicated, and is utterly senseless at this moment," reported the doctor. "I am amazed, but it is true."

The painful fact was commented upon at some length, and then the captain explained his relations with Morley, and his belief that the second lieutenant had some powerful influence over the vice-principal.

"Why do you think so, Captain Wainwright?" asked Mr. Primback.

"Because Morley spent an hour in his cabin last evening, and to-day comes the order to sail for Constantinople before the arrival of the Young America. I think the orders were, that whichever vessel arrived at Cowes first should wait for the other."

"Is that your only reason for thinking Morley influences Mr. Tompion?" inquired Dr. Crimple.

"No, sir; when I suspended Morley for neglect of

duty and disobedience of orders, Mr. Tompion re-stored him without hearing me."

"That looks more like it," added Mr. Primback, who was the senior instructor. "Now, what do you wish us to do about it?"

"Nothing at present, sir. I had some words with the second lieutenant this afternoon; I shall not be surprised if Mr. Scott and myself are suspended from duty."

"If this is done, we shall be convinced that Morley has a mortgage on the vice-principal," added Scott.

The captain explained all that had occurred on deck.

"I expect trouble, gentlemen, and I want your ad-vice," continued Wainwright.

"I don't know much about nautical affairs, but I don't think the vessel ought to be directed by a man in liquor," said Mr. Primback.

"I think it is coming on to blow, sir. My barome-ter indicates a change of weather," the captain pro-ceeded. "I cannot handle the vessel if my officers do not obey my orders. If Morley or anybody else does not do his duty I shall suspend him. The trouble may come on in this way; or I may be suspended my-self. Shall I submit to the suspension, or shall I dis-obey the vice-principal?"

"This is, indeed, very serious business. Do you think there will be a storm, captain," asked the senior professor, with evident alarm.

"I think we shall have a gale within twenty-four hours, sir."

"It is a bad time to have any trouble in the management of the vessel, then," added Mr. Primback, nervously.

"It is; we are about off The Needles now, and I think we shall have rough weather before morning," replied Wainwright. "Shall I obey the orders of the vice-principal, or not?"

"I don't know what to say," answered the puzzled professor.

"Perhaps you would like to talk it over with the carpenter and boatswain. They are old sailors and reliable men," suggested Scott.

"I should," said the doctor.

"So should I," added Mr. Primback.

The old salts were sent for, and Wainwright and Scott retired, in order to permit them to discuss the question in all its bearings. The boatswain and carpenter believed in the captain and first lieutenant, for Mr. Rimmer had witnessed the difficulty which resulted in Morley's suspension, and believed that Wainwright was right; and the boatswain readily adopted his opinion. The result of the conference was, that the orders of Mr. Tompion, if they changed the organization of the ship's company, or altered the vessel's course, should not be obeyed. The suspension of the captain and executive officer was not to be tolerated. The opinion of the council was communicated to the captain, who agreed that nothing should be done as long as Morley performed his duty.

As the captain had predicted, but not till his opinion had been fortified by that of Marline, a storm was approaching. The wind came very fresh from the south-east during the night, and the Tritonia carried only her jib, foresail, and mainsail. Everything went on very well during the night. Possibly the conference with the professors, and the calling of the boatswain and carpenter below, all of which had been noticed and reported to Morley, had some influence upon him, and deterred him from any overt act. He did not know what had transpired in the professors' state-room, for Wainwright and Scott kept their own counsel, and said nothing even to their friends.

Already the nine officers were divided into two parties, and had been since the suspension of Morley. The captain had but three adherents, including Scott, while Morley had four; but the crew, who had done the most of the voting, were believed to be on the captain's side in a much greater proportion. However, it was not expected that Morley's friends would follow his lead.

In the morning the wind freshened to a gale. The foresail had been taken in; but the Tritonia labored heavily, rolling down in the trough of the sea, so that the water poured in over the bulwarks. The whole port watch under Morley was on duty from eight o'clock. The captain had ordered life-lines to be extended across the deck to insure the safety of the crew. The vessel was off Guernsey, having passed The Casquets three hours before. The wind came fierce and gusty from the Bay of Biscay.

"Put two reefs in the foresail, Mr. Morley, and have it ready to set," said the captain, who was holding on at the life-line.

"In the foresail?" growled the officer of the deck.

"I said so," replied the captain, sharply.

"She don't lay to under a close-reefed foresail," muttered Morley, in surly tones.

"I don't purpose to lay her to."

"What are you going to do, then?"

"When you have obeyed my order I will give another."

"I don't intend to risk my life by driving the vessel ahead in the trough of the sea. The proper thing to do is to lay her to under close-reefed mainsail, and lash the throat down if it comes too heavy for her," said Morley, impudently.

"I didn't ask your advice, and you will obey my order," replied the captain.

"I am used to the Tritonia. I have been in her in more than one gale, and I know she don't work under a close-reefed foresail. I decline to obey the order, and have given my reasons."

"I suspend you from duty," said the captain. "Mr. Scott!"

"Here, sir!"

"You will take the deck, and close-reef the foresail at once."

"Yes, sir."

Scott gave the orders to reef the foresail, and the work was promptly done. The jib and mainsail were taken in, and the reefed foresail was set. The foretop-gallant-yard and mast had been sent down early in the morning. The captain then ordered the vessel to be headed west-south-west, which made the true course about west, so that she had the wind on her quarter; and this took her out of the trough of the sea, relieving her very much. It was a heavy gale, but not a hurricane, and the Tritonia went along very well.

Morley retreated to the cabin as soon as he was suspended, and knocked at the door of the vice-principal, who was just waking from his inebriate sleep. He stated his case, and charged the captain and first lieutenant with disrespect to the vice-principal, in speaking evil of him on the quarter-deck.

"Send the captain to me," said Mr. Tompion.

"I am suspended, sir."

"I restore you; report to the captain for duty, and send him to me."

"Besides disgracing the quarter-deck by scandalous speech in regard to you, sir, I am afraid he will founder the vessel," added Morley.

"I will go on deck myself."

"I had hoped you would take more decided measures, sir."

"What?" demanded the vice-principal, with a stare.

"Suspend the captain and first lieutenant. In my opinion we shall all go to the bottom if you don't," added Morley, with emphasis.

"I will get up immediately, and see you in the cabin."

The conspirator retired, and Mr. Tompion got out of his berth. His nerves were in fearful commotion, and he drank half a tumblerful of brandy to quiet them. He made his toilet, and then drank again. The strong liquor took immediate effect, and even then he was not in condition to settle the serious question referred to him. He tried to walk, but the uneasy motion of the vessel defeated him. Opening the door, he called Morley.

"I think you are right, Mr. Morley. I am quite

sick, and do not feel able to go on deck. I suspend the captain and first lieutenant."

" Will you give me a written order to that effect? "

" You may write it, and I will sign it."

Morley wrote the order, which not only suspended Wainwright and Scott, but put himself and Greenwood in their places. With difficulty Mr. Tompion signed the order, and armed with this document the conspirator went on deck.

CHAPTER XI.

THE STREETS OF CONSTANTINOPLE.

DE FORREST and Beckwith, after the pleasant interview with Mr. Englefield at the banker's, were utterly dissatisfied with the situation. The detective was certainly very considerate that he did not commit them to prison, or in some other way secure their attendance on board of the Young America when she arrived. He did not appear to trouble himself enough about them to keep a watch upon their movements. He had not interfered to prevent them from drawing money at the banker's, as he might have done, and he permitted them to depart, even after they knew the whole truth in regard to his mission.

The runaways walked up the steep hill to Pera. They were silent for a time, though they occasionally glanced at each other, as if to read in the expression of the face the effect of the detective's revelation. They took no notice of the Turks, Arabs, Armenians, and other nationalities that were represented in the passers-by. Indeed, they reached the hotel without speaking a word. They passed through the corridor, and went up stairs to their room. One of them seated himself in a chair, and the other stretched his limbs on a sofa.

" Where are we now, De Forrest? " said Beckwith.

" In Constantinople, of course," replied the chief runaway, petulantly.

" Shut in, the gates closed, so that we can't get out."

" Well, is it my fault? "

" Of course not. I don't hold you responsible for our mishap."

" O, I didn't know but you did ! " growled De Forrest.

" You needn't be so touchy about it. We are in the same boat."

" I wish we were in any boat."

" You seem to have abandoned hope."

" What's the use? We are trapped."

" Don't give it up yet. The ship will not be here for two or three weeks."

" What can we do? That blasted Britisher says we can't go on board of a steamer without being stopped ; and all we can do is to struggle like a fly in a spider's web."

" The Britisher thinks he is smart, and perhaps he is ; but suppose we try a hand in this game with him."

" What do you mean? "

" I don't intend to give up the ship."

" And the ship don't intend to give you up, either ; and in my opinion the ship will get the better of you."

" Very good, De Forrest ; we can look about us, and study up the chances. If we find an opportunity to get away, we can improve it," said Beckwith. " I have my letter of credit, and plenty of cash, and I don't intend to cry baby yet."

" What are you going to do? " asked De Forrest,

somewhat encouraged by the hopeful view of his friend.

"I haven't the least idea. I don't know what to do; but let us look around, and ascertain. As Mr. Englefield says, I have no doubt that all the regular steamers are closed against us. But I saw an American flag flying at the peak of a bark in the port to-day. Perhaps we can do something with her. Never mind now. We will see the sights of Constantinople, and keep an eye on the situation also. We may be able to show this Britisher that Yankees are smart sometimes."

And so they spent nearly a week in seeing the wonders of the City of the Sultan. They met Mr. Englefield two or three times a day; but he appeared to take no precautions in regard to them. Merely to ascertain which way the land lay, as Beckwith expressed it, and doubtless he meant the " land of liberty," they applied at the office of the Messageries Impériales for tickets to the Piræus. When their names were asked for, they gave in " Samuel Smith" and "Jacob Jones." The clerk then asked for their passports. This time the runaways had these documents with them; but after giving fictitious names, they dared not show them. Then there was a great deal of talk among the clerks and others in the private office, and finally the young gentlemen were invited to enter this apartment. A man who spoke English was sent for.

" We are forbidden to sell tickets to you. You are runaways from your ship," said the interpreter.

" But we are students, not seamen," replied Beckwith. " We are the sons of gentlemen, and have the money to pay our passage."

" Where do you wish to go ? "

" To the Piræus ; and we want first-class tickets."

The price of a ticket was sixty-five francs ; and for a Frenchman to sacrifice one hundred and thirty francs in those dull times, while the war was keeping all travellers at home, was more than his nature could stand.   The man who had forbidden the agent to sell the tickets was only a detective, though he had the power to give the boys a great deal of trouble.

" Come to me to-morrow, and I will get you on board," said the agent ; and this answer was interpreted, though Beckwith understood it very well. " The steamer sails at four in the afternoon ; but you must go on board in the forenoon, and the captain will keep you out of sight."

The runaways were satisfied with this arrangement, paid their money, and received their ticket, which was only a receipt, and answered for two persons.   They gave their real names this time.   The next morning Mr. Englefield smoked his pipe in the reading-room, and the boys pretended that they were going over to Scutari, to see Miss Nightingale's hospital, and get the fine view from the hill.

" All right, my lads ; go where you please, but don't forget to come back before night," laughed the detective.

They left the hotel, but it was only to seek a shelter from observation in one of the narrow alleys, where they waited till Mr. Englefield came out.   He walked up the Rue de Pera, and entered a *café chantant*, where English beer was sold during the day.   He was fond of beer, and the boys were satisfied he would

stay in the *café* an hour or two, at least. They returned to the hotel, and asked for their bill, saying
they wished to pay it before it became too large. Like
honest Americans, the Greeks in charge of the house
never refuse to take money when it is offered, and
sometimes when it is not offered. The bill was paid,
and the runaways went up to their rooms.

" Now, how shall we get these confounded bags out
of the hotel? " said De Forrest.

" We can wear the pea-jackets," said Beckwith, as
he put on his own.

De Forrest followed his example. Beckwith then
transferred all the small articles in his bag to the pockets of the overcoat, and his companion did the same.
The pair of shirts were placed inside of the back of
the coats, each assisting the other in laying them
smoothly. This additional thickness made them look
rather round-shouldered ; but they were not aiming at
symmetry and beauty on the present occasion. The
bags were then flattened out as much as possible, and
placed on the breast, the coats being buttoned over
them. If any one of their friends, especially Mr. Englefield, had seen them then, he might have congratulated them on their rapid growth, or suspected that
they were stuffed for the part of Falstaff. Thus prepared, they went down stairs, and got out of the house
with all possible haste. No one appeared to notice
them. As they walked down the steep hill to Galata,
they congratulated themselves on the smartness with
which they had managed the affair ; and probably Mr.
Englefield's beer tasted better than it would if he
had known what they were doing. The agent of the

steamer took them off to the vessel in his own boat, and they were politely received by the captain, who laughed prodigiously when they unbuttoned their coats. He took them to his own room, and locked them in. Of course the obliging Mr. Englefield could not expect them from Scutari till late in the afternoon; but in spite of this fact, he went on board of the French steamer just before her hour for sailing. He looked over all the passengers on board, and remained on deck till the order was given to heave up the anchor. He examined the passenger list, and looked into all the state-rooms in the first and second cabins. He did this every time a steamer sailed; and he went ashore assured that his charge were still safe.

The runaways did not appear at dinner. Possibly they had taken a longer jaunt in Scutari than they had intended. At dark they had not arrived, and Mr. Englefield applied at the office for information. The boys had paid their bill in the forenoon, but only that it might not become too large. Alexis and Dimitri, the Greek guides, were called up. Neither of them had been over to Scutari, or had seen the missing guests. The room of the absentees was then visited, and it was found that their meagre baggage had been removed. Mr. Englefield was both annoyed and perplexed. Possibly he concluded that he was not so " clever " as he had supposed, though this was hardly probable, for men like him seldom " go back " on themselves. The next day he went to the agent of the French steamers, who was utterly ignorant in regard to the movements of the runaways. There was the passenger list; he could read for himself; and it

was an imputation upon his own " cleverness " to suppose they had escaped in that way, after his visit to the
vessel.   The one hundred and thirty francs paid to the
Frenchman concealed everything.   For the next week
the detective was very busy, but he became no wiser.
When the ship arrived, he went on board of her; but
he was a sad and bewildered detective then, and was
very sorry he had not " committed " the runaways
when they reached Constantinople.   But he had a
theory.   The American bark, which Beckwith had
noticed, sailed a few days after the French steamer,
and he was confident that the runaways had been concealed on board of her.   Mr. Lowington was willing
to accept this theory, since there appeared to be no
other explanation of the departure of the boys.   If
the young gentlemen had gone home, he was satisfied,
and let the matter drop from his mind.   Mr. Englefield was paid for his services and expenses, and departed by the next steamer for Vienna.

The students on board of the ship were impatient
to go on shore, and after Mr. Mapps's lecture they
were permitted to do so.   The boats had been lowered, and made fast to the swinging boom, and in regular order the ship's company embarked.   Captain
Cantwell invited Dr. Winstock to take a seat in his
gig, and the surgeon was the *chaperon* of the first
three officers during their stay in Constantinople.

"What is that tower, sir?" asked the captain,
pointing to a structure which was planted in the
water near the Asiatic shore, and opposite the mouth
of the Golden Horn.

" Europeans call it Leander's Tower, and it is so

laid down in many books, but is a misnomer. Leander swam the Hellespont, which is the Strait of Dardanelles, to meet Miss Hero; and of course there is no sense in calling this tower after him. The Turks call it *Kiz Kulassee*, or Maiden's Tower, though there seems to be no fitness in this name, unless we accept the romantic story told about it, which is utterly devoid of truth."

" What is the story? " asked Sheridan.

" It is said that one of the sultans had a beautiful daughter, to whom he was devotedly attached. The Moslem oracle declared that this fair girl would lose her life by the bite of a venomous serpent. The prediction troubled the fond father sorely, and he looked about him for the means of averting her dire destiny. He rebelled against Fate, to which the Turk generally yields himself in blind submission, and caused this tower to be erected for her residence in the sea, where no serpent could possibly reach her. But Fate was not to be cheated by any human devices. One day Fatima — for this, I believe, was her name — saw a boat passing the tower, loaded with baskets of the most delicious grapes, such as you will see as soon as you go on shore. She desired one of her attendants to purchase a basket of fruit, which was done. When Fatima helped herself to grapes from the basket, a small serpent darted from the rich clusters, and stung her. Before a leech could be brought from the shore she died, and Fate claimed its own. But all this is a silly fiction."

" It is not a bad story," laughed Murray.

" No; but history and romance should be separated,"

added the doctor. " In ancient times the tower was called Damalis, the name of the wife of the Athenian general Chares. She died at Chrysopolis, now Scutari, and her husband buried her in a mausoleum erected on the rocks where the tower now stands. On the column above it was an inscription, in which the deceased claimed to be a heifer, but not the one for which the Bosporus was named; for you know this word means the ford of the heifer, after the animal that swam across it. The close of the inscription was as follows: ' I, the remains of an Athenian woman, was the wife of Chares when he sailed here to meet the fleet of Philip. I was then named a heifer, but now the consort of Chares, and I enjoy the sight of both continents.' But this story is almost as foolish as the other. The tower was originally built by Manuel Comnenus, one of the emperors of the East, in order to pass over it a chain, by which the Bosporus could be closed against vessels. There was another tower for the same purpose on the other side. This has been destroyed and rebuilt several times, the last by Mahmoud II."

The boats landed at Galata, where the custom-house officials lie in wait for travellers. A fat Turk challenged the doctor and his party, speaking in monosyllabic French. Dr. Winstock said they had nothing, and took no further notice of him.

" Why is this called Galata ? " asked Murray.

" Because that's its name," laughed Sheridan.

" That is perhaps the best answer that can be given to the question, but it is properly a suburb of Constantinople, as is Pera, at the top of the hill; Tophana, farther up the Bosporus; and Eyub, at the head of the Golden Horn. Galata was built by the Genoese, and surrounded by a wall and moat, which still exist. It is the seat of all the foreign commerce of the city, and the custom-house is here. The round structure you see yonder was built by the Genoese for a watch tower. It is one hundred and forty feet high, and our best way is to ascend it, for it commands a fine view of the city."

The party climbed to the top, and were amply rewarded for the labor of doing so.

"Those are odd bridges," said Murray, pointing to the two floating structures which connect Galata with Stamboul.

"They are floating bridges — built on boats," added Dr. Winstock.

"There are two humps in this nearer one."

"Those are parts raised up to permit the passage of boats beneath. A section of the pontoons can be removed, so that large vessels may go through. At Kassim Pacha, the suburb next above Galata, on the Golden Horn, are the Turkish arsenal and navy-yard. Though we call the city and suburbs by the same name, only the triangular section between the Golden Horn and the Sea of Marmora is properly Constantinople, or Istamboul, as the Turks call it. That part was the Byzantium of the ancients. The walls extend across the peninsula from water to water."

"Shall we see them?" asked the captain.

"Yes; one excursion will be in the boats by the Sea of Marmora to the Castle of the Seven Towers, and another up the Golden Horn to Eyub, and the

Valley of the Sweet Waters, where the sultan has a summer palace, At the point of the peninsula is the Old Seraglio, which contains a considerable portion of the interesting edifices of the city, including the Mosque of St. Sopha. Over in Scutari there are miles of burying-grounds. Near us you see the new palace of the sultan, which is a splendid affair, and not at all Oriental, though there is rather too much gingerbread work about it for good taste. Now we will go down and take a tramp through the streets. There is no regularity or order about them. They twist and wriggle about in every conceivable direction, and it is very easy to get lost."

From Galata the party walked up the hill to Pera. The street was very narrow, and as it had rained the day before, it was very wet and muddy. It was crowded with people in a vast variety of costumes.

"Steady!" said Murray, suddenly. "There comes a lady. I must stop and look at her."

"Be civil, lieutenant," added the doctor.

In spite of this warning, the three officers stared at the lady with all their eyes. She was dressed in loose, flowing robes of brown material which might have dragged upon the pavement if she had permitted them to do so. She wore white cotton socks, dropped down into a heap above her shoes, which were of yellow morocco. The 'yashmak,' or muslin, which Turkish ladies wear upon the head, covered all her face, except the eyes and a part of the nose.

"Is that a houri?" asked Murray, as the lady passed on.

"Hardly," replied the doctor.

"She is as homely as a broken brickbat," laughed Sheridan. "She is pale and yellow. Her face is almost the color of her shoes."

"The women eat too many sweetmeats to be healthy. About the streets and in the bazaar you will see vast quantities of pastes, gums, candies, and other stuff of the sort, of which the females are large consumers."

"Her head-gear was very thin," added Captain Cantwell. "I saw her face plain enough."

"I think you will find that the prettier the lady, the thinner will be the veil."

"Then this one ought to have a thicker one," added Murray.

"Here are a lot more."

A great, fat, slouchy-looking woman next waddled by them.

"She's a beauty!" exclaimed Sheridan, as he glanced at her ankles, below which her socks were rolled up in a heap.

"That is the Turkish standard of beauty," added the doctor.

"Are these the beautiful houris we read about in the Arabian Nights," asked Murray, with an expression of disgust.

"Certainly not. These are Turkish women of the ordinary class. On Friday you will probably see some Circassians."

The Turkish women who are seen in the streets and in the avenues of the bazaar are far from attractive to an American. They are not simply very plain, but are positively homely. They are dirty, in spite of the baths; they are untidy, their white socks being almost invariably rolled down on the top of their shoes; and their loose robes permit no idea of symmetry of form. There is no poetry in their motion, for they all waddle.

"Hallo! How's this?" shouted Murray. "Shall we run or face the music?"

"Face the music," laughed the doctor, as he dodged into a doorway, the rest of the party following his example.

The occasion of this demonstration was the approach of a donkey loaded with half a dozen joists, about twenty-five feet in length. They were crossed over his back, one end of them projecting far beyond the animal's head, and the other dragging behind him on the ground, close up to the houses on each side of the narrow street. He cleared the street as effectually as a Persian war chariot armed with scythes could have done it, as the passers-by were compelled to retreat or seek shelter in the doorways and alleys. At the same moment, farther up the hill, could be seen a large mule, with two immense panniers dangling at his sides, filled with cord-wood. Like the donkey, he swept the street, the panniers nearly touching the houses on each side.

"The donkeys and the mules seem to have the right of way here," said Cantwell.

"Where the streets are not more than eight or ten feet wide, it is no use to contend," replied the doctor, as the party resumed their walk.

"Are there no vehicles in this city?" asked Sheridan.

"Very few indeed. Down on the street which leads to Tophana, you will find an excellent road, by which the sultan often goes to mosque; and a few carriages are to be seen there, in which the wives of the pachas and others take their morning airing. You can go over to the Seraglio, and out to the Seven Towers in a vehicle; but by far the larger number of the streets of Constantinople are impassable for carriages."

"What's that going up the hill ahead of us?" inquired Murray.

The strange object appeared to be a pile of trunks, valises, and other travelling articles, mysteriously provided with a pair of legs. A nearer approach explained the mystery. It was a *hamil*, or porter, carrying a traveller's baggage. He was a dark-skinned fellow, wearing a turban instead of a fez. Slung over his back by ropes across his shoulders was a kind of cushion or saddle. Upon it was placed a good-sized sole-leather trunk; on this a valise, an overcoat, and a leather hat-box; while the man carried in his hands two bags and two umbrellas. He bent forward under his load, but his face looked cheerful, and he did not seem to labor so hard in toiling up the hill with his burden as Dr. Winstock's party.

"When I first came to this city, I had two such trunks as the one that porter carries," said the surgeon; "but the hamil carried them both up to Misserie's at one load; waited some ten minutes in the corridor, until my room was assigned to me, and then went up two flights of stairs with it. He did not seem to be tired after he had put down his load."

" Why don't they have wagons? "

" This street isn't wide enough for a wagon, in the first place ; and if it were, how much load do you think a horse could pull up this steep hill?   The wag-on alone would be enough for him."

" How do people get about who can't walk?" asked Sheridan.

" In many places in the city, you will find saddle horses to let.   There is one," added the doctor, as they passed from the narrow street into the Grande Rue de Pera.   " The man in charge of him is an Arab, and if you hire the horse, the keeper will run after you all day, whipping up your steed, if he needs it."

" But how do ladies get along? "

" Do you see that sedan yonder?" continued the surgeon, pointing to it, near the hotel.

" I see."

It was a kind of box, large enough to seat a single person.   It had doors, and small windows provided with curtains, and was borne on two poles, by as many men.   At that moment a handsome hooded phaeton, drawn by two horses, dashed along the *Grande Rue*, which was so narrow that the foot-passengers were obliged to flee for their lives into the alleys, doorways, and shops.   Some places are wide enough for two vehicles to pass, but generally the wheels are within a foot of the buildings on either side.   On this street are the principal hotels, and the winter residences of the ambassadors, — very plain structures, — and most of the diplomats have villas on the Bosporus for the summer.   The principal foreign stores are on this thoroughfare, though the bankers are generally in Galata. Perhaps half the people seen in Pera are foreigners, and the aspect of this quarter is more European than Oriental.

Our travellers walked through this street till they came to the vast space which had been ravaged by the great fire of 1870, only three months before. The loss was estimated at twenty-five millions of dollars; seven thousand houses were destroyed, among them many of the best in the city; and about one thousand persons perished in the flames. This vast territory, blackened with piles of ruins, presented a sad spectacle. In some places men were clearing away the rubbish, preparatory to the erection of new buildings, and the students were much interested and amused at the operations of the Turkish laborers. They brought up the dirt from the cellars in baskets, instead of shovelling it out, and it was carried away in panniers by donkeys and mules. It is safe to say that an Irish laborer, well superintended, would have accomplished as much as four of them. All the tools were clumsy, and the operations ungainly.

From the scene of the fire, the party retraced their steps through the Rue de Pera, and descending a flight of broad steps, or rather paved terraces, they came to Galata again. The pavement in the old avenues of Constantinople is precisely the same as that found in the streets of Pompeii, and consists of irregular blocks of stone, with the flattest side laid uppermost. The excursionists crossed the lower floating bridge, over which a vast tide of humanity is always sweeping in both directions. On the way they inspected a fleet of caiques, which are by no means so graceful as they are usually represented to be. They look somewhat like "dugouts," or canoes, with attempts at carving or other ornamentation in and upon them. They are round-bottomed, and boatmen and passengers sit on cushions placed on the bottom of the craft, for they upset almost as easily as a bark canoe. On the lower side of the bridge, half way over, was the landing-place of the ferry steamers to Scutari, in no way noticeable except for the lattice partition on the quarter-deck, which separates the women from the rest of the passengers.

The party wandered about Stamboul for an hour, and the appearance there was truly Oriental. They looked into the stores, coffee-rooms, and houses, all of which were decidedly Asiatic. Many of the buildings were of wood, with a kind of "overhang" above the first floor. The shops contained curious wares, whose use the strangers could not even surmise. They obtained an outside view of a mosque, with a beautiful fountain near it. The streets were full of peddlers, vending all manner of wares. Those who sold grapes were the most interesting. Each of them carried a large basket, and sold the fruit by weight. The boys purchased some, — for they had procured a supply of Turkish change, — and they were delicious. Returning to the other side, they embarked for the ship.

CHAPTER XII.

THE VICE-PRINCIPAL'S WRITTEN ORDER.

IN spite of the protest of Morley, the Tritonia made very good weather under a close-reefed foresail, and Captain Wainwright was entirely satisfied with the action he had taken in regard to the vessel. After his orders had been executed, he walked forward, and inquired for Mr. Marline, the adult boatswain, and a midshipman was sent below to call him. Wainwright was uneasy, and expected a tempest other than that of the elements; but the safety of the vessel was his first consideration.

"On deck, sir," said Mr. Marline, reporting to the captain.

"I wish to speak with you privately," replied the captain, as he led the way to the quarter-deck, and then below to his state-room, while Morley was in the vice-principal's cabin. "Sit down, if you please, Mr. Marline."

The boatswain seated himself, satisfied that the trouble had already commenced.

"I have just suspended the second lieutenant for refusing to obey my order," continued Wainwright.

"Indeed! I am sorry for that," replied the boatswain.

" Sorry for it?"

" Sorry that it should be necessary, I mean. Of course, after the talk we had with the professors, I expected it."

" I ordered Mr. Morley, as officer of the deck, to put two reefs in the foresail, and he declined to obey the order."

" Then you did quite right to suspend him," promptly added Mr. Marline.

" There is no doubt in my mind about that; but Mr. Morley declared that the Tritonia would not work under a close-reefed foresail. Is that so?"

" No, sir, it is not so. She will work under anything that any vessel will."

" You are an old sailor, and know the Tritonia better than I do, for I have not been in her in heavy weather before. Do you think I have done the right thing?"

" Certainly you have, Captain Wainwright," answered the boatswain, heartily. " The vessel is doing very well, and behaving like a lady. You have got her out of the trough of the sea, where she was laboring heavily. There were two ways to do it, one of which you have chosen; and, on the whole, I think it was the best way."

" Morley said she ought to be laid to under a close-reefed mainsail, with the throat of the gaff lashed down," added the captain.

" There is no kind of need of that," laughed the boatswain. " It don't blow heavy enough to require anything of that sort."

" That was just my opinion."

"It blows a smart gale, but not heavy enough to keep the captain on deck. We are running off our course; that's the only objection I have."

"That's of little consequence, compared with the safety of the vessel."

"Why, she is in no more danger than if she was in one of the Liverpool docks."

"If she were in peril, of course I should not be in my state-room."

"When it comes heavy enough to blow the foresail out of the bolt-ropes, it will be time enough to talk about laying her to. She would be safe enough on her course to the sou'-west, in the trough of the sea, but she isn't comfortable on that tack. I think she would carry a double-reefed mainsail and storm-jib, close-hauled on the wind."

"But that would bring us in among the islands and rocks off the shore," suggested the captain. "Our present course gives us the open sea."

"You are quite right. I should keep her as she is. If the gale holds for twenty-four hours, I should brace her up at the end of that time, for then she will have the open sea ahead as well as astern."

"I find we are perfectly agreed on this point. I told you I expected trouble, Mr. Marline."

"Yes, sir; and I expected it myself."

"By this time Morley has reported his suspension to the vice-principal, who will probably restore him to duty, and very likely suspend me."

"I talked all that over with the philosophers —"

"With whom?" inquired the captain.

"I beg your pardon. I mean the professors," said

the boatswain. "I dare say it is very wrong to do so, but Mr. Rimmer and I always call them the philosophers."

"I see nothing wrong in it, for the term is hardly disrespectful."

"Well, sir, I talked the matter over with the philosophers — I mean the instructors. They sent for the carpenter and me in order to get a salt opinion. I told them, fair and square, and Mr. Rimmer told them just the same, that the captain of the Tritonia was all right, and Mr. Morley was all wrong. The philosophers agreed with us that the captain must be sustained; that's what the philosophers called it; Rimmer and I say backed up. We are ready to do it. When you say the word, Captain Wainwright, we will clap Mr. Morley into the brig, and any one else who don't obey orders."

"I am very sorry to have this trouble, Mr. Marline. It is not of my seeking," added Wainwright.

"Of course it isn't. Mr. Morley is mad because he wasn't elected captain, and he has made all the trouble. This voting on board ship is a nuisance."

"I begin to think so myself. I rather liked the excitement of the elections, though Scott and I opposed the thing in the beginning. I will go on deck now, and wait for the earthquake, for there will be one."

"No doubt of that."

"But suppose Mr. Tompion should come on deck himself," suggested the captain. "I can't very well resist him."

"The philosophers have agreed to take care of him. The fact of it is, Captain Wainwright, Mr. Tompion is no longer fit for his business. He is drunk all day long. I was always afraid of it," added the boatswain, seriously.

"Afraid of what?"

"That he would take to drinking again."

"Why, did he ever drink hard before?"

"Bless you, yes. A man never drops all at once into tippling as hard as he does. I never said a word about it before, but he was obliged to resign his place in the navy on account of his habits. His friends got him out, or he would have been court-martialed and ruined. Yes, sir; he was a lieutenant in the navy, and as promising an officer as there was in the service. I was in his watch one cruise, and in his gun division, too."

"I am surprised!"

"He left off drinking, and I don't believe he touched a drop for three years. Mr. Lowington, who is a sort of salt-water angel, encouraged him, helped him, and stood by him. He got a ship for Mr. Tompion, and he made two voyages in her. Then he gave him this place, which pays better. But when a man gets the appetite for rum fixed in his body and bones, it is pretty hard to get it out of him. It is a very sad case, and Mr. Lowington will feel as though he had lost his mother-in-law when he hears about this business."

"I am glad to know the whole story, and I really pity him. I hope some way to save him will be found," added the captain, as he left his room, and the boatswain went forward through the steerage.

Wainwright ascended the steps to the deck. The Tritonia was pitching and rolling violently in the heavy sea, and a great wave occasionally combed over her bow or quarter, washing the decks with a barrel or two of water, which swashed out at the scuppers. It was simply exciting, not perilous. The whole port watch was still on duty, with Scott as officer of the deck in the place of Morley. The weather was too rough for the regular recitations, and all school work had been suspended. The captain seated himself on the settee at the side of the companion-way to wait for the expected event of the day. It was not long delayed, for Morley had been on deck some time, waiting to deliver the order from the vice-principal to the captain. Mr. Marline and Mr. Rimmer were in the waist, as near the mainmast as the etiquette of the ship permitted them to go. When they saw Morley hand his document to the captain, they stepped upon the quarter-deck.

"Captain Wainwright, here is an order from the vice-principal," said Morley, touching his cap, as he held out the important paper.

The captain took it, opened it slowly, and with no appearance of excitement, though his looks certainly belied him, he read the order. He saw at the first glance that it was in the handwriting of the second lieutenant. It was as follows:—

"Mr. Morley, second lieutenant, suspended by Captain Wainwright, is hereby restored to duty.

"Captain Wainwright and Mr. Scott, first lieutenant, are hereby suspended from duty, and forbidden to appear on deck till further orders. Mr. Morley is hereby appointed captain of the Tritonia, and all vacancies are hereby ordered to be filled by the other officers in the order of their rank.

"F. TOMPION, *Vice-Principal.*"

"Did you write this order, Mr. Morley?" asked the captain.

"By order of the vice-principal, I did; but of course he signed it himself," replied Morley.

"I have no doubt he did, though, comparing it with his ordinary signature, any one would be justified in doubting the genuineness of it."

"Do you think I signed it?" demanded Morley, laboring to keep cool.

"I told you I had no doubt Mr. Tompion signed it."

"Then, of course, you are ready to obey it."

"On the contrary, I have concluded not to do so," replied the captain, quietly.

"Do I understand that you refuse to obey this order?" exclaimed Morley, amazed, and apparently unwilling to believe the evidence of his own ears.

"You have correctly understood me, I think; if you have not, I distinctly and explicitly declare that I will not obey the order."

"Let me remind you that this is an order from the vice-principal," added the astonished Morley.

"I am aware of it."

"Is it not in due form?"

"I do not object to the form."

"Will you tell me if there is anything irregular about the order?" asked Morley, who had never dreamed of such a thing as any one disregarding an order from the vice-principal, for he would not have dared to do it himself under any circumstances.

"I know of nothing.   I grant that the form is quite correct.   If it were not, I should not quibble about that.   I decline to obey the order."

"May I ask your reason for this extraordinary conduct, Captain Wainwright?" asked Morley, still struggling to keep cool.

"The vice-principal has no right to restore you or to suspend me without a hearing."

"Then you shall have a hearing."

"He is not in a condition to hear and judge upon the merits of a question which involves the safety of this vessel and all on board of her."

"Mr. Tompion is sick."

"Mr. Tompion is drunk."

"What!"

"Mr. Tompion is drunk, and while he remains in this condition, I shall decline to obey his orders, either verbal or written."

"Such a charge is a disgrace to the quarter-deck," said Morley, in a loud and violent tone.   "Mr. Tompion is sick, and is confined to his state-room.   Here is his written order, which you admit is in proper form; and you do not doubt the genuineness of his signature."

"I do not."

"Then I insist that you obey the order."

"I refuse to do so."

"*Mr.* Wainwright, I shall no longer recognize your authority as commander of the Tritonia," added Morley, savagely.   "I propose to read this order to the ship's company."

"I forbid the reading of it to the ship's company," replied Wainwright.

The captain, who still held the order in his hand, tore it in pieces, and threw it overboard.

"What do you mean?" stormed Morley, astounded at the audacity of Wainwright. "How dare you destroy an order from the vice-principal?"

"You are excited, Mr. Morley. We will not argue the matter."

"This is an outrage. By that order you and Mr. Scott are suspended from duty, and I am appointed captain of the Tritonia. I hereby take the command of the vessel; and I order you into the cabin."

"I refuse to yield the command, or to go below," answered the captain, rising from his seat.

"Then I will enforce the order."

Morley sprang at the captain, in the fury of his anger; but he sprang upon the wrong fellow, for, before Mr. Marline could interfere, he toppled over and rolled into the lee scuppers, under the influence of a single blow from Wainwright's hard fist.

"Shall I commit him to the brig?" asked the boatswain.

"No; not yet."

Morley knew very well that, physically, he was not a match for Wainwright, and his fall only reminded him of what he had long known. He did not, therefore, renew the assault. He picked himself up, and looked at the captain, who seemed to be too ready for a second attack.

"You will hear from me again!" howled he, and then retreated to the cabin, where he was followed by his friend and supporter, Greenwood.

"What under the canopy are you doing, Morley?"

demanded the third lieutenant. "Didn't you know any better than to pitch into the captain?"

"He is not the captain now," replied Morley. "He and Scott are suspended; I am captain, and you are first lieutenant."

"What do you mean by that?" asked Greenwood, who had not seen his fellow-conspirator after his suspension, though he knew his programme.

"I mean just what I say. Did you see Wainwright tear up the vice-principal's order?"

"I saw him tear up a paper, and throw it overboard."

"That was Mr. Tompion's order, suspending Wainwright and putting me in his place."

"Is that so?"

"Wainwright read the order, and he will tell you so. I am the captain now; and I pitched into him when he refused to obey the order."

"It was stupid to do that."

"Perhaps it was; but I was mad. I am going to write out that order again, get Mr. Tompion to sign it, and then read it to the ship's company."

"That's the right way to go to work. You ought to have done that before."

"I told Wainwright I was going to do it, but he forbade my doing it, and destroyed the order. Now talk the matter up with the officers and seamen, and have all hands on deck in half an hour to hear the order read."

"I will do all that;" and Greenwood left the cabin.

The affray on the quarter-deck, and the events which led to it, were already under discussion. Every officer and seaman, except Morley, was on deck, for even the drenching spray could not drive the students below when there was a prospect of an exciting time. Some of the officers had heard the whole conversation between Wainwright and Morley, and the merits of the question were pretty well understood. Among the officers, the four friends of the second lieutenant took sides with him, and declared that Wainwright ought to obey the order of Mr. Tompion, even if he was intoxicated, while Scott, Allyn, and Campbell sustained the captain. None of them, however, knew that the professors and the adult forward officers had taken counsel together, and decided what should be done in the difficult emergency. Perhaps, if they had known this, it would have changed the views of those who sided with the conspirators. The seamen held all sorts of opinions, and it was impossible to determine the strength of either party among them.

Morley rewrote the order precisely as it was before, and then entered the state-room of Mr. Tompion. It was some time before he could rouse the inebriate to his senses, so deep was his drunken slumber. He had in a measure slept off the effects of his last dram. The conspirator did not attempt to explain the situation on deck to the vice-principal, fearful that he might refuse to sign the duplicate order. He only said that the first one had been destroyed, and with trembling hand Mr. Tompion signed the paper.

"I am very sick, Mr. Morley," said he, as he gave up the pen.

"I am sorry, sir. Shall I ask Dr. Crimple to come in and see you?"

"No, no. I don't want to see anybody," he added, lying down in the berth again.

Morley left the room, satisfied now that he had the key to the situation. He paused in the cabin to consider the matter. Then he looked into the steerage. It was empty of students, and he was sure that Greenwood had assembled the crew on deck, as he had requested. He went to the quarter-deck himself, and the gaze of every one was turned to him as he appeared.

"Mr. Wainwright, I have procured another order from the vice-principal, which I intend to read to the ship's company, who are now assembled on the quarter-deck," said Morley.

"I forbid the reading of it," replied the captain.

"I don't care if you do forbid it; I shall read it," added Morley, as he moved towards the waist where the crew were assembled.

Wainwright followed him. The seamen were all in position to hear the order, and grasping a life-line, Morley unfolded the paper.

"Officers and seamen, I have an order — "

"Mr. Marline," called the captain, "you will commit Mr. Morley to the brig."

Before the conspirator could begin the order, the heavy hand of the boatswain was placed upon his shoulder.

"No, no!" shouted some of the officers and seamen.

"Commit him to the brig," said Captain Wainwright, firmly.

Mr. Marline dragged his prisoner through the knot

of seamen gathered in the waist, and in a moment more had turned the key of the brig upon him.

" I protest ! " shouted Greenwood.

" Let us hear the order ! " called some one from the waist.

" Young gentlemen," said Professor Primback, taking position at the mainmast, and raising his voice above the howling of the gale, " I feel obliged to make an explanation.   It is a very painful duty, but I am compelled to do it ; and that is, to declare that the vice-principal of this vessel is intoxicated, and unfit to discharge his duty.   Mr. Morley, taking advantage of Mr. Tompion's condition, has obtained from him the order which he attempted to read to you.   Dr. Crimple and myself, with the head steward and the forward officers, have had a consultation over this matter, and we have decided that the vice-principal's order, suspending the captain, and putting Mr. Morley in his place, ought not to be obeyed ; and Captain Wainwright acts in accordance with our advice.   I hope you will see the necessity of obeying your rightful officers, and doing your duty faithfully until we join the ship, and Mr. Lowington can decide who are right and who are wrong."

A few hisses greeted the speech of the professor, as he retired from the stand, but they were immediately drowned in the applause of Wainwright's friends, who were evidently more numerous than his enemies among the seamen, though it was otherwise among the officers.

Captain Wainwright then stepped forward.

" I appoint Mr. Greenwood second lieutenant, in place of Mr. Morley, suspended," said he.

"By the vice-principal's order, I am first lieutenant," Greenwood interposed.

"You are appointed second lieutenant. If you refuse to obey any order given you as such by Mr. Scott or myself, I will suspend you at once, and commit you to the brig, if necessary," added the captain, very decidedly.

"Well, I don't refuse, but —"

"We will not argue the matter," interposed the captain, who then proceeded to make the rest of his appointments, by which all the officers below the second lieutenant were temporarily advanced one grade.

Though the friends of Morley were still discontented, they offered no further objection, and for the present, at least, order seemed to be restored.

CHAPTER XIII.

THE DANCING DERVISHES AND THE DOGS.

"ALL hands ready to go ashore!" shouted the boatswain of the Young America, after a shrill pipe on his whistle.

This call was to enable the students to dress themselves properly for a trip to the city. On the quarter-deck, talking with Mr. Lowington, was a man in a fez, who had just come on board. Except the covering of his head, his dress was entirely European. Many people who are not Turks wear the fez, especially the Greeks, of whom there are great numbers in the City of the Sultan. This fez is a red felt cap, in the shape of the frustum of a cone, with a long silk tassel fastened in the middle of the top, and hanging down even to the neck of the wearer. It is worn by all classes of Turks, from the sultan down to the shoe-black.

The man in the fez was Dimitri, a *commissionaire*, or guide, from Misserie's Hotel. He spoke English and French fluently, and was thoroughly posted in the sights of the great city. He had been engaged to procure a firman from the sultan, which is necessary in order to visit the mosque of St. Sophia and other notable buildings in the Seraglio, and to attend the students in other excursions.   It was Friday, the Mohammedan Sunday, and the sultan, as usual on this day, was to visit one of the mosques in state.   This occasion furnishes almost the only opportunity for tourists to see the Ottoman sovereign.   He visits different mosques on this day, sometimes going over to Stamboul in his barge, and sometimes riding on horseback to one nearer his palace.   The particular mosque his majesty will attend is usually known during the forenoon, and a crowd always gathers near the palace gates to see the show.

The students seated themselves in the boats, each of which shoved off as it was loaded, until the whole six were in line.   Dr. Winstock and Dimitri were in the captain's gig, and the fleet pulled for Tophana, where the palace is located.   The Greek guide indicated the landing-place, and the party went on shore, marching in proper order, to the intense astonishment of the Turks and others, to the broad avenue on which the palace is located.   One side of the royal residence faces the Bosporus, and there are kiosks and landings on the water, where the sultan may embark in his state barge, which is a magnificent affair, pulled by a whole regiment of oarsmen, who drive it through the water at steamer speed.   With the exception of his new palace, there is hardly one on the Bosporus which a New York *millionnaire* would condescend to occupy.   We do not call them palaces in republican America ; but there are thousands of dwellings on the Hudson, on the Delaware, and in the suburbs of our great cities, which would be so designated in Europe, and which are vastly more elegant and costly than thousands so pretentiously named on the other side of the ocean.

On the avenue, near the palace gate, a considerable collection of people of all nations had assembled. On one side of the street, behind a rail, a battalion of the Imperial Guard was waiting the coming of the sultan. They were fine-looking men, of splendid *physique*, and rather large stature. They were dressed in full Turkish costume, made of blue cloth, and wore the fez. Their appearance was decidedly picturesque, and the students gazed upon them with admiration, until something still more attractive engaged their attention. Several carriages, most of them of the English pattern, were driving up and down the avenue, all of which were occupied by ladies, some old and ugly, and some young and pretty.

" Who are these ladies, Dimitri? " asked Captain Cantwell.

" I don't know just who they are, but they belong to the pachas, I suppose. This building on the street here, with no windows near the ground, is the harem of the sultan ; but none of his ladies are to be seen abroad."

" Don't they go out? "

" They go to the summer palace, and return, but they are shut up in the vehicle so that no one can see them."

" There are four ladies in that carriage," said the captain, as a vehicle, which had passed several times, came before them. " Two of them are young and pretty."

" Very likely they are a couple of the wives of some

pacha.   It isn't prudent to take much notice of the ladies in Constantinople," said Dimitri, with a significant smile.

" I suppose not; but I had no idea that they rode out in the streets, as we see them doing here.   One of those ladies in the carriage is a beauty."

" A Circassian, I suppose."

" Her veil, or whatever you call it — "

" Her *yashmak*," prompted the Greek; " the muslin they wind around the head to conceal their faces."

" Jaw-crack, you mean," laughed Sheridan.

" Her yashmak is very thin, and I can see the whole of her face almost as well as though she didn't wear it. The thing is the merest gauze," said the captain.

" But the old ladies don't wear gauze," added Sheridan.

" I noticed that the material of theirs was quite thick."

" The older and the uglier, the thicker the yashmak," replied Dimitri.   " Here comes the same carriage again."

Cantwell and the other officers gazed with admiration at the beautiful Circassian, if such she was.   The captain thought she smiled very faintly as she looked at him; he gazed at her beautiful but pale face, and he smiled in return, though the women on the front seat watched her like duennas, as probably they were. Presently the vehicle returned again.   The fair lady smiled beyond the possibility of a doubt this time, and the captain smiled, too, just as certainly.   Again and again the carriage passed the spot, and at last Cantwell was bold enough to raise his cap, and bow slightly. The Circassian smiled again, and the old ladies looked very ugly. It was evident enough that the pretty lady was getting herself into hot water, for she had no right to look at anything of the masculine gender, except her husband, if she had one, whose affections, perhaps, she shared with two or three hundred others. For about an hour Cantwell kept up this silent flirtation with the houri of the carriage. She was the only one in the dozen vehicles that passed up and down the avenue who was noticeable for her beauty. The oftener she came, the more loosely was her *yashmak* bound about her face, and the more coquettishly she smiled upon the young stranger. There was mischief in her eye, and she seemed to have forgotten all the precepts of the Koran.

While waiting for the pageant, the captain and Dimitri walked down to the palace gate. A fat pacha came out, and everybody bowed low to him. Cantwell touched his cap with dignified politeness, and the fat official as politely returned the salute, though he took no notice of the rabble that fawned for a glance. An ugly-looking negro, also dressed in rich costume, appeared at the gate, and the crowd bowed to him.

" What's that fellow ? " asked the captain, who, being a conservative in politics at home, took no notice of the black official.

" He is one of the eunuchs of the harem," replied Dimitri.

" One of the black-guards."

" Just so ; but in rank he is equal to the pachas, and the chief eunuch, the Kyzlar-Agassi, is the equal of the grand vizier."

This man was elegantly dressed in the costliest of cashmere, and, like the negro race the world over, his taste ran to bright colors. His fez was of bright scarlet, with a blue tassel, his jacket was striped with gold lace, and his boots and overshoes were of the daintiest of patent leather and the gayest of morocco. He was a thick-lipped, flat-nosed, woolly-headed negro, but he was a dandy of the first water. His manner was full of importance, languid, and apparently he was weary of life; in fact, Mr. Mantalini in a black mask and Oriental costume, tricked out for a Cremorne masquerade. He walked to a carriage near the gate, which seemed to be waiting for him. He spoke to the footman, and his voice was like the squeaking of a cornstalk fiddle. He seated himself in the carriage, and drove off, and Cantwell returned to the spot where the ship's company were stationed.

Presently a stir along the line indicated the appearance of the sultan. The troops formed a stiff line, and the band began to play a melody, which contained some wildly barbaric strains. The officers gave a sharp order, and the soldiers presented arms as the head of the procession appeared. A line of cavalry stretched along each side of the avenue, with prancing horses, leaving the centre of it open and unobstructed.

" That's an odd way for an escort to march," said Sheridan.

" But no man must go in front of the sultan," replied Dimitri. " That's the rule of the road in Turkey. There he is."

The sultan was on horseback, all his attendants keeping at a respectful distance from him. He was

THE SULTAN GOING TO THE MOSQUE   Page 227.

rather a stout man, forty years old, and quite good looking. His hair and beard were sprinkled with gray. He wore the fez, with frock coat and pants in European style. His breast was covered with orders and decorations. The saddle-cloth and other trappings of his horse were richly ornamented with gold. His appearance and manner were decidedly impressive. As he approached, the battalion of soldiers gave one wild, sharp yell, which was their greeting; but the sovereign did not notice it even by a nod. He glanced rather languidly about him, especially at the ship's company of the Young America, which seemed to give him a slight sensation of surprise. All the officers and seamen, as well as the principal and instructors, took off their caps, and bowed to the Oriental potentate; but he made no sign of recognition to this salute, and immediately turned his gaze in another direction, lest his royal dignity should be compromised by too great familiarity, even of his eyes, with these Yankee "infidels." His imperial majesty was followed by a string of pachas, all richly dressed, and well mounted.

"There is Omer Pacha," said Dimitri.

"Who's he?" asked Murray.

"He is the commander-in-chief of the second *corps d'armée*."

"And fought the battle of Oltenitza with the Russians, and beat them badly," added Cantwell. "He distinguished himself in the Crimea in 1852."

"That's the sultan's son," continued Dimitri, as a pale youth of thirteen, mounted on a small horse, passed the students.

Cantwell and his companions raised their caps to the distinguished young gentleman, and he, having more manners than his royal papa, returned the compliment with a military salute.

" His father ought to learn politeness of him," said Sheridan.

" It isn't etiquette for the Ottoman sovereign to take any notice of the people in the streets."

" Just so ; he is the brother of the sun, grandfather of the moon, and first cousin to the planet Jupiter," laughed Sheridan. " He ought to change his manners. If I meet him again in the street, or anywhere else, I shall take no notice of him. I shall cut him clean."

" Don't do that," interposed Cantwell. " He will feel badly about it, and you ought not to hurt his feelings."

" He hurt my feelings ; in short, he cut me, and I don't stand such treatment from anybody."

The rest of the procession consisted of richly-dressed officials, the most nobby and elegant of whom were the Albanians, who were decidedly genteel and stylish. The whole show was certainly magnificent. Gold lace and bright colors were the ruling elements of the pageant, and nothing finer was ever seen in any first-class circus.

" Now, come ; we must hurry up to Pera," said Dimitri, when the last of the procession had passed. " We can see the Dancing Dervishes to-day, for this is Sunday."

" Friday, you mean," suggested Murray.

" It is the Mohammedan Sunday. We have three

Sundays altogether in Constantinople. Friday is the Moslem's, Saturday the Jew's, and Sunday the Christian's."

"And about the same attention is paid to each by all the people," said Dr. Winstock. "The Turks are generally about their business to-day, as usual."

The party walked up the hill to the Rue de Pera, on which the monastery of the Dancing Dervishes is located. They are variously called by Europeans the Dancing, Whirling, and Turning Dervishes. Passing through a court-yard, the tourists came to the vestibule of the monastery. Dimitri produced several pairs of large slippers for the instructors, which they slipped on over their boots, but there was not a sufficient supply for the boys.

"Put off thy shoes from off thy feet!" said Sheridan.

"What for?" demanded Murray.

"No one must enter a mosque with his boots or shoes on," added the guide. "You mustn't touch the floor with anything which has been in the dirt outside."

"Is that the idea?"

"Precisely," added Dr. Winstock. "Formerly, no one was allowed to enter a mosque unless the shoes were actually taken off; but the wealthiest Turks now compromise with their consciences by wearing overshoes, which they slip off when they go to church."

"We have no overshoes to take off, and no slippers to put on; for the rule seems to work both ways here. What shall we do?" inquired Cantwell.

"The floor is covered with mats and sheep-skins,

and as no one enters with his dirty boots, the place is quite clean. Go in your stocking feet," replied the surgeon.

The students left their shoes in charge of the porter at the door, ranging them along the wall in such a way that each could readily find his own. This man takes charge of boots and shoes, umbrellas and canes, and exacts a small fee for it, as is done in most of the theatres and picture galleries of Europe. Dimitri led the way into the room where the performance, or rather the service, was to take place. The main building was in the form of an octagon, and the audience-chamber is rather suggestive of a circus. All the floor, except a space ten feet wide or so next to the walls, was enclosed by a lattice fence, and used for the whirling. Columns connected by this rail extended to the roof, and supported a gallery above the audience-space on the lower floor, the rear portion of which was latticed for the use of women, who are permitted to see, but not to be seen. A portion of the front gallery was occupied by a reader and by the music. The dancing floor was clean and smooth, and opposite the door was spread a prayer carpet for the sheik, or head of the monastery. The visitors squatted on the floor behind the rail, all around the enclosure, in a very uncomfortable posture for Christians.

The dervishes entered singly or in groups, and squatted on the floor opposite the prayer carpet, until about twenty of them had assembled. They were dressed in loose, brown robes, and looked as solemn as though they " meant business." Presently the sheik, a bowed and venerable old man, with a long, white beard, dressed like the others, entered and squatted upon the prayer carpet. Like all the others, he wore a hat shaped just like an inverted flower-pot. The material seems to be very thick, and the color was a lightish brown. The dervishes were of all ages, from the boy of twelve up to the sheik of eighty or ninety, though hardly any of them were over forty. They all had precisely the same expression — that of solemnity and religious enthusiasm.

The old sheik, as soon as he was seated on his carpet, began to repeat, in a low and mumbling tone, some sentences from the Koran. Then one in the front gallery read, or rather intoned, something from a book, which, of course, none of the non-Mussulman portion of the audience could understand. The sheik next mumbled something more; and then the dervishes, headed by one who appeared to be the chief marshal, marched several times around the circus, pausing at the prayer carpet of the sheik, and bowing low. This bowing is somewhat ludicrous, and reminds the spectator of Baron Pompolini in the opera of Cinderella. Two dervishes, with arms crossed on their breasts, bow facing each other first, then " right about face," and bow to the next two in the line ; and this process is repeated until all have passed the carpet. When the last of the bowing was accomplished, the music in the gallery, which appeared to consist of a banjo and some other instrument, struck up a monotonous tune, and the head of the line of the dervishes slid off towards the middle of the circus, and began to whirl or waltz. Their example was followed by all the other dervishes, until the whole of them were whirling in two circles around the circus. As they commenced the exciting part of the performance, they slipped off their brown robes, and appeared in white jackets and skirts, the latter, like petticoats, reaching nearly to the floor. On some occasions this dress is dark.

The waltz was kept up about half an hour, without any cessation whatever. There were no collisions, as is sometimes seen in Christian ball-rooms, and not even the skirts were brought into contact, though they were spread out as those of little girls when engaged in the game of " making cheeses." The movement is emphatically graceful, is perfectly timed, and there is no hurrying or confusion. The dancers are barefoot, and keep the left foot on the floor, whirling on the heel, while the right is continually thrown over the instep of the left. It makes one dizzy to look at them, yet they never seem to be giddy. Sometimes the music increases in rapidity, and the dervishes conform to the time. The position of the body and limbs is uniform, the left arm elevated a little above the horizontal, the hand turned down, while the right, with the palm of the hand upward, is raised to an angle of forty-five degrees.

When the dance was finished, the dervishes again defiled before the sheik, more sentences from the Koran were drawled out by the reader in the gallery, and the service for the day was closed. The audience consisted largely of Turks or other of the faithful.

" What does it all mean ? " asked Sheridan. " It looks very ridiculous."

" Does it look any more ridiculous than the services of the Shakers at home ? " said Dr. Winstock.

" Perhaps not; but I don't see where the religion comes in."

" Certainly the expression of those men was that of pious enthusiasm," added the doctor. " Though we may not be able to appreciate the religious manifestation of these dervishes, or the Shakers, or the Methodists in camp-meeting, we ought to be respectful, and even reverent, as we witness them. I do not understand the significance of this service, but I am told that it is an imitation of the revolving motions of the heavenly bodies. Whether this is true or not, I cannot say, and thus far I have been unable to find any satisfactory explanation of the performance."

The party retired from the room, claimed their shoes in the vestibule, and walked down to the boats.

" I suppose you have already noticed the dogs of Constantinople, Captain Cantwell," said the surgeon, as they came upon a group of these animals.

" It would have been impossible not to notice them," replied the captain. " I haven't read a book about this city yet which had not a chapter about the dogs, and before I came here I had begun to think they were a big institution. They are the meanest class of dogs, taken as a whole, that I ever saw. In fact, they are all yellow dogs."

" A large portion of them are, and I confess they are not attractive, though they form an interesting class of the population. I staid here a month on my first visit. My health was rather poor, and I did not sleep well at night. It seemed to me there was a battle among the curs every hour or two between sunset and sunrise; and if you notice it, you find about the same number during the day, indicated by the barking, yelping, and howling of the beasts."

" What makes them fight so much?" asked the captain.

" It is said that all the dogs have their own territory; that, like the human inhabitants, they reside in and belong to certain streets and squares. The canines of this locality claim the monopoly of it, and do not permit other curs to invade their territory. When they do so, the regular residents pitch into them, and drive them out. This makes the row, which disturbs us by night and by day."

" Why don't they stay at home, then?" asked Murray.

" I suppose all the claim they can have upon particular localities is for the garbage or other food to be obtained within its limits. Of course the whole business of these dogs is to obtain enough to eat, and I doubt whether any one of them was ever yet satisfied. When they are hungry, and their own territory does not furnish them with food, they are driven into other localities in search of sustenance, which brings on the war."

" Look at that fellow!" exclaimed Sheridan. "Lodgings are scarce with him."

The dog pointed out was lying on a quarter sheet of brown paper, which he had found on the soft mud; and this was the dryest bed the poor fellow could obtain. Indeed, the make-shifts of these dogs for a resting-place are often ludicrous; and not only may they be found on pieces of paper not more than six inches square, but curled up on projecting stones in the walls, clinging to the narrowest of thresholds in a doorway, and coiled away on the sill of a cellar window. The top of a box or cask is a princely lodging for them; an old mat or a bundle of straw is a luxurious bed, hardly to be had more than once in a dog-life.

"What do these dogs live on?" asked the captain. "I saw a couple of them quarrelling over an old boot, yesterday."

"I think they live principally on old hats, old boots, grape skins, and garbage generally," replied the doctor. "I don't think they eat mud, for there would be less of it if they did. They feed upon all the refuse matter thrown into the streets. The Turks do not regard a swill-pail as a necessary article in their houses, but throw everything they don't want into the streets. The dogs are not dainty, and do not seem to discriminate between a crust of bread and an old shoe."

"All the dogs are lean and lank, as though they got but little to eat. But I see that a great many of them have no hair on portions of their bodies. I saw one just now whose back was entirely bare," said the captain.

"They are covered with fleas, and perhaps they rub off some of their hair in fighting these vermin," answered the doctor. "They also have an eruptive disease, something like the itch, called *mange*, which takes the hair off. These dogs have no care, as you perceive. They roll in the mud, and their coats are matted with filth, so that they are particularly liable to this disease. They are owned by no one, and their condition is very deplorable."

"Why don't the government kill them off?" asked Sheridan.

" The last sultan attempted to do so ; but the effort had nearly created an insurrection in the city, for the Turks are superstitiously afraid to destroy them. Doultless they do some good, for they are about the only scavengers in the streets.   They eat every-thing composed of flesh, as I have heard one say, from a dead cat up to a dead pacha.   It is even said that they dig up the dead in the burying-grounds, but I do not care to believe this.   When I was here before, I used to stand for a while at the door of Misserie's Hotel in the morning, observing the passers-by.   One day, a couple of rather small, yellow dogs, which were only puppies, came up to the door.   They were cleaner than most of their kind in this city, and had a pleas-ant expression on their faces.   I was pleased with them, and bought a loaf of bread in the baker's shop opposite, which I fed out to them.   The next morn-ing I saw them again, and fed them as before.   Every morning after this, I found them at the door when I went down, and it cost me a loaf of bread every day to get rid of them.   But I was interested in them, and very willing to support them.   I found that they lived under a doorstep at a wooden house near the hotel. I got them quite fat before I left, and I am afraid they missed me after I was gone.   If I were the sultan, or even grand vizier, I would either cause all the dogs to be killed, or sell out half a dozen of the useless pal-aces, and feed and shelter them with the proceeds."

" Give them to the dogs."

" Yes, literally."

" Don't these dogs bite?" asked Murray.

" I presume they do, if they have a sufficient excuse

for doing so; but I must say that, in all my wanderings through the city, I never saw one bite or attempt to bite a man. I never hesitated to pass through a drove of them, and never met one that was ugly. The fact is, they are so miserable, that they have lost all life and spirit," said the surgeon, as they reached the place where the boats had been secured in charge of the adult forward officers.

The tourists went on board of the ship, and spent the rest of the day in looking up interesting and valuable information in regard to the great city.

CHAPTER XIV.

MR. TOMPION AND HIS BOTTLES.

SUMMER gales are not usually of long duration ; and on the morning after Morley was committed to the brig, the Tritonia had hardly wind enough to give her steerage-way. There was, however, an ugly swell, which kept the vessel threshing about in a very uncomfortable manner. What breeze there was came from the southward, and she was close-hauled on the starboard tack, unable to lay her course. The weather was cloudy and muggy, with thick fog-banks lying all around, which must soon close in upon her. She was not making a knot an hour, and at the rate she was going, it would take a week to recover what she had lost in the gale.

The friends and adherents of Morley were utterly astounded by the event which had transpired on board, and twenty-four hours afterwards they had not come to their bearings. All the officers, except Scott, were moved up one grade, and each one's position and duties were somewhat changed, so that he was obliged to give some extra attention to them. The situation had been thoroughly discussed, but the malcontents had not yet concluded what to do. Morley, in the brig, was sullen and silent, for no one was allowed to communicate with him. Mr. Marline, who had the custody of him, was inflexible in the discharge of his duty. Greenwood was now regarded as the leader of the opposition party, and the others looked to him for counsel and guidance.

The temporary fourth midshipman was Ward, the highest petty officer in rank. He was an important dignitary in the Bangwhangers, and a particular friend of Scott and the captain. The removal of Morley and the promotion of Ward gave the majority of one in the cabin to the Wainwright party. If the Morley-ites should conclude not to recognize the captain as the rightful commander, there would still be two officers in each watch to sustain the present order of things.

Greenwood and his companions were entirely unde-cided, and while the gale continued they had not much opportunity, or much inclination, to come to a conclusion. Both of the professors and both of the adult forward officers had counselled the captain to disregard the order of the vice-principal, and of course they would sustain him. If it was true that Mr. Tompion was intoxicated, it was not supposed that he would remain in this condition for any great length of time. They were not satisfied, however, that the charge against him was just, for they had not seen him in this condition. He was sick, and this was the reason he was confined to his state-room ; but whether drunk or sick, he would probably soon re-cover, and certainly he would not permit his authority to be set at nought. He was a strict disciplinarian, and believed obedience to be the first duty of an officer or a seaman, under all circumstances. The vice-principal had sympathized with Morley and Greenwood, when their rank was reduced by the advent of the officers from the Young America. He had decided in their favor, and Greenwood for this reason, if for no other, believed in Mr. Tompion, and was very unwilling to accept the theory that he was intoxicated.

So far as Greenwood knew, the vice-principal had not been informed of the subversion of his authority on board. He desired very much to see him; but, as he had virtually submitted to the present authority, he was not quite ready to report the facts to him. He wished to establish his own loyalty before he did so. He had about made up his mind to refuse to obey the captain, and the other Morleyites would follow his example. Then he should be able to address Mr. Tompion, in a little speech he had turned over in his mind, to the following effect: —

" I am very sorry you are ill, Mr. Tompion. You are looking very pale; but I hope you will soon be better. Mr. Morley delivered your order to Captain Wainwright, who, tearing the paper in pieces, threw it overboard, and refused to obey you. When Mr. Morley attempted to read the second copy of the order to the ship's company, he was dragged off, and committed to the brig, where he is now a prisoner in charge of Mr. Marline. As the wind was blowing a gale at the time, I submitted to the captain rather than endanger the safety of the vessel by refusing to do duty; but as soon as the gale subsided, I insisted that the order of the vice-principal should be obeyed, and his authority respected. I declined to acknowledge Mr. Wainwright as captain, or to obey his orders as such. I called for the release of Captain Morley, and did what I could to restore your authority. I am happy to say that I have been fully sustained by Midshipmen Sherman, Walker, and Prescott."

Of course Mr. Tompion would go on deck, even if he was sick; certainly if he were only drunk, provided he was able to handle his legs in the uneasy state of the deck. Morley would be released, and Wainwright and Scott sent to the brig in his place. The professors and the forward officers would " catch fits," for the vice-principal was a positive man, and would not stand any nonsense from anybody. The " oldsters " could no more stand up against him than they could against a hurricane or an earthquake, and certainly the youngsters could not. There would be a " jolly row " just as soon as he set the ball in motion.

The conning of his speech, and the train of thought which followed it, convinced him that he *ought* to set the ball in motion. The starboard watch, under Scott, were in charge of the deck; and Greenwood sat in the cabin considering the situation. He had begun to turn over in his mind the difficulties in the way of the execution of his plan, when Sherman, now acting fourth lieutenant, came into the cabin from the steerage. The professors had attempted to carry on the school work of the vessel in the morning, but the dead rolling of the Tritonia, added to the disinclination of the students to study, had prevented them from doing so successfully. An interior tempest was expected

16

next, and the boys had not learned their lessons. They rolled off their stools, and tumbled over upon each other, probably on purpose, though the vessel was really too unsteady for work.

"Sherman," said the chief malcontent, as the former entered the cabin.

"Well, what's up?" demanded the fourth lieutenant, as he seated himself on the transom at the side of his friend.

"Nothing yet," replied Greenwood, who then proceeded to deliver himself of the plan he had formed, and of the speech he had conned, becoming quite eloquent when he described the jolly row that was to ensue when Mr. Tompion came on deck, and established his authority again.

"You are to refuse to do duty before all this can come to pass — are you?" said Sherman.

"Yes; we must set ourselves right before we appeal to Mr. Tompion. We must prove that we are faithful ourselves before we complain of the captain," added Greenwood.

"Precisely so. I see the point; but just how is this to be done?" asked Sherman.

"In the first place, we must talk the thing up with Walker and Prescott. They are in the starboard watch on deck now. You see Prescott, and I will see Walker, before noon."

"They will consent to anything you and I agree upon. They told me so this morning."

"All right; but we must see them, and have the matter fully understood, for we must go together. 'Union is strength,' you know, and all that sort of thing."

"We will stick together, if we can agree upon anything; but I don't want to get into a row that is to amount to nothing."

"Nor I; but don't you see we have Tompion on our side? and when he gets the idea, he will tiger the thing through."

"But if he is as drunk as the fellows say he is, he can't do anything."

"Don't you believe all you hear, Sherman."

"Professor Primback said he was in a state of intoxication — said it out loud to the whole ship's company, you know. There must be something in it."

"Well, grant that he is as boozy as an owl, he isn't going to stay so till we get to Constantinople. There couldn't have been over half a dozen bottles of liquor in that valise he brought on board at Cowes, for that's where the fellows say he got his rum. Six bottles won't keep him drunk many days."

"Perhaps not; but suppose you get him on deck when he is too tipsy to stand up. He can't do anything then."

"You are right," answered Greenwood, musing. "That would make a bad failure of the whole thing. I can't believe he is so drunk as the fellows say he is."

"You must make sure that he is all right before you attempt to do anything."

"I will see to that. I will go into his room, and satisfy myself. They say he came out to breakfast this morning, but I didn't see him."

"Go and see him, Greenwood. If you find he is 'over the bay,' look about you for any rum lying around loose, and throw it overboard."

" Good !   I'll do that.   I will look into that valise, if he is far gone, and pitch the bottles through the port.   Then he will be all right by to-morrow, and we will wait till that time before we do anything."

" Right !   You are sensible to the last," said Sherman, heartily approving the plan, as modified, up to this point.

" If we get him sober, we are all right."

" Let's look a little further, Greenwood.   Suppose the vice is all right, and in good condition to support his body and his dignity on the quarter-deck.   What's the next step ? "

" If it is to-day, I shall take the afternoon watch at noon.   When I am called, we will all be on deck together.   As the trumpet is handed to me, I shall decline to take it, and refuse to obey the orders of Wainwright any longer.   How's that ? "

" Scott will report to the captain, then."

" To Wainwright, who, I claim, is not the captain."

" Then you will state your position to him."

" Exactly so."

" And he will order Mr. Marline to commit you to the brig," added Sherman.

" Do you think so ? " asked Greenwood, with a startled look.

" I know it.   Didn't he say yesterday, in the row, that he would commit you if you refused to obey any order given by him or Scott ? "

" I don't think he would do that, now the excitement has died out."

" I think he would ; and instead of going to Mr. Tompion with your story and speech, you would be looking through the bars of the brig, or talking it over with Morley."

Greenwood was puzzled, for he realized the force of his friend's argument. Wainwright and Scott were both very decided in emergencies.

"Well, suppose he sends me to the brig — what then?" he asked, wishing to see to what the captain's anticipated action would lead.

"If I step forward, then, and follow your example, I shall be sent to the brig, too."

"That will make three of us in limbo, under the eye of the big boatswain," replied Greenwood.

"And if Walker and Prescott follow suit, they will make five, which is about a complement for the brig, rather crowded at that," laughed Sherman.

"This won't do."

"Of course it won't. It may take a month for the Tritonia to get to Constantinople, and I don't care to look through the oak bars for so long a time."

"Nor I; but Tompion hasn't rum enough to keep boozy a month, and he would very soon find out what had been done. Then we should have a chance to state the case. Why, look at it. As the matter stands, it is mutiny for the officers to take the course they have, for the vice is the real captain of the vessel."

"Not too fast, Greenwood. I have been reading up on this matter a little," said Sherman, going to the library, and returning with a book, which proved to be Dana's Seaman's Friend. "'The master may so conduct himself'" — Sherman read from the book — "'as to justify the officers and crew in placing restraints upon him, to prevent his committing any act which might endanger the lives of all the persons on board.' But it adds that the crew run a great risk in interfering."

"Does anybody pretend that making Morley captain, and me first lieutenant, instead of Wainwright and Scott, endangers the lives of all the persons on board?" demanded Greenwood, with a palpable sneer.

"Well, I don't know what view the professors take of it; but the boatswain and carpenter believe it," added Sherman.

"They don't believe any such thing!" protested Greenwood, with strong contempt. "They know that Morley is a better seaman and a better navigator any day than Wainwright is; and if I am not as good as Scott, I will jump overboard in the Bay of Biscay O! You can't pour any of that molasses down my back."

"Mr. Rimmer says that Morley left his station the night after we sailed from Copenhagen, and by his neglect of duty, had nearly caused a collision; that there would have been a collision if the captain had not been on deck at the time, and taken the command out of his hands. Both he and Mr. Marline say they wouldn't trust such a fellow."

"I think myself that Morley was a little lame there; but he acted as he did only because Wainwright was watching him, and looking for a chance to trip him up," added Greenwood, apologetically.

"He tripped himself up."

"He was in the wrong that time, but he can handle the Tritonia better than any other fellow on board.

Never mind that; this question is going to be settled by Mr. Lowington, and not by the courts of law."

"You don't expect him to excuse the vice for getting drunk — do you?"

"No; he can settle that with Mr. Tompion; but he says that every one should obey his superiors, and complain afterwards," replied Greenwood.

"Be that as it may, it seems to be not exactly prudent to put your plan into operation. In my opinion, we should all be in the brig, perhaps for the rest of the cruise. It looks to me like a dead lock at this point," said Sherman, who was evidently as much interested in the success of the project as his companion.

"I don't believe he would send five of us to the brig," protested Greenwood.

"He will send you there, at any rate, and your cake will be dough as soon as you move."

"If it is, I shall not knead it any more," added the chief conspirator, with a sickly smile. "But we must get round this trouble somehow."

"Well, how? That's the question."

Greenwood scratched his head, and fumbled over his cap for a time, and then his face brightened up all of a sudden, evidently with the flash of a bright idea.

"I'll tell you," said he. "We are both in the port watch. I am the officer of the first part, and you of the second."

"That's so; and the quarter watches are to stand from noon to-day, I heard the captain say."

"I'm rather sorry for that; but no matter. I will refuse to do duty till Captain Morley is placed in command according to the order of the vice."

"Just so; we have been all over that before. Then I am to step forward and follow your illustrious example, and also follow you into the brig," added Sherman, impatiently. "I thought you had something new to offer."

"So I have, if you will hear me. Don't interrupt me, if you please, and then I shall not have to go over it again."

"Blaze away! You have the floor, Greenwood."

"I decline to do duty, and am sent to the brig."

"That's plain enough; and I —"

"You will hold your tongue, if you can, long enough for me to state my programme," laughed Greenwood. "You will not follow my example; but like a good, patient, obedient officer, you will take the trumpet and serve as officer of the deck, in the place of your refractory superior in the port watch."

"What do you mean by that? Just now you preached that union is strength, and all that sort of thing, you know. Now I am to lick the dust and bow down to the tyrant of the quarter-deck."

"Well, if you like it any better, you shall decline and I will submit. I don't care a fig which way you do it; only our two fellows in the starboard watch must follow your or my example, as we agree, and refuse to do duty, and be sent to the brig."

"I don't see the point," added the puzzled fourth lieutenant.

"Shall I be the obstinate one, or will you? Let us settle this point first."

"That depends upon circumstances. I don't comprehend the plan, and therefore can't decide."

" One of the four must submit, so as not to be sent to the brig. Don't you see? "

" Hang me if I do! Is he to have a soft thing, while the other three are battering their heads against the oak bars of the brig? As this is your plan, I think you had better be the obstinate one, refuse to obey the order, and be cast into the brig, as Daniel was into the lions' den."

" Good! I am perfectly satisfied; but I think your skull is thicker to-day than usual."

" Thank you. It is too thick to be cracked against the oak bars. Why don't you open up your idea ? "

" Because you don't hold still long enough. Now I will tell you just what to do as soon as I and the other fellows are in limbo. Like a good boy, you will keep your watch, and as soon as you are off duty, you will call upon Mr. Tompion, make the little speech to him that I have just rehearsed, and report to him just the condition of affairs on board. Inform him that his tried and trusty friends are languishing in the brig for their loyalty to his cause. Talk to him with tears in your eyes."

" O, ho! I see why one of us is to be obedient!" exclaimed Sherman, delighted with the scheme.

" I knew I could beat it into you if you would hold still long enough. Now you understand it, and know just what to do."

" But as you have prepared your speech, and have something on the side of your face, so that a fall on it wouldn't hurt, I think I had better go to the brig, and let you get off your own oration," suggested Sherman.

" On the whole, I think not. You have behaved

very well on this cruise, while I am known to be a friend and supporter of Morley, the traitor. If you hold out and I cave in, they will suspect something — smell a mice. You will see the vice, as soon as I am caged, or as soon after as you can. If Tompion is able to go on deck, we shall not stay long in the brig. If he isn't able, we will wait till his rum is all used up. I will ascertain about that myself. But there will be fun when we get the wires laid and touch off the earthquake."

The plan was restated and carefully matured. Sherman went on deck to prepare the two midshipmen of his party for the performance of their part of the exciting drama. It was a dead calm by this time; the last breath of wind had died out, and the sails of the Tritonia were banging furiously, as the heavy sea rolled and pitched the vessel. But half an hour later, a light breeze from the westward rippled over the waves, and the fog and the clouds began to drift away. The wind freshened, and knocked down the sea. Sherman found Walker and Prescott favorably inclined to any plan which their superiors might adopt, and he explained to them the operation of that which had been devised. They approved it, and declared that not less than a dozen of the crew were ready to stand by them; perhaps more, though they had not sounded them any further.

In the mean time, Greenwood watched his opportunity in the cabin to enter the state-room of the vice-principal. The improved weather had lured all the officers to the deck, as the fog rolled away, to discover whatever might be in sight. The cabin steward was busy in the pantry making a potato salad for dinner; and any one who has been to sea knows how agreeable a salad of any kind is. Improving his chances, he opened the door of the vice-principal's cabin. He used all this strategy because he believed that his visit, even to the highest power on board, would be regarded as treason by the captain and first lieutenant, and perhaps by the professors.

Mr. Tompion was in his berth, and was snoring heavily. The second lieutenant examined him, looked him over thoroughly, and if he had any doubts before, as he professed to have, he could have none now, that the principal was drunk, blindly, stupidly drunk. In accordance with the programme, he looked about him for liquor. He found a bottle, half full of brandy, stowed away between the berth-sack and the partition, which, however, he did not disturb. The valise which Mr. Tompion had brought on shore from Cowes was in one corner of the room. It contained two full bottles of brandy. Unscrewing the port, he opened it and dropped both of them into the sea, though a big wave partially drenched the interior of the cabin during the operation. He carefully searched the apartment for any more liquor that might be there, but he found none. The half bottle in the berth was all that remained; and he decided not to disturb this, lest he might excite the suspicions of the invalid. Having executed his mission, — which was practically a benevolent one, whatever the motives of the missionary, — he retired as cautiously as he had entered. The earthquake could not be touched off that day, and must be deferred till the next, when the vice-principal would certainly be sober enough to sustain his dignity as the chief authority of the Tritonia. He reported what he had discovered to Sherman, and the other two officers of the party were duly informed of the postponement of all action till the following day, at eight bells in the morning, when the port watch would take the deck.

In the afternoon the sun came out, and with a fresh breeze the Tritonia sped on her course towards the Straits of Gibraltar. The recitations were resumed; and Morley, within the bars of his prison, listened to the busy hum of the school-room, and perhaps wished he was a diligent student, as he had been before his ambition led him astray.

Mr. Tompion waked as the influence of the brandy fumes subsided; but again and again he drank, till the bottle in his berth was empty, and then he was sufficiently inebriated to sleep all night long. In the morning he awoke sober, but with haggard face and shaking nerves. He rose from his berth and opened the valise, in order to obtain another dram to quiet his quaking frame. The valise was empty, and he wondered what had become of the bottles which his clouded memory half assured him he had left there. He was certain of nothing, and he concluded that he had consumed all his stock of liquor. If the suspicion had occurred to him, he would not have believed that any one on board could have had the temerity to destroy his brandy. He was fearfully muddled, and could not comprehend the situation. It mattered little whether he could or not. He was sober, and he had not the means of getting drunk again. At seven bells he went out into the cabin, and took his tea and toast with the officers off duty, including Greenwood and Sherman, who observed him with the deepest interest.

After breakfast he retired to his room, and thoroughly searched it for the missing bottles. They were not to be found. He was restless and uneasy; his nerves disturbed him terribly; and he ordered the steward to get him some wormwood tea, which is a specific for men recovering from a spree. It came, and he drank freely of it. It improved his condition, and seeing that he was very dirty, he shaved himself, washed, and put on a clean shirt; which made him look like another man.

On deck the exciting drama had actually commenced. Greenwood touched his cap to the first lieutenant, and declared that he could no longer obey the orders of Wainwright, who had been suspended by the vice-principal.

"It has taken you a long while to make up your mind," said Scott.

"I do not like to be hasty in a matter of so much importance," replied Greenwood, meekly. "I do not think it is right to disobey the vice-principal, and I have concluded that we shall get into trouble if we continue to do so."

Scott reported the case to the captain, and he attempted to reason with the malcontent, who, of course, was determined to discharge what he called his duty.

"Very well, Mr. Greenwood. If you insist, I shall be obliged to commit you to the brig."

"I insist that Mr. Morley, the rightful captain of

the Tritonia, be released and placed in command, according to the order of the vice-principal. I decline to do duty till this is done."

" Mr. Marline, commit Mr. Greenwood to the brig ;" and the big boatswain obeyed the order without a question.

" Mr. Sherman, you will take the deck."

Sherman obeyed the order ; but Walker and Prescott, according to the arrangement, stepped forward and declined any longer to act in opposition to the order of the vice-principal. They also were sent to the brig.

Sherman served his watch out, and then went down into the cabin, where he found Mr. Tompion reclining on the transom in the main cabin. He told his story, made Greenwood's speech for him, and, as anticipated, the vice-principal was fiercely indignant at the disobedience of Captain Wainwright.

CHAPTER XV.

THE SULTAN'S FIRMAN AND THE BAZAAR.

"WHAT is the population of Constantinople?" asked Captain Cantwell, as the boats were pulling to a landing-place in Stamboul.

"The last estimates I have seen place the number at over one million," replied Dr. Winstock. "It is therefore the third city of Europe."

"Can you tell me in what language the Koran was written?" asked Sheridan, who was thinking of something else.

"In Arabic, which is the church language of the Mohammedans, as Latin is of the Roman Catholics, and Slavonic of the Orthodox Greek."

"Who wrote it?"

"According to the Moslem doctrine, Mohammed received it from the angel Gabriel; but it is generally understood to have been composed by the prophet himself. The writer was well acquainted with the Old and New Testaments; and Mohammed is regarded by his followers, who know anything of the Bible, as the promised Messiah. The unity of God is continually asserted in the oft-repeated sentence, 'God is God, and Mohammed is his prophet.' The Moslems believe that Jesus Christ was a great teacher, but not the equal of Mohammed. The precepts of the Koran are generally good, and he who follows them will lead a virtuous life, though it contains some doctrines abominable in themselves. It forbids the carving of the human figure in wood, stone, or other material. Consequently you find that the ornaments of fountains, mosques, and other structures are of flowers, vases, and diagrams."

The ship's company landed near the floating bridge. Dimitri and several other guides were with them, one of whom was armed with the sultan's firman, to visit St. Sophia, and other mosques and public buildings. This document is the official permission of the sultan, who is the head of the church; and the name of *firman* is applied to all his edicts, civil as well as ecclesiastic, as *ukase* is to those of the Czar of Russia. Though it costs nothing at the Porte, the persons who obtain it charge a heavy sum for doing so, and the cost to tourists is from ten to twenty francs each, depending upon the number. An officer of the government accompanies the party, and he receives half of the perquisite.

Near the bridge the students saw a number of boys selling newspapers. They were small sheets, and looked as though a spider fresh from the inkstand had been promenading over them.

"What newspapers have they, Dimitri?" asked Cantwell.

"Turkish, Greek, and Armenian," replied the guide.

"Will you buy one of each for me?" added Cantwell, as he took from his pocket several of the great coppers, on which the sultan's monogram is placed, instead of the forbidden head, and Dimitri bought them.

"What's the news, captain?" asked Sheridan, as Cantwell turned over the Turkish sheet.

"It is all about wars, and rumors of wars."

"But you are reading the wrong way," laughed the doctor. "A Turkish book or paper begins at the end, reads backward, and ends at the beginning."

"I see that the title of the paper is on the fourth page. I think I will keep the sheet, and read it at my leisure. This Armenian looks as though it had been struck by lightning. It is all in zigzags."

There was something new to be seen every moment, and Dimitri was sorely tried to answer all the questions put to him.

"What's that fellow?" asked Murray, as the small party which attended the doctor paused before a stand, shaded by a huge umbrella.

"That's a sherbet-seller."

"Let's have some;" and the Turk dipped the portions called for from a large earthen bowl, in which currants, lemon-slices, and other fruits were swimming in a reddish fluid.

"Humph! Is that the sherbet we read about in the Arabian Nights?" snuffed Sheridan. "It's nothing but shrub."

"Nothing more nor less," added Dr. Winstock. "That is lemonade in the other bowl."

"What's that fellow over there?" demanded Murray, pointing to a bearded, turbaned Turk, squatting upon a low platform, with a box before him.

17

"He is a letter-writer," answered the doctor. "He is doing a job for the customer at his side."

Near him was a man at a high stand, on which was a stack of bread, made in rings, covered with sesame and coriander, which looked rather tempting, but which, on trial, had a strong taste of rancid grease. Certain localities were infested with peddlers of grapes, lemonade, almond paste, and other wares.

After wandering for some time through the narrow and crooked streets, over the rough pavement, or through the deep mud, the party arrived at the Seraglio. It is at the point of land between the Golden Horn and the Sea of Marmora, triangular in shape, and nearly three miles in circumference. It is filled with gardens, shaded by the melancholy cypress, with mosques, palaces, kiosks, and castles, though a considerable portion of the buildings was destroyed by fire in 1865. Across the peninsula extends a wall, which encloses the Seraglio. It is entered by three gates, the principal of which — a high, narrow, Arabesque archway — is the imperial gate, — the Sublime Porte, that gives its name to the Turkish government. Near it is a beautiful marble fountain, which is rather a temple, and there are many of these fountains in and about the city. Near this gate is the Mosque of St. Sophia, or Ayia Sofia, as the Turks call it. It is two hundred and sixty feet long, by two hundred and forty-three broad, in the form of a Greek cross. It was built by the Emperor Justinian for a Christian church (A. D. 531–538.) Its cedar came from Lebanon; its porphyry columns from the ruins of the Temple of the Sun, at Baalbec; others from the Temple of Diana at Ephesus. It has one grand dome in the centre, clustered around with a score of inferior ones on the main building or its dependencies, with four minarets towering far above the highest dome, each provided with three galleries for the Muezzin, and crowned with the crescent. As at other mosques, the buildings which surround it are for the educational and charitable institutions connected with it.

The students entered a door in a tower, and walked up an inclined plane, circling round a centre, to the gallery of the church, which commanded a fine view of the interior of the magnificent structure. The floor was of large marble slabs, cracked and badly settled, and much of the masonry above and around bears the marks of age. But the students were more interested in the place as a mosque than as a temple of antiquity, and they looked more at the people below than at the columns from Baalbec and Ephesus. On one side is a carpeted platform, on which is the Caaba, where the grand mufti says his prayers. It is on the Mecca side of the mosque, and at prayer all the faithful face towards it. The principal floor in this, as in other mosques, is covered with straw matting. On the right of the platform is an elevated pulpit, which looks more like a band-stand, in which a priest was squatted, engaged in expounding the Koran to a small group, composed mostly of women, who were seated on the floor. Suddenly he raised his voice to a high key, and glanced up at the visitors in the gallery. Dimitri said he was denouncing the infidels; but all guides tell the same story to excite the interest of the tourist, and it is probable that he only waxed eloquent over the beauties of the Mohammedan scripture. On two great green circles was inscribed, in gigantic characters, some sentence of the Koran, which was something like the " legends " on a tea-chest.

The party descended to the floor of the mosque, and wandered all over it. The storied pillars were pointed out to them ; but they cared but little for them, and turned to the Turkish boys, who were studying the Koran in some enclosures near the walls. They were bobbing their heads up and down, as children intensely engaged sometimes do in America ; but in this instance the movement was the requirement of their religion, which compels them to bow as they read the sacred names and certain passages. They were jabbering aloud, and the sight was rather ludicrous, for they took no notice of the young infidels who surrounded them. From the ceiling above are suspended, by long wires a great number of lamps and of ostrich eggs, the latter being ornamental, as well as having some religious significance.

The travellers left the mosque, and the doctor's little group decided to have a lunch on the Turkish plan. Seating themselves on some stools by the side of a *café*, they ordered coffee. It was brought to them in little thimbles of cups, holding about a swallow. The beverage was thick and black, with a teaspoonful of grounds at the bottom. It is drank without milk or sugar ; and the students were satisfied forevermore to let the celebrated Turkish coffee severely alone. Crossing the street, they entered a restaurant, in the window of which were specimens of the viands to be obtained within. The cooking was done in sight of the customers, at a furnace in the rear of the shop. Two hemispheric copper kettles were on the fire. One contained boiled rice, tinted pink by some Oriental condiment, and the other was half filled with bits of mutton, swimming in a gallon or two of melted grease. Dimitri called for a dish from the furnace, and the cook rounded up a portion of the rice on a small plate, and then made a hole in the summit of the pile, into which he ladled a gill of the melted fat and a few bits of the meat. A Christian who was half famished would doubtless have eaten the mess with a good relish; but a mouthful or two satisfied Sheridan, whose curiosity had led him to order the dish. In the window was a large plate of dough-balls, looking like New England pancakes, fried brown, probably in the kettle with the meat. Some of these were ordered as an experiment, for they appeared to be very nice. The experiment was a failure, for the balls were soaked with grease, and were as unpalatable as they were indigestible. Disgusted with these specimens of Turkish cookery, the party ordered a large portion of the delicious grapes, which were a decided success.

After the lunch, the excursionists visited two other mosques, those of Solyman the Magnificent and of Achmet. They were built by these sultans, who were entitled by their conquests to do so; for in order to save the faithful from the burden of over-taxation, no sovereigns who are not conquerors are permitted to build churches. The Mosque of Solyman, or Suleiman, contains four immense columns, and in that of Achmet are also four, not less than twenty feet in diameter, which support the dome in each. The former was built by the Turks, and they are justly proud of it, for it is the most beautiful in the city. In the court-yard of the Mosque of the Sultan Bajazet are vast flocks of pigeons, or doves, which are fed by the alms of the pious; and the Mohammedans are more tender to beasts and birds than to man. Some of the party, prompted by Dimitri, gave an old Turk, who sat at a chest filled with grain, a few piastres, upon which he cast a couple of measures of the grain upon the pavement. Instantly thousands of the birds darkened the air, as they flew down for the food. They piled themselves up and rolled over each other in their efforts to reach the pavement. Dr. Winstock gave the man more piastres, and his example was followed by the officers with him. The grain was spread all over the court, and still there were pigeons enough to pack the pavement two or three deep. They are very tame, and it is difficult to walk about in the vicinity of this mosque without treading upon them. As the party left the mosque, the Muezzin appeared in one of the galleries of a minaret near them, and, in a shrill cry, called the faithful to prayers.

" What does he say, Dimitri? " asked Cantwell.

" In the first part, he calls upon God three times; then he acknowledges that there is no other, and that Mohammed is his prophet. He closes with, ' Come to prayer, come to prayer! Come to the temple of salvation. Great God, great God! There is no god but God.' This he says four times, looking towards the four points of the compass.—I suppose, gentlemen, you don't care to see any more mosques. You have visited some of the finest in the city."

" How many are there? "

" Fourteen imperial mosques, and sixty others. They are all very nearly alike. We will go to the Hippodrome now, if you please."

This is an open space, and was the circus used for races, games, and other sports in the time of the early Greek emperors, five or six hundred years after Christ. It is about a thousand feet long and four hundred wide. It contains the granite obelisk, brought from Thebes, in Egypt, where it had stood for two thousand years, by Theodosius, A. D. 390. It rests on a pedestal whose four sides are sculptured with figures of this emperor in several of the important events of his life. The obelisk itself is sixty feet high, and is covered with Egyptian hieroglyphics. The spiral pillar, half gone, formed of three copper serpents entwined, held the tripod from the Temple of Delphi. The third column is the broken pillar of Constantine, and is composed of square stones. In ancient times it was covered with sheets of gilded copper, which were stripped off by the conquering Turks when they captured the city. The Hippodrome was also ornamented with four famous bronze horses, which, after travelling about Europe for six hundred years, may now be seen over the door of St. Mark's Church, in Venice.

" Where is the ' Burnt Column '? " asked one of the boys, who had been coaching himself for the occasion.

" That was the column of Constantine the Great, in the forum of this emperor," replied Dr. Winstock. " On the top of it was a statue of Apollo, to whom it was dedicated; but Constantine stole it, erased the name of Apollo and the inscription, and modestly substituted, ' To Constantine, whose justice shines like the sun.' "

" But why is it called the Burnt Column?"

" Because it has been singed so many times in the great fires that have ravaged the city. The statue was thrown down by an earthquake, and the height reduced from one hundred and twenty to ninety feet."

The party then went to the Armory, which contains the ancient Church of St. Irene, a curious and interesting relic of the past, as are the old implements of war used in the crusades. In the Museum is a large collection of wax figures, made by order of Mahmoud II., to preserve the knowledge of the costumes, the manners and customs, of the Janizaries in particular, and of other curious people of his realm. Pages, porters, boatman, eunuchs, priests, and other people are represented; but the exhibition is vastly inferior to Madame Tussaud's, in London. A walk to the pretty little marble palace near the point, to the old palace, built by Mohammed II., and to what the fire has left of the structures erected by his successors, finished the day. Some remains of the Oriental magnificence of the sultans may be seen in the beautiful kiosks, the fountains and baths; but the students went on board of the ship with the feeling that the grandeur and elegance described in the Eastern tales was more in the imagination than in the reality.

The next day they pulled up the Golden Horn to Eyub, which means Job, after a Arab general who was buried here in 672. It formerly contained several Christian churches, but is now celebrated for the royal mosque within its limits. Three days after the capture of Constantinople by Mohammed II., in 1453, a sheik, beloved by the sultan, came to him and told him somebody had prophesied that a Turkish emperor who should conquer the city would find the tomb of Eyub, and make it glorious in the eyes of the whole world. Mohammed went out and found the tomb, built a mausoleum, and then a mosque over it. He was so delighted by these incidents, that he ordered all his successors, on their accession to the throne, to be girded with the sword of state within this mosque, which has always been done. The students walked up the hill beyond this structure, in a path through a burying-ground. They examined the stones that marked the resting-places of the dead. They were tall and narrow, many of them ornamented with a turban at the top, and were inscribed with sentences from the Koran in blue, yellow, and gold. Some of the tombs were elaborate kiosks, or temples, containing cenotaphs surrounded with flowers. There are miles and miles of these burying-grounds in and around Constantinople, all adorned with multitudes of the solemn cypress. It was formerly a Moslem custom for parents to plant one of these trees on the day a child was born to them; and the children planted one at the head of the father's grave. This practice accounts for the vast number of them.

It is a tradition, among the followers of the prophet, that when the Moslem is dying, the angel of death, Azrael, comes to his bed with a drawn sword, at the point of which are three drops of gall. These the sick man swallows: the first turns him pale; the second kills him; and the third commences the decomposition of his body. When he is buried, two black angels, with great iron maces in their hands, subject him to an examination. When they come the dead man sits up, and, one at his head and the other at his feet, they demand the defunct's opinions as to the truth of the Koran, the prophetship of Mohammed, and the Unity of God. If he is all right on his creed, — for they do not ask him if he practised what he believed, — the angels leave him, and the faithful departed one falls asleep to wait for the resurrection and paradise. If his belief is not satisfactory, the angels pound him on the head with their maces till his cries ring through the whole world. His heavy sins become snakes and dragons with seven heads, and his minor ones scorpions. He is thrown among these reptiles, stung and tormented by them till the last day.

While the excursionists paused on the hill to view the beauties of the City of the Sultan, which, like Rome, has seven hills, Dr. Winstock rehearsed some of these sepulchral traditions, but added that the Turks were not united in their belief in these stories. While they were thus engaged, a funeral procession passed over the hill at a full run. The boys could hardly avoid laughing, in spite of the solemnity of the occasion, it was so strange to see the bearers running with a corpse. The body was under a sheet, with a turban hung on a stick at the head.

"What's their hurry?" asked Murray, amazed at what appeared to be the levity of the Turks at a funeral. "They evidently mean business by the way they go at it."

"Probably the friends of the deceased believe the

traditions I have related to you, and that the soul of the departed is in pain until after the examination is over," replied the doctor.

"They hurry to the grave that their dead friend may the sooner fall asleep in the hope of paradise. You see over these graves, instead of a mound, as in our country, a cavity, where the grave has sunk down. The Turks do not use coffins, but cover the corpse with a few sticks to prevent the earth from resting too heavily upon it. They leave a hole from the head of the dead to the surface of the ground, said to be done in order that the departed may make any communication with the living, if he desires to do so; but more probably it grew out of some ancient custom. After a time this hole is filled up, and the decay of the body causes the earth to sink down, as you see in many places around you. These bearers, you noticed, were quite cheerful, because the Koran promises the expiation of certain sins to those who carry the corpse of a true believer even forty paces. The Turks bury their dead at one of the hours of prayer, generally at noon or sunset. The body is carried into a mosque, and after this followed by a portion of the congregation to the grave."

"Can't we go down and see what they do?" asked Murray.

"Decidedly not; it would not be proper to do so, for the Moslem considers that the grave of the faithful would be polluted by the presence of an infidel. They are less strict now than formerly, for Christians were not permitted to enter a mosque or other holy place, and now not even a firman can procure admission to this sacred mosque of Eyub."

The party resumed their walk, and soon reached the Valley of the Sweet Waters, above Eyub, for there is another locality with the same name on the Asiatic side of the Bosporus. Doubtless the water is sweet when there is any, and the fountains and cataracts very beautiful when there is enough of the aqueous fluid to run them. The stream was nearly dry, in spite of the heavy rain which had recently fallen, and it was nothing but a dirty puddle. The palace of the sultan is of wood, and a very mean affair. The enclosure contains a mosque, and a garden not well cared for. On the bank of the stream, in sight of the cataracts, is a pretty kiosk, in which the sultan takes tea with some of his ladies. Oriental splendors received another shock in the minds of the students on this occasion.

The country around the city is far from inviting. It is hilly, and at this season was brown and dried up. There is not a decent road to be found; indeed, no roads at all, except the one built by the sultan, to enable the Empress Eugénie to reach the palace set apart for her use, in a carriage. There is little cultivation, and no fine gardens gladden the eyes of the visitor, as in most other countries. The students returned to the boats at Eyub, disappointed, and with the feeling that, in the hands of enterprising Christians, this region would bloom like the gardens of paradise, which the Moslems dream of, but do not yet possess.

The next day the ship's company landed at Stamboul, and walked up the steep hill to the Seraskier, a watch-tower, in which persons are kept day and night, to signal the locality of any fire that may break out. This is done with colored balls in the daytime, and with colored lanterns in the night. The structure is connected with the new palace of the war office, which has a magnificent gateway. The view from the tower, which is ascended by a circular inclined plane, amply compensates for the labor of going up.

"Though this is a city of fires, there is no fire department worthy of the name," said Dr. Winstock. "From here you can see what a vast territory was swept over by the fire of last spring. When I was here before, the only fire engines were those which were carried on the backs of men."

"They couldn't do anything with steamers here," added Sheriden. "They could never get them up and down these hills and through these narrow streets."

" A few of them might be serviceable, for there are many places where they could go, as along the Grand Rue de Pera, and by a street along this side of the Golden Horn. I have been to the walls and to the Seraglio in a carriage, and engines could be drawn over the same route."

After enjoying the view for an hour, the excursionists visited several other objects of interest in Stamboul, the first of which was one of the seventeen ancient cisterns. They were built by the Greek emperors to contain a supply of water for the people during the summer, which is a dry time in Constantinople. They were filled in the wet season by aqueducts from distant places. One near St. Sophia is called the " Subterranean Palace,"and contains three hundred and thirty-six granite columns ; the vast apartment being elaborately ornamented. The one visited by our tourists is called the "Cistern of the Thousand and One Columns;" but this number is an Oriental exaggeration, for there are only two hundred and twenty-four. They are of marble, and were formerly beautiful enough to be above ground. This vast space is reached by a long flight of steps, and is occupied by silk-spinners, who are lighted in their work by apertures in the roof above them. Some of these cisterns are still used for their original purpose.

The party next paid a visit to two of the mausoleums of the sultans, of which there are several in the city, for the monarchs are not buried in a common sepulchre, as in most other countries. They are elegant chapels, high, circular apartments, with lofty windows, richly finished in costly marbles. The cenotaph is also of marble, generally with a kind of sloping top, like the roof of a house. It is adorned with emblems, as the turban with feathers studded with diamonds, and with rich Persian shawls. Without regard to the position of the room, the coffin is placed in a line with the direction to Mecca. The tomb of Mahmoud II. is the most elegant in the city, and contains the remains of some other members of his family. From this place the tourists went to the great Bazaar, which is one of the chief attractions of Constantinople to the stranger. Like many other Oriental novelties much talked about and much written about, it mocks the expectations of the visitor. Instead of a place fitted up with Eastern magnificence, and stored with glittering merchandise, the buildings are rude, and the apartments and courts utterly lacking in harmony or symmetry. It is, in fact, only a number of streets walled in and covered over. The pavements of them are rough and dirty, as they are outside.

But the novelty of the scene inside of the Bazaar is irresistible, and the stranger may wander through it all day finding enough to interest and amuse him. The avenues are covered by arches of stone. The true Oriental shop is only a box, hardly big enough for a peanut-stand. It is closed by two horizontal doors, which are locked at night. When the shop is opened, the upper door is turned up and fastened in its place, and from it are suspended specimens of the merchant's wares. The lower door is dropped upon some posts set for the purpose, so that its surface forms a shelf about two feet above the pavement. On this the shopkeeper squats and lights his pipe. In the little box behind him, which contains the bulk of his goods, is usually an attendant, who passes up whatever articles his employer requires. The Turk himself is too lazy to get up. He is in tremendous contrast with the supple salesmen of Paris or New York, who bows and scrapes, and leaps about all day long. He is slow of speech, and apparently indifferent, which, however, is far from the truth. As infidels are fair game, he usually asks four or five times the value of the goods. If one hundred piastres are demanded, it would not always be safe to offer him twenty. If he will cheat an infidel, it is no more than just to infer that he will cheat the faithful.

There are all kinds of shops in the Bazaar. Some of them are very like European stores on a small scale, and some are merely stands. Each class of merchandise has its favorite locality. One avenue will be crowded with shoe-shops filled with red shoes, yellow shoes, spangled shoes, satin shoes; indeed, the display is an exhibition of bright colors, in strong contrast with a Christian establishment. Another street is given up to dry goods, where rich silks and cloth of gold dazzle the eyes, even where the fair customer has to wear wooden clogs, which are a very common and necessary article in the city, to keep her dainty feet out of the mud-puddles in front of the shop. Jewellers, diamond merchants, and dealers in Turkish fancy articles cluster in another locality, and often their whole stock is contained within a small chest. Here is a pipe-shop, where the chibouk is the speciality; another has its whole trade in amber mouth-pieces. Here is a collection of nargilehs, and there of all the varieties of tobacco. Here is an avenue which abounds in copper kettles and pans, and there one which is equally rich in merchandise of brass.

The Bazaar is generally crowded with people; a considerable portion of them are, no doubt, mere " loafers," who do not go there to buy or sell. Some are on the lookout for a job, and others for a chance to cheat a Christian or a Jew. Certain parts abound with women, mostly of the middle and lower classes. Their picturesque and flowing robes, their veiled faces, and their socks down at the heels, challenge the attention of the European. The blackest and ugliest of negresses are as carefully veiled, and it would seem to a better purpose, as the fairest and whitest. The faces of some of these Nubian females are positively disgusting, and the less one sees of them the better. Turkish slops, such as sherbets and lemonade, though the latter is often very palatable; pastes, often in ropes yards in length, and cut off by the foot to the customer; confectionery, coffee, and similar refreshments are sold at stands throughout the Bazaar.

The students spent half the day wandering through the avenues, and examining the merchandise. They were continually entreated to purchase by drummers and touters outside of the shops, being sometimes accosted in pigeon English. On their way to the boats, they passed through a narrow street, where they had an opportunity to observe the Turkish manner of carrying heavy merchandise. A box of goods, four feet square and the same in depth, was slung by ropes to a long pole, which was "manned" by eight porters. They bore their heavy burden a rod or two, and then paused to rest. They took up the whole street, and yelled for the people to get out of the way when they moved. The boys laughed at them, and regarded the Turks as utterly lacking in inventive power.

18

CHAPTER XVI.

THE EARTHQUAKE ON BOARD OF THE TRITONIA.

"IS any reason assigned by Captain Wainwright for this disobedience of orders?" asked Mr. Tompion, when Sherman had informed him of the subversion of his authority on board of the Tritonia.

"Not that I am aware of, sir," replied the acting fourth lieutenant.

"And four of the officers are shut up in the brig?" added the vice-principal, whose indignation had somewhat subsided as he thought of his own condition during the last two days.

"Yes, sir; four of them."

"Who has the deck now?"

"Mr. Scott, sir."

"Very well; I will attend to the matter at once;" and Sherman retired, ready for the earthquake which he had touched off himself.

But Mr. Tompion was not so desirous of prompt action as he had been in the beginning. It looked as though he had been ignored, and his authority set aside because he was not in condition to do his duty. His reflections were very painful, and the situation, so far as he himself was concerned, was exceedingly unsatisfactory.   More than this, he was in a state of actual suffering.   Though somewhat improved by the treatment of the steward, he was still in a miserable condition.   His nerves were shaken and his stomach demoralized; probably he had what is called the "horrors."   He craved another dram, and no doubt another dram would have quieted his nerves and rekindled that deleterious excitement of the system on which he had been living for several days.   He searched his cabin again for a bottle of brandy, but with no better success than before; and he was convinced that some one — perhaps the mutinous captain of the vessel — had removed his liquor.   Then it occurred to him that the medicine chest might contain some liquor.   The key hung in the state-room of the professors, for Dr. Crimple was the ship's surgeon. He procured it, and opened the chest.   Mr. Lowington, though very strict in his temperance principles, was not a fanatic, and there was a pint bottle of brandy among the medicines, which the vice-principal conveyed to his cabin.

He was conscious, agonizingly conscious, that he had fallen from the high estate of manhood which he had struggled to maintain for so many years; that he had relapsed to the state which had compelled him to leave the navy, and that unless he immediately renounced the bottle, it would be fatal to him.   He resolved to do so, but not immediately.   He satisfied himself that he could not do so at once, his nerves were so fearfully shaken; but he would gradually restore his system to its wonted tone, and then once more and forever abandon the use of liquor.   What drunkard ever reformed himself in this manner? Not one, for the first dram breeds the necessity for another; it upsets the moral as well as the physical equilibrium. To yield a little to the craving of this insidious appetite is to destroy all power of resistance, at least for the time. Mr. Tompion convinced himself that a dram was a present necessity to him, and he drank half a tumbler full of the raw, fiery brandy. Certainly it did quiet his nerves for the time, as the freezing cold that kills the body first benumbs and banishes pain. He returned the bottle to the medicine chest, and placed the key where he had found it, before he felt the effects of the liquor he had drank. If he had waited ten minutes before he did so, he would have drank again.

The dram steadied his frame, and in a measure restored his powers for the time. If he could have stopped here, perhaps it would have been well. Thus fortified, he returned to the subject which disturbed him, and having disguised his breath with cloves, he went on deck, determined to re-establish his authority, and to commit the captain and the first lieutenant to the brig.

"Mr. Wainwright," said he, careful to disregard the title which the captain had forfeited by the order.

"On deck, sir," replied Wainwright, touching his cap.

"Where is the captain?"

Mr. Tompion was not violent, or even indignant, in his manner, for he had decided to bring about the tempest in a natural way, and without exposing the fact that Sherman had informed him of the insubordination on board.

"I am the captain, sir," replied Wainwright, glancing first at the vice-principal and then at Scott, who simply nodded at Campbell.

This glancing and nodding evidently meant something, for Campbell at once hastened to the steerage. He had been absent but a moment when both of the professors appeared on the quarter-deck, the head steward and the two adult forward officers in the waist, while all the officers and seamen came on deck, having been suddenly dismissed from recitations when Campbell had delivered his message to the instructors. Of course this was all arranged beforehand, for the professors had agreed to do the talking with the vice-principal if he attempted to disturb the present order of things on board.

"You are not the captain," replied Mr. Tompion, rather sternly.

Wainwright bowed and made no reply, but he looked anxiously for the coming of the professors.

"By my written order you were suspended. Where is Captain Morley, who was placed in command by the same order?"

"I am instructed to refer you to Professor Primback for an explanation," replied Wainwright. "Here he comes, sir."

"I beg your pardon, Mr. Tompion," the instructor began; and he was more agitated than the captain. "Will you oblige me with an interview in my room or your own?"

In his turn the vice-principal was startled, for Sherman had not said a word about the professors or the forward officers. The conspiracy looked much more formidable than he had anticipated, for he had not suspected that any others than the students were concerned in it. But Mr. Tompion felt at this moment that his dignity must be maintained. He had begun to discipline the captain, and all the Morleyites were rejoicing at the prospect of witnessing the effects of the earthquake which Sherman had promised. The vice-principal did not like to retire till he had made himself felt.

"I will see you in a few moments, Mr. Primback," replied he, his face even paler than before. "I asked you, Mr. Wainwright, where Captain Morley was. You did not answer me."

"In the brig, sir."

"I desire to speak to you about this matter, and to explain it," interposed the professor.

"I will enforce my authority first, and hear the explanation afterwards. By whose order was Captain Morley committed to the brig?" demanded the vice-principal.

"By mine, sir," answered Wainwright, firmly.

"You will instantly order his release," added Mr. Tompion, sternly.

Wainwright bowed, but said nothing.

"Who else is in the brig?"

"Mr. Greenwood, Mr. Prescott, and Mr. Walker, sir."

"Release the whole of them at once!" commanded the vice-principal.

The captain made no movement to obey.

"Do you hear me?" roared Mr. Tompion, so angry by this time that he shook his fist at the captain;

MR. TOMPION ASSERTS HIS AUTHORITY. Page 279.

whereat Mr. Marline and Mr. Rimmer began to move aft.

"In whose charge are the prisoners?" he added.

"In Mr. Marline's, sir."

"Mr. Marline!"

"On deck, sir," replied the boatswain, touching his cap.

"Release your prisoners at once, sir."

The old salt stood like a statue on the quarter-deck.

"Do you hear me, sir?" cried Mr. Tompion, savagely.

"I do, sir."

"I hope, Mr. Tompion, before this business proceeds any farther, that you will grant me an interview below," said Professor Primback.

"I beg you will do so, sir!" added Dr. Crimple.

"This is mutiny!" thundered Mr. Tompion. "Are you concerned in it, gentlemen?"

"We are; and the farther you proceed with the business in this way, the more disagreeable it will become," replied Professor Primback, who was provided with a backbone.

"Will you obey my order, Mr. Marline?" roared the vice-principal.

"No, sir; I will not," answered the boatswain, bowing.

"Let me add, Mr. Tompion, that this is very serious business," interposed the senior professor.

"You will find that it is!" retorted the vice-principal.

"All that you do complicates the matter, and I beg you will go below with us," added Dr. Crimple. "No one will obey your orders."

Mr. Tompion was utterly astounded. It was plain, even to him, that the control of the vessel had been wrested from him; but it was not in his nature to submit without a struggle. The fact that four of the officers were in the brig for disobedience to the captain, and the fact that Sherman had given him information of the state of discipline on board, assured him that the ship's company were not a unit in their action.

"All who are ready to obey the orders of the vice-principal will walk up to the weather side of the vessel," said he, anxious to know his strength.

Sherman and about a dozen of the Morleyites among the crew started for the weather rail.

"To the weather side, every one of you!" called Scott, leading the way; and in an instant the whole ship's company were on the side indicated.

"All others go down to leeward!" shouted the vice-principal; but Scott determined that no expression of opinion should be had in this way, and the command was not heeded.

"We are prepared for the worst, Mr. Tompion," said Professor Primback, "even for violence."

"What do you mean by that, sir?" demanded the vice-principal.

"If you proceed any farther in this direction, we shall be obliged to interfere."

"I think you have interfered already; but I propose to restore order in this vessel."

"Let me say plainly, then, Mr. Tompion, if you don't retire at once to the cabin, the forward officers will lay violent hands upon you."

"Has it come to this?" gasped the vice-principal, who now realized that he was utterly powerless.

"We will stand by you, sir," said Sherman, greatly excited. "Come, fellows, let's break down the brig!" he added, rushing forward.

"Mr. Marline, commit Mr. Sherman to the brig," interposed the captain.

The boatswain sprang to obey the order; but Sherman showed fight, and the old salt threw him upon the deck. The Morleyites rushed forward to assist him, but Scott and his friends were there also, and for a moment a sharp *mêlée* raged, though the conspirators were immediately overwhelmed. The refractory officer was carried to the brig and locked in with his companions, where he had an opportunity to tell them the exciting news.

Mr. Tompion was satisfied by this time that he could accomplish nothing on deck, and he sullenly retreated to the cabin, followed by the professors. He rushed into his own room, and remained there till the middle of the afternoon. The instructors decided not to disturb him, and were confident he would resort to his bottle again for strength and comfort. His liquor was all gone; and he wanted it now more than ever before. The fierce excitement had nearly worked off the effects of the dram he had taken. He tried to reflect, but he could not. He was crazy for liquor. He knew that he had two bottles in the valise the day before, and he came to the conclusion now that the professors had taken them away. He determined to find them, and in the middle of the afternoon, when they were engaged with their classes, he visited their room. The bottles were not there, but the key of the medicine chest was, and he obtained the brandy from that. Before night he was stupidly drunk again, and the bottle was empty.

In the mean time, the Tritonia had been making a fine run, and was approaching Cape Finisterre.

In the brig, the case looked as hopeless as it did in the cabin of the vice-principal. The day of deliverance had come and gone, but Morley and Greenwood were still prisoners. Prescott and Walker were dissatisfied with the situation, for they had been assured that they could be confined to the brig only a few hours, and there was not the least prospect of their getting out for a month.

" I have had enough of this thing," said Walker.

" You haven't been here six hours," replied Greenwood.

" Don't grumble," added Morley. " I've been here two days, and I don't complain yet."

" It's none of my funeral, in the first place," continued Walker.

" Nor mine," said Prescott ; " and I have no idea of staying in here two or three weeks."

" Don't back down yet," begged Morley.

" Greenwood told us we should be in here but a few hours," said Walker. " Now Sherman has come, and says the vice-principal has lost the battle, and Wainwright's fellows are having it all their own way. What's the use? I expect they will put Tompion in the brig next. — Mr. Marline !"

" Well, my lad, what do you want?" replied the boatswain, who was on watch to see that the prisoners had no communication with the seamen.

" I want to get out."

" So do I," added Prescott. " I was all wrong, and I want to set myself right. I thought before that I ought to obey Mr. Tompion."

" Come out," said the boatswain, unlocking the door, and permitting Prescott and Walker to leave their prison. " You will report to the first lieutenant on deck at once. I am authorized to release any one, except Morley and Greenwood, who is willing to do his duty."

" Then you may release me," said Sherman. " I didn't fully understand the matter, and I thought I ought to obey the vice."

Sherman came out, and went on deck to report himself.

" All backed down," said Morley.

" I don't know that I blame them much, since this last news came," replied Greenwood. " Mr. Tompion is counted out."

" So it seems. I had no idea the professors would carry the thing so far," added Morley.

" If the vice is gone up, our game is played out."

" Well, I suppose it is. But the principal can't blame us for obeying the orders of the vice," continued Morley, who began to feel that his cause was lost.

They discussed the subject in the brig for the rest of the day; but both of the conspirators were obliged to confess that the " earthquake " was a fizzle, and that they were hopelessly defeated. Yet they were not quite ready to humble themselves, and promise obedience to the captain.

The three officers who had been discharged from

the brig reported to the first lieutenant, and their cases were referred to the captain. They were willing to do their duty and obey their superiors, and this statement was all that was required of them. All of them claimed to have been sincere in their belief that it was their duty to obey the vice-principal. Sherman, the most violent and impulsive of the trio, said that he had really pitied the vice-principal when he saw him deserted by everybody, and he was honest enough to describe his interview with Mr. Tompion, as he had arranged it with Greenwood.

"Doubtless it was a difficult matter for you to arrive at a correct conclusion, Mr. Sherman," said Professor Primback, who had been called to hear the statement of the fourth lieutenant. "I can see that you might have been entirely sincere."

"O, I was, sir!" protested Sherman. "I was in the Tritonia with Morley and Greenwood before this cruise. I thought it was a hard case for them to be put down, and I sympathized with them before these troubles; but I never would agree to do anything I thought was wrong."

"You may redeem yourself by your future conduct," added the professor. "When the day of reckoning comes, you will be judged by that."

"I mean to do my duty, as I always have."

"You were not committed to the brig as a penalty for your opinions, but to place you where you could do no harm. Will you answer me one question now?"

"If I can."

"In what manner did Morley obtain that written order from Mr. Tompion?"

"He told us all about his relations with Mr. Tompion, while we were in the brig. I haven't the same opinion of Morley that I had before; and if I had understood him and Greenwood, I wouldn't have followed their lead. I didn't know that they were laboring to bring about this row, so as to get the highest places in the vessel."

"You didn't answer my question," said Mr. Primback, gently.

"I will answer it, sir. On the first night out of Copenhagen, Morley caught the vice-principal drunk, and helped him to bed. Mr. Tompion had sense enough to know that he had exposed himself, and made Morley promise not to tell of it. He says he shouldn't have dared to make that row in the fog, and get suspended, if he hadn't known that he had a mortgage on the vice, as he called it. He induced the vice to sail before the ship came, and got suspended again, on purpose to have Mr. Tompion sign that order removing the captain and first lieutenant."

This was about what the professor, the captain, and others supposed was the secret of Morley's influence over the vice-principal. The penitent officers returned to their duty, and all went well on deck. The next morning Mr. Tompion was necessarily sober again, but thirsting fiercely for his dram. The Tritonia was off the coast of Portugal, sixty miles from Lisbon. The inebriate desired to go into port, in order that he might obtain more liquor. He called Mr. Primback into his room. The professor explained the situation, and related Morley's confession to him. He was astonished and apparently indignant, and expressed his willingness to drop the matter where it was.

"But I think the Young America will go into Lisbon," said he; and he mentioned half a dozen reasons for this belief.

The instructor was not a nautical man, and could not appreciate these reasons.

"At any rate, we had better run in. If she is not there, we shall find in the ship-news some report of her. I am no longer in authority here."

"But your counsels will be heeded, and I hope you will soon be restored to your position."

Mr. Primback consulted the forward officers and the captain, and it was finally decided to make a port at Lisbon; and at sunset the Tritonia was at anchor in the Tagus.

CHAPTER XVII.

SCUTARI, THE WALLS, AND THE HOWLING DERVISHES.

ALL aboard for Scutari!" said Sheridan, as he went down the accommodation steps of the ship to the captain's gig, where Dr. Winstock and several of the officers were already seated.

The oars were up, and at the order they fell, and the boats all went off. The day was to be devoted to an excursion to Scutari, which is in Asia, opposite Constantinople. The boats passed near the Turkish men-of-war, which were anchored in the Bosporus, with the Ottoman flag at the peak. It is red, with a crescent and star upon it.

" I never knew till yesterday the origin of the crescent," said Murray.

" What was it?" asked the surgeon.

" One dark night, Philip of Macedon, having besieged Byzantium, attempted to undermine the walls; but the new moon came out, and enabled the defenders of the city to see what was going on, and Philip was thus defeated. The Byzantines were so grateful that they adopted the crescent as the symbol of their city."

" That may be true, and may not. The crescent

was used more than a thousand years before Christ, and two thousand years before the Ottoman empire was founded. The word comes from the Latin *crescere*, to increase, and was used in this sense in Greece, in Rome, and in Syria. The idea was symbolized by ornaments in the form of the new moon. Such are mentioned in the Book of Judges. When the Turks conquered Constantinople, they found the crescent there, and adopted it as their national symbol. You see it on all the mosques, and it is to Mohammedanism what the cross is to Christianity, though it was a religious emblem long before the time of the prophet of Islam."

The party landed at Scutari with no little difficulty, for the wind was blowing fresh from the south-west, and driving in a heavy sea. The ferry-boat which had just arrived was pounding against the rude pier at which she landed her pa-sengers. The students entered the town, which is even more Oriental than Stamboul. A score of Arabs and others, with horses to let, waylaid them as they entered the square. Some of the boys wanted to ride for the " fun of it," and they were permitted to engage horses through Dimitri, who bargained for the lot at a reduced price — about three francs apiece. While the Greek guide was dickering with the Arabs, the captain and Sheridan entered a coffee-room with Dr. Winstock. It was a small shop, with seats all around it about two feet wide, so that the Turkish customers could squat upon it. The proprietor stood in the rear, at a large brass dish or brazier, containing a charcoal fire, on which stood a coffee-pot. Half a dozen Turks reclined on the settee, smoking nargilehs, drinking coffee, and carrying on a conversation. They were ragged, dirty fellows, and doubtless laborers.

"I suppose they are talking politics," said Cantwell.

"Probably not," laughed the doctor. "Turks don't meddle with politics, except in times of insurrection. More likely they are talking about their work."

"They smoke first-class pipes, for these nargilehs must cost a good deal."

"These pipes are let out for a smoke by the keeper of the shop. Will you take some coffee, for we cannot patronize the shop by hiring a pipe."

The doctor ordered coffee by making a sign, as if pouring off the contents of a cup.

"I think that smoking looks nasty," said Sheridan, turning up his nose. "That bubbling noise is enough to make me sick, and the odor here is vile. Let's get out as quick as we can."

The party drank the thimbleful of muddy, black coffee, and the doctor held out a handful of the big copper piastres, to which the keeper of the shop helped himself, doubtless taking four times as much as was his due.

"There's a team!" exclaimed Cantwell, as they went into the square.

Six mules, loaded with fruit and vegetables from the country, were strung in a line; a cord from the bridle of each, except the leader, was fastened to the saddle of the next ahead of him. The driver occasionally rapped one of them with his stick, and he leaped forward, crowding those ahead, and jerking those behind, to the great amusement of the boys.

At last the procession was ready to move, and horse and foot commenced the ascent of the hill behind the town. Many such mule teams as the one described were seen, most of which were loaded with grapes.

" Do they make wine here?" asked Murray.

" Certainly not; the Moslems are forbidden to drink wine as well as to eat pork," replied the doctor. " But I am afraid some of the Turks are falling from grace, for it is said the sultan frequently gets boozy on champagne, which he probably does not call wine. If he sets the example, the true believers will find sufficient excuse for following it."

The excursionists visited the hospital and the burying-ground used by the English during the Crimean war. Scutari was the scene of Florence Nightingale's devoted sacrifice and labor for the sick and wounded soldiers. At this place there is an extent of about three miles of burying-ground used by the Turks, and the students saw several funerals at noon, all of them going to the grave as though they were running a race. The view from the hill above the town is magnificent. In the town the party entered a khan, which is an Oriental hotel. There are two hundred of them in Constantinople, provided by the government for the encouragement of the merchants who visit the city. The khan is a square containing a fountain, and sometimes a garden surrounded on all sides by buildings, with galleries from which open the rooms. On the ground floor are the stables for the horses and mules of the travellers. The apartments are unfurnished, for the Oriental carries his bed with him. A coffee-room is attached to each, and provisions and feed for the animals are sometimes sold.

"How's that?" asked Captain Cantwell, as he stood comparing the time by his watch with that of a large old-fashioned clock, in the coffee-room of the khan.

"What's the matter, captain?" inquired the doctor.

"This clock seems to be going, but it is about two hours too slow."

"Turkish time," laughed the surgeon. "Noon when the sun sets."

"Noon when the sun sets!" exclaimed Murray.

"Just so; they use the astronomical day of twenty-four hours, instead of the civil day of twelve hours, and one o'clock is one hour after sunset. It was formerly the custom to reckon time in this way in Italy, where it could be half past twenty-three o'clock."

"But the sun sets at different times."

"Do you see that calendar?" asked the doctor, pointing to a card covered with Turkish characters, which was attached to the clock. "It is to enable the Turk to know when the day begins, so that he can set his clock. At one hour after sundown it is one o'clock. Now it is twenty-two o'clock; and as it is so late, it is time to return to the boats."

One day the ship's company made an excursion in a steamer up the Bosporus, and into the Black Sea; but their opinion of it was about the same as that of De Forrest and Beckwith. Another day they made a boat trip into the Sea of Marmora, to the walls of the city. They landed near the Castle of the Seven Towers, which was the first place they visited. It is nothing but a ruin, and the original structure was erected so far back in the past that the date cannot be given.

It has been rebuilt several times, once by Mohammed II., who used it as a place of safety for his valuables, and his successors as a prison for Greek Christians and foreign ambassadors in time of war. The party entered the round tower, which Dimitri said had been the prison of a French envoy for years. The walls enclose a large space, which is now improved by the erection of several wooden buildings, to accommodate a school for orphan girls. The boys went through the eating-room, and the work-shop in which the girls were making fringe, tassels, parts of harness, and cartridge cases for the Turkish army.

Leaving the castle, the party took a long walk across the peninsula, to the Golden Horn, following a rough road near the walls, which consist of three lines. The inner one is the highest, and is crowned with frequent lofty towers, round, square, and octagonal, which were quite picturesque, and would make a whole series of drawing-cards. The walls are eighteen feet apart, and the spaces are generally filled with rubbish from the ruins, though an occasional fig tree lifts its heavy foliage to relieve the desolation of the place. Along the line there are thirteen gates, each having its name and history. The walls are full of interest, and as the party walked along, the instructors related to the students several stories from ancient history.

"The town was founded by Byzan, a Greek fisherman, who built a few huts here. The name of Byzantium comes from him," said Dr. Winstock. "Constantine started the walls, but Theodosius, in 413, enlarged the city, and probably laid the foundation of the present inner line. Greeks and Turks had a hand in the work till they were completed. The Sea of Marmora, you know, was the ancient Propontis. Constantine obtained marble for his walls and buildings from an island in the western part of it ; and the modern name of the sea comes from *marmor*, plural, *marmora*, the Latin for *marble*."

Part of the country along the road was cultivated, and the students observed with interest several rude machines for raising water to irrigate the land. Fig trees grew in abundance, and the grapes hung in rich profusion on the vines ; but there were no improvements on the land ; it was in its primitive state, and everything seemed to be in keeping with the ruined walls on the other side of the road. The gardens were soon passed, and for miles on the left was a burying-ground, covered with gravestones, leaning at all angles, falling or fallen, as though the dead were forgotten. It was desolation on both sides there. In some places where the street had been improved, and towards Eyub, where a sidewalk had been built, some of the gravestones were worked in for curbs and for pavements, though the boys looked in vain for any inscription on these pieces ; for no Turk would be wicked enough to step upon a slab on which a verse from the Koran was inscribed. In the pleasantest spot they could find, the party picnicked on the ground from the provisions brought from the ship. It was dark when they reached the boats, and it was a long pull to the ship, but the oarsmen were frequently changed. The water in the Bosporus and Golden Horn was covered with boats, most of them caiques, or, in Turkish, " kijik " which carried lamps on each side of the rowlocks.

The boys slept well that night, and the next day did not go on shore till afternoon, when a portion of them visited a monastery of the Howling Dervishes. There is one of these in Scutari, and another in Pera, the latter of which was selected by Dimitri because the ceremonies were less hideous and disgusting than those at the former. The party went up and down steep hills in the outskirts of Pera, in a dirty region, till they came to the monastery. It was a mass of irregular wooden buildings, on a side hill, and they had to descend a flight of stairs to enter it. The structure was no better than a barn in this country — not so good as many barns. The porter at the entrance took charge of coats, canes, and umbrellas, and sold coffee, candy, confects, and tobacco to visitors. Dimitri led the way to the chapel, which was a room forty feet long by twenty wide, finished with unpainted boards. At one end and along a part of one side was a gallery. They heard the "singing" as they entered, and saw a dozen men squatted on the floor, who were behaving in the most extraordinary manner, as judged by the European standard. The party went into the gallery, and reclined upon the sheep-skins spread on the floor; but not without a suspicion that Moslem fleas would bite as hard as any others.

The dervishes were mostly in one corner of the room. They wore no distinctive dress, and one was in the uniform of a soldier. Poverty seemed to be one of the conditions of the order. They were chanting a monotonous strain, and bowing and swinging wildly as they sang. The burden of the song was a constant repetition of the words "la illah — illah la." The double l, as in Spanish, sounded like *ilyah*. At the first syllable they bend forward, with a jerk; at the second, they straighten up; at the third, they throw their heads back; and so on. The movement is convulsive, and as the ceremony proceeds they warm up, and the tones become wild and savage. Once in a while they give a yell in concert, which sounds like " hoo!" but it is really " Ya-hu," or Jehovah, with the accent on the last syllable. This chant was kept up for half an hour, and the party in the gallery began to weary of it; but the worst of the performance was yet to come.

In this preliminary exercise, the object is to repeat the name of God, " Allah," or " Illah," three hundred times. When this was done, the dervishes ranged themselves, standing in a line against the farther wall of the chapel, where they began to sway their heads up and down, and to the right and left, making with each motion a heavy breathing sound, not unlike that made by a man chopping wood. The sound soon became more guttural, and the motion more violent. The noise and the gestures indicated the most agonizing sensations, and most of the dervishes grew very pale. The spectators expected to see some of them drop senseless on the floor. In front of these active ones, five others had seated themselves on a praying carpet, chanting the old strain, and one of them was gesticulating at the others.

The aspirate sounds were at last a savage grunt, and it looked as though the fanatics intended to shake their heads off. The sight was painful and disgusting to behold. Occasionally a shout was heard, but there was

not much that could be called " howling." This pa t
of the performance lasted about half an hour more,
and they stood still again. An old man repeated some
sentences, the others frequently shouting a single word,
Ya-hu, which sounds like " hoo ! " This wild yell was
given with so much emphasis that a couple of ladies
present were alarmed, and retired. At the close of
the ceremonies, the old sheik came in, and the sick
were brought before him to be healed. A little child
was placed upon the floor, and he put his foot upon
it. A cripple took the same position, and the old
man actually stepped on him with both feet. Others
were touched and pressed with the hand on the head,
chest, and arms. Whether the " healing " was effected
or not, the students had no means of knowing. The
performance was ended, and the party withdrew from
the chapel.

" I don't know what all that means," said Murray,
as they walked up the steep hill.

" Neither do I, unless it is to mortify the flesh, for
those men suffered intensely during that heavy breathing and rapid motion. If you should do it for a moment it would make you dizzy; and in five minutes
you would faint away," replied the surgeon.

" I couldn't do it."

" I wouldn't try. These men used to torture themselves by other means, such as cutting themselves with
knives, and burning their bodies with hot irons; but
the sultan, as the head of the church, forbade these
practices."

Before dark the students were on board of the ship
again. This was about the last of the sight-seeing in

Constantinople, though small parties went on shore every day, and visited minor objects of interest. Mr. Mapps delivered another lecture on ancient geography and history, and indicated the localities of prominent events in the vicinity. He told them that Hannibal was buried on one of the Prince's Islands, which could be seen from the ship.

Mr. Lowington heard nothing more of the Tritonia, or of the runaways, and he was naturally very anxious about both. He had used the telegraph freely, but it had as yet afforded him no relief.

CHAPTER XVIII.

FROM THE TAGUS, TO THE GOLDEN HORN.

AFTER entering the Tagus, the Tritonia, in obedience to Portugeuse law, was obliged to heave to and take on board a custom-house officer, though there was nothing for such a functionary to do. When the vessel was opposite the city, an officer in a boat directed her where to anchor, and she had a berth off the Marine Arsenal. The purser paid the pilot, who was about to go on shore in a boat which put off for him, when Mr. Tompion came on deck with his valise in his hand.

"I wish to go on shore," said he to Professor Primback. "Am I permitted to do so, sir?."

His tone was bitter, and the professor was annoyed by it.

"Certainly, Mr. Tompion. The captain will provide a boat for you."

"I will not trouble him. I shall ascertain where the ship is, and will report to you in half an hour or an hour," replied the vice-principal, as he went over the side into the shore boat.

"Clear away the first cutter," called the captain, who had heard this conversation. "You shall have a boat in a moment, Mr. Tompion."

The vice-principal paid no attention to him, but the captain sent Sherman in the cutter with directions to report to him, and bring him off when he was ready to return. The fourth lieutenant landed, and found Mr. Tompion at the Hotel Central, near the water, looking over the English papers. Sherman reported that the first cutter was at his service. As he did so, the odor of the vice-principal's breath indicated that he had already been drinking. In half an hour he came to the landing, with some newspapers in his hand, and stepped into the boat. He had drank brandy twice in this time. The cutter was soon alongside the Tritonia, and Mr. Tompion went on deck.

"I find that the ship arrived at Cowes the day we sailed, and left on the following day," said he to the senior professor. "Probably she will be here by to-morrow."

"Is it certain that she will stop here?" asked Mr. Primback.

"I think she will. Now, sir, I have communicated with the American consul at this port, and I intend that my orders shall be obeyed," said Mr. Tompion.

The professor saw that the vice-principal had been drinking again, and the situation was exceedingly trying to him.

"No one can regret these difficulties more than I do," he replied, as by mutual consent they went below and entered the professor's room. "We have endeavored to treat the case as delicately as possible."

"Is it delicate to get up a mutiny, sir?" demanded Mr. Tompion, sternly.

"Last evening you expressed your willingness to

drop the matter where it was," added Mr. Primback, though the smell of his companion's breath was a sufficient explanation of his present conduct.

" By which I meant that I was not disposed to punish any one for his conduct. If Wainwright acted under your advice, he is more excusable than if he had done it out of his own head."

" We advised him in the matter."

" I intended to commit him to the brig for his disobedience. I will remit that penalty, but he cannot retain the command of the vessel. Both he and Scott must be relieved."

" And Morley placed in command, I suppose."

"Certainly; he is the next in rank. I have been insulted, and I cannot submit," added Mr. Tompion, warmly. " Morley and Greenwood must be released at once."

" I hope you will not insist upon this, sir."

" But I do insist. It must be done."

" We cannot consent to it," answered Mr. Primback, decidedly.

" You don't understand it, sir. I am in actual command of this vessel, and no one but the owner can remove me."

" We will take the responsibility. Dr. Crimple and myself have thoroughly examined the subject, and we have come to the conclusion that a man in a state of intoxication is not in proper condition to control the movements of the vessel."

" Intoxication! What do you mean by that, sir?" demanded Mr. Tompion, angrily.

" Surely you are aware, sir, that such was your own condition for several days."

"I am not aware of it.   I was sick, and I did take some brandy ; but I was none the worse for it."

"We think the evidence is quite strong enough."

"I will not discuss a question of this kind.   The charge is an insult to me," said the vice-principal, violently.   "To-morrow morning I shall remove Wainwright and Scott, and place Morley in command.   I shall have a file of soldiers here to enforce my orders, and to arrest any one who disobeys me.   I have nothing more to say."

Mr. Tompion abruptly left the room, went on deck, and over the side into the first cutter, which he had ordered to wait for him.   The boat shoved off, and in a short time returned without him.   Mr. Primback, startled by the declaration of the vice-principal, immediately called a council in his room, consisting of Wainwright, Dr. Crimple, and the forward officers, to whom he related the substance of his interview with Mr. Tompion.

"I am willing to be removed," said Wainwright.

"We are not willing to have you removed," replied Dr. Crimple.

"He has the weather-gage of you, gentlemen," said Mr. Marline, shaking his head ominously.   "He is the actual captain, for his name appears as such in the vessel's papers.   He can do all he said he would, and the police here, at the request of the consul, would enforce his orders."

"What then?"

"We should all have to be tried for mutiny.   There is a United States ship of war in port, I think, and I suppose we should be sent on board of her, to be conveyed home. I have no doubt we should be fully justified; but we don't want to be sent home in irons."

"Where do you suppose the ship is?" asked the doctor.

"Up the Strait, by this time. She was at Cowes on the day we had the gale, and the next she had a fair wind."

"Perhaps we could overhaul her," suggested the captain, anxiously.

The boatswain shook his head.

"What shall we do? That's the question," said Mr. Primback. "If we were in the wrong, it would be easy to recede."

"In my opinion we came to this port to enable Mr. Tompion to obtain a supply of liquor," added Dr. Crimple.

"I don't see but we must submit," continued Mr. Primback. "We cannot hold out against the Portuguese government, and Mr. Tompion certainly has the technical advantage of us."

The subject was discussed for an hour, but no satisfactory solution of the difficulty was reached.

"I will go on shore, and lay the case before the consul," said Mr. Primback; and this course was assented to by all.

The professor took Mr. Marline with him, and they were sent on shore in the second cutter. They found the consul, who heard the case patiently, and then enlarged upon the difficulties it presented. He could only advise them to settle the matter among themselves.

"You have seen Mr. Tompion?" said the professor.

"No, sir; I have not seen him."

"But he told me he had communicated with you," added Mr. Primback.

"He certainly has not. Where is he now?"

"On shore, but I don't know where."

"I think we had better see him. I will use my influence with him. Probably he is at one of the hotels, and we will endeavor to find him."

They went to the Hotel Braganza first, and then to the Central, where the vice-principal was found. It was early in the evening, but he had retired to his room. The party were shown up to his apartment. The consul knocked, but there was no answer. He tried the door; it was not locked, and he entered, followed by his companions. On the table were a lighted candle and two bottles, one of which was empty. In the valise on a chair were six others, packed in a quantity of soiled linen. Mr. Tompion was on the bed, utterly senseless. The consul shook him, but was unable to obtain a word or a look from him.

"It is a plain case," said he; "this man is not fit to command a vessel."

"We are satisfied on that point; but what can be done?"

"The case is anomalous, and I shall be obliged to look it up," replied the consul, as they left the hotel. "It is a pity you came into port."

"I see that now; but Mr. Tompion intimated that he was satisfied to let things remain as they were," added the professor.

"Possibly you may be able to redeem this mistake," said the consul, significantly.

"Perhaps we may; but the custom-house is closed."

"I will see Mr. Tompion in the morning. I shall take good care of him, and I don't think he will be ready to go on board before noon," laughed the official.

Mr. Frimback and the boatswain returned to the ship with the hint they had obtained. In the morning they went on shore again; the formalities of a clearance were gone through with, the dues paid, and the Tritonia was ready to sail, having the permission of the Portuguese government to do so.

"Call all hands, and get up the anchor," said Captain Wainwright to the first lieutenant; and to the astonishment of the ship's company, the boatswain sounded this call through the vessel.

Mr. Tompion was not on board, and the Morleyites forward could not understand it. In a few moments the Tritonia was standing down the river. The consul had called upon the tippler at the hotel in the morning, but he was still unfit to do anything. Belem Castle was passed, and the vessel went out to sea. The knot of difficulties had been unsnarled by cutting it.

"Did you hear what the fellows in the steerage were saying, Morley," said Greenwood, in the brig.

"Yes, I heard it," replied the conspirator, gloomily. "They have left Mr. Tompion on shore."

"I don't understand it. But I suppose the vice is on another spree. I am ready to cave in now."

"I am not. We can't be blamed for obeying the vice."

While they were talking about it, Mr. Marline opened the door of the brig, and directed them to report to Mr. Primback in the cabin. They obeyed the order.

"Mr. Morley, are you ready to do your duty?" asked the professor, who was now the acting vice-principal.

"I have always been ready to do it," muttered Morley.

"I think not; you evidently do not understand the case;" and to the astonishment and indignation of the conspirator, Mr. Primback recited to him his own confession, reported by Sherman. "You made the trouble with the captain because you had a mortgage on Mr. Tompion, and knew that he would restore you. You obtained the written order from him while he was in a state of intoxication. But we leave all these matters to be adjusted by the principal. We do not wish to keep you in the brig. Will you submit to the present order of things?"

"I can't help myself," growled Morley.

"So long as you do not interfere with the discipline of the vessel, you shall remain at liberty. If you attempt to meddle with the order on board, you will be sent back to the brig. I say the same to you, Mr. Greenwood."

"I am willing to return to my duty, and obey all the officers above me," replied Greenwood, promptly.

"Then you may report for duty; for technically you were right, as I do not know that you were concerned in the conspiracy with Morley," added the professor.

"He was not. I didn't even tell him that I had caught the vice-principal drunk," said Morley.

For the present the trouble was settled. Greenwood apologized to the captain for all he had done amiss, and endeavored to redeem himself, as far as he could, by his good conduct. The Tritonia continued on her voyage, with light winds, and it was a week before she reached the Strait of Gibraltar. From this point she had good breezes for a week, and then a succession of calms, followed by contrary winds. It was the 10th of September when she entered the Bosporus, and dropped her anchor in the Golden Horn. Her arrival created a decided sensation in the Young America, and Mr. Lowington hastened on board of her. He was greeted with hearty cheers as he went over the side, and respectfully saluted by the officers on the quarter-deck.

"Where is Mr. Tompion?" asked the principal, after he had shaken hands with the professors.

"We left him at Lisbon," replied Mr. Primback.

"So I was informed by telegraph; and I have been very anxious about you," added Mr. Lowington.

The banker at Lisbon had written him all the particulars of the Tritonia's visit to that city; and the letter, not properly directed, was waiting in the British post office at Galata to be claimed.

"It is a long and painful story," continued the professor; "and we had better tell it in the cabin."

The professor summoned the captain, Dr. Crimple, and the adult forward officers, to attend the conference; and when they were seated in the cabin, he related the incidents of the voyage after the parting of the two vessels. When he had finished, the others put in what they thought had been omitted, and the whole story was brought out. Mr. Lowington was, of course, surprised, for he had been confident of the reformation of Mr. Tompion; but he was gratified that the consequences were no worse. He approved the conduct of the professors, of the captain, and of all who had assumed the responsibility. While the party were still together, Morley and Greenwood were sent for. The latter had behaved very well, in spite of the reproaches of the former.

"Morley, I have listened to the charges against you. What have you to say?" said the principal.

"What are the charges against me, sir?" he asked.

"Disobedience to your superior officers; insolence and insubordination in your relations with Captain Wainwright."

"He picked upon me, dogged me, and watched his chance to pick me up."

"And you gave him the chance?"

"I couldn't help it."

"Yes, you could," said the principal, sternly. "When did he pick upon you?"

"The night we sailed from Copenhagen, he staid on deck about all night on purpose to pick me up."

"Were you on watch all night, Morley?"

"No, sir; of course not. I had the deck with the first part of the port watch from twelve till two."

"The captain was up when you relieved the second part of the starboard watch — was he?"

"Yes, sir."

"He seems to have treated the other officers the same as he did you. Who had the deck before you?"

"Greenwood, sir."

" Did he pick you up, Greenwood? "

" No, sir ; he didn't say a word to me. I didn't give him the chance."

" But he staid on deck? "

" Yes, sir."

" He did his duty ; he was where he ought to have been ; and I commend him for his fidelity. He was fully justified in suspending you, and would have been when you left your station to talk with the midshipman forward. Mr. Tompion's conduct in restoring you without hearing the captain was emphatically wrong, though his action is explained now. You boasted that you snubbed and insulted the captain because you knew the vice-principal would restore you. The second time you tried it was during a gale, and then you disobeyed in order to be suspended, so that you might procure the removal of Wainwright."

" I acted under the orders of the vice-principal," growled Morley.

" Mr. Tompion was not in condition to give orders. I censure you for your own conduct, not for his. Captain Wainwright, pipe all hands to muster, if you please."

The captain left.

" Wainwright and Scott came on board of the Tritonia, and shoved us down," added Morley.

" I have heard all that story before, and I have told you it is not a particle of excuse for you," replied Mr. Lowington, sternly, as he led the way to the deck.

The ship's company had assembled : the principal briefly reviewed the events of the cruise, and heartily commended the conduct of the captain, the professors, and the forward officers. He then pulled off Morley's shoulder-straps, reduced him to a common seaman, and transferred him to the ship. Greenwood was censured; but the principal said his subsequent conduct entitled him to consideration, and he would retain his position as second lieutenant.

Morley was sent on board of the ship, and the troubles were finally settled. The squadron remained a week at Constantinople to enable the Tritonia's students to see the city, and to await the arrival of the Josephine, which had passed the Strait, according to the ship news. Within the week she arrived, and the three vessels sailed for the waters of Greece. The passage was a delightful one; the sea was smooth, and the wind was light all the way. On the morning of the second day the squadron entered the Dardanelles, and the students on deck observed the shores with deep interest. Lofty mountains, some of them snow-capped, were seen at a distance from the shore, in Asia. Several towns were passed, and some strong fortifications. The boats used by the people were odd craft, with the leg-of-mutton sail, and the men in them had a peculiarly savage look. The entire day was spent in passing the Strait, which in the narrowest place, at Abydos, is a mile wide. At this point Xerxes built his pontoon bridge across, — which was carried away by a storm; whereupon he flogged the sea with three hundred lashes for its bad conduct, — and built two others, which stood longer. Here Leander swam over to see Miss Hero, and Lord Byron followed his example. Half a dozen of the students desired to attempt the same feat, but Mr. Lowington

did not believe in " sensations," and would not permit it.

Towards night the squadron passed out of the Strait
into the Ægean Sea, or Archipelago. The Island of
Tenedos was seen on one side, and Imbros and Lem-
nos on the other, with several smaller islands in the
vicinity. They were mountainous and bare, of a reddish color, with not a tree upon them. The course
was laid about west-south-west, and in the morning
the vessels were off Scyros, with islands in every
direction. The weather was perfect, with the bluest
of skies and the clearest of atmospheres. At night,
Cape Doro, on the Island of Negropont, or Eubœa,
was on the starboard bow. Its hills were red and
bare ; and Greece looked like the meanest country in
the world, though its scenery is bold and rugged. As
the sun rose on the following morning, the professors,
full of classic enthusiasm, were on deck, quoting Byron
as they gazed upon the promontory of Sunium, or
Cape Colonna, on which are the remains of a temple
of Minerva.

> " Save where some solitary column mourns
>   Above its prostrate brethren of the cave ;
> Save where Tritonia's airy shrine adorns
>   Colonna's cliff, and gleams along the wave."

The cape was doubled, and the squadron stood
along the shore of the classic land till the middle of
the afternoon, when pilots were taken, and the vessels
passed in single file through the narrow channel, between two ancient moles, into the harbor of Piræus,
where they anchored.

CHAPTER XIX.

ANCIENT AND MODERN GREECE.

THE students of the squadron were not so enthusiastic as the professors, but they were deeply interested in the classic shores which surrounded them; and as soon as the vessels were put in order, they devoted themselves to a survey of the scenery and the town. The Piræus is the port of Athens, five miles distant. The harbor is land-locked except at the narrow entrance between the ancient piers, and not much over half a mile in length. The country is hilly, though the slope is very gradual near the water. The houses of the town, like those of all Greek places, are intensely white; indeed, seen from the sea, in contrast with the brown hills, these towns look like dabs of whitewash, carelessly dropped upon the landscape.

At the entrance to the port was a yacht station, where an English cutter was hauled up to the pier. Near the squadron lay a small Greek man-of-war, with her blue checker-board flag at the peak. Several steamers and many vessels, from full-rigged ships down to the small craft with mutton-leg sails, that run to the islands, were at anchor, for the town has considerable commerce, and, like many American places, sprang into existence all of a sudden, when the court of King Otho was established at Athens.

"I see it!" shouted Captain Cantwell, who had ascended to the mizzen-top to examine the surroundings.

"What?" demanded Sheridan, on deck.

"The Acropolis!"

It could be seen, even from the deck of the ship, faintly in the distance; but it was the first sight of the Acropolis, and the students gazed upon it with interest. While they were doing so, a Greek custom-house official, in the full costume of his nation, came on board. It was Albanian, such as the party in Constantinople had seen in the sultan's train, though by no means as rich and elegant. He wore an embroidered jacket, and from the waist reaching to the knees, a very full, white skirt, which the students called a petticoat. It was composed of a profusion of material, like the robes of a *danseuse*, and was kept in place by a broad belt or sash. Greek dandies affect small waists, and draw this sash so tight that it produces the same consequences as tight lacing among the followers of Parisian fashions. The legs are encased in leggins, and on the head this man wore a fez with a blue tassel. In the belt was a whole arsenal of weapons, as though the officer had come to take possession of the ship by force and violence. There was nothing for him to do, though, as he insisted upon remaining on board, he was politely treated, and invited to supper in the main cabin, where Professor Badois talked with him in his own lingo.

The darkness came on, and shut out the view of

the classic land. Immediately after breakfast the next morning, all hands in the squadron were called to the ship to attend lecture. When they were all assembled in the steerage, Mr. Lowington made a long address upon the evils of the elective system, as he termed it, and announced that the present officers would retain their positions until the first of October, when the old method of appointing them by the merit-roll would be restored. This announcement was received with applause, but there were many who preferred the elective method.

Morley appeared among the crew of the ship in the dress of a common sailor. There was an expression of satisfaction, if not of vengeance, on his face, as he listened to the remarks of the principal. He was a fine scholar, and he determined to win the place which the elective plan had prevented him from obtaining. His position was similar to that of some of the ablest statesmen of our country, who have aspired to the presidency, and died without attaining the goal of their ambition.

On the foremast hung a map of Greece; and Mr. Mapps taking his stand as soon as the principal had finished his speech, commenced his lecture.

" The ancient Greeks called themselves Hellenes, and their country Hellas; and the modern Greeks still retain these names. The official title of the present sovereign is the King of the Hellenes. Græcia was the Roman name, but after it became a Roman province it was called Achaia. In the East the Greeks were known, in early times, by the Hebrews, as Javan; by the Persians, as Iuna; and by the Egyptians, as

Uinim.   I shall presently have something more to say of these names.

"The modern kingdom of Greece is small in territory, having an area about equal to that of Vermont and New Hampshire, or hardly more than half as much as Portugal.   In ancient times continental Greece, though greater in extent than the modern kingdom, was small indeed, compared with its fame.   Yet, in one point of view, it was of vast extent; for with the old Greeks Hellas reached wherever their people had settled and their language was spoken.   As early as the fifteenth century before our era, the Greeks began to form settlements in foreign countries; and they continued to colonize through the whole period of their history. At the north-eastern corner of the Sea of Azof was the Greek town of Tanais; on the eastern shore of the Black Sea were Phasis and Dioscurios; away to the west, beyond the Pillars of Hercules, — which were pointed out to you as you passed through the Strait of Gibraltar, — Greeks were also settled.   Between these extreme points, on every coast, in the Crimea, along the western and southern shores of the Black Sea, on the Sea of Marmora and the Dardanelles, on the west coast of Asia Minor, in Egypt, Africa, Italy, Spain, and Gaul, in Sicily, and the numberless other islands of the Mediterranean and the Archipelago, Greek colonies were planted; and some of them became richer and more populous than any state of the parent land. Miletus could count over eighty colonies; and the cities of Agrigentum and Syracuse were among the largest in their time.   Southern Italy was long known as *Magna* Græcia, or Great Greece, so numerous and so widely extended were the Greek cities there.

"We are not to suppose, however, that all these colonies were under one home government, for this never was true while the Greeks were their own masters.   Each colony, each city, with a beach on the sea, or a surrounding border of farms inland, was generally an independent state.   This was as true in Greece proper as in the colonies; for when several towns recognized a single city as their capital, the case was simply an exception to the rule.   The patriotism of the Greek embraced only his own city; and for that he was willing to lay down his life.   In any other city he was an alien and a stranger; he had no share in the government, he could own no houses or lands, and he could not sue in any of the courts of justice.   There was no political union among them till the people were subject to a foreign power.   They could never unite even against a common danger.   In the wars with the Persians, with the Macedonians, and with the Romans, the Greeks were divided; and when they were at peace with the rest of the world, they were at war with each other.   And thus it happened that nothing was more common than for 'Greek to meet Greek.'

"In the earliest times, the people were already divided into several tribes — the Dorians, Æolians, Ionians, and Achæans, being the most prominent.   In the fabulous history of the country, Hellen, the son of Deucalion and Pyrrha, is said to be the common progenitor of the people; and from him they were called Hellenes.   Of course this is an invented explanation, and at first the name was given only to a tribe, being afterwards taken by all the inhabitants.   We are told that the tribe administered the worship of Zeus, or

Jupiter, at Dodona, in Epirus;" and the professor pointed out the location on the map, in the north-western province. "This place was the central seat of the Græci before the Greeks and the ancestors of the founders of Rome separated; for the Greeks and the Romans are of the same race.

"The Ionians were the first to make sea voyages; and it was from them that the Greeks were called Ionians; for Javan, Iuna, and Uinim, are only different pronunciations of this word.

"Very early in Grecian history, there was a long period of migrations, during which one tribe often displaced another, and finally the Ionians and Dorians became the representative people, Athens, in Attica, being the most influential city of the former, and Sparta, or Lacedæmon, in Laconia, of the latter. Still the number of Greek states, instead of becoming smaller, increased. Homer enumerates thirty, while at a much later date there were several hundred. Divided and at war with each other as these states always were, they regarded themselves as, in a certain sense, a single nation. They were all of the same race, they spoke the same language, and accepted the same religion. In their view the whole world contained but two classes of men — Greeks and Barbarians. The poems of Homer — those wonderful poems that have been recited and read for three thousand years, and are still the delight of students as well as of poets and statesmen, — represent the Greeks as engaged in a common enterprise against a foreign power. These poems were considered a common inheritance, and did much to keep up the national spirit.

"The last, but by no means the least, bond of union among the Grecian states was the great national games, which afforded each Greek, as often as once a year, the opportunity of meeting all other Greeks in friendly rivalry.   The four great national festivals were the Olympic, Pythian, Isthmian, and Nemean.   The most ancient, as well as the most famous, of these was the one celebrated at Olympia, in Elis;" and the professor pointed to the western part of the Morea.   "It was established, according to tradition, by Hercules; but as it was somewhat neglected in the course of time, it was revived B. C. 776, we are told, by Iphitus, king of Elis, and Lycurgus, the Spartan legislator; and when the Greeks began to reckon time by Olympiads, they counted from this revival.

"At first the games consisted of foot-races only, and lasted only a single day; but afterwards the time was increased to five.   During the month in which it occurred, all warfare was suspended, and it was sacrilege for an armed force to enter Elis with hostile intent. Besides the foot-race, there were wrestling, boxing, horse-races, and chariot-races.   The last, with four horses, was the most highly appreciated, and became the most popular of all the amusements.   Victors in these matches were present from all parts of the country, from Magna Græcia, the isles of Greece, and the most distant colonies.   To win the prize in any of these games was no idle task, for the Greeks were a nation of gymnasts.   No city of theirs was without its gymnasium, which was a great square, with porticos, and avenues of plane trees.   Some cities had several of them.   Old and young gave a large portion of their time to exercise. No one could enter the arena at Olympia unless he had exercised without interruption and with care for the last ten months before he applied for admission. Some of the games combined various trials of skill. The Pentathlum, for instance, included jumping, running, wrestling, throwing the javelin, and pitching the discus, or quoit.

"After the leaping, the strength of the arm was tested in throwing the spear; and those who made the four best throws were entitled to share in the next contest. The number of competitors grew less at every trial. The three best runners joined in throwing the quoit; and finally, when the number was reduced to two, they tried their strength in a wrestling match for the prize, which was only a wreath of wild olive. But this garland, simple as it was, meant a great deal; for the victor's name was proclaimed before the assembled nation, and at home new honors awaited him. He entered his native city in a triumphal procession, while his praises were frequently sung in the loftiest strains of poetry. Generally he was relieved from the payment of taxes, and had the right to a front seat at public games and spectacles. By one of Solon's laws at Athens, a victor at Olympia received a prize of five hundred drachmas, or nearly ninety dollars, in silver; and this was at a time when an ox could be bought for eighty-five cents, and a sheep for fifteen. His statue was generally erected in the sacred grove of Zeus at Olympia. Such a statue was in the best of company, for this grove of olive and plane trees was a temple of the arts, such as the world had never seen elsewhere. Most prominent here was the Temple of the Olympian Jupiter, containing the statue of the god in gold and ivory, sixty feet high, the masterpiece of Phidias, and one of the seven wonders of the world. Throughout the grove were many beautiful pleasure houses, built by the Greek cities, and statues of gods, heroes, and victors in the games. Pausanias, a Greek writer, counted two hundred and thirty statues erected to Jupiter alone; and Pliny estimated the number remaining there in his time, after Greece had been a Roman province for two centuries, at three thousand.

"The first state to become prominent, and take a leading part in the Greek family of nations, was Crete. The history of Greek commerce begins with piracy. The tribes which dwelt along the coast were accustomed to look upon this gravest of modern crimes on the sea as a natural occupation, quite as respectable as hunting or fishing. As late as Homer's time (B. C. 1000), when strangers landed on the shore, they were asked whether they were traders or pirates, as we ask a man whether he is a farmer or a mechanic. Minos of Crete was the first to make war upon the freebooters, and drive them from the waters of the Ægean Sea. Under the protection of the numerous fleets of this king, the Cretan mariner pursued his voyage in comparative safety. The age of Minos is rather dim and shadowy; but it was a recognized truth among the Greeks, that law and order, the foundation of governments, came to the rest of Greece from Crete.

"The next state to become prominent was Argos,

from which, according to tradition, went forth the colonists who made settlements in various parts of the Morea, or the Peloponnesus. For three or four centuries Argos was the great power of the peninsula south of the Gulf of Corinth. At first the government was an absolute monarchy, in which the sovereign was lawmaker, judge, and king; but afterwards it was almost a republic, and continued so for several generations. This liberal rule was disturbed by Pheidon, (B. C. 780–744), a very remarkable man, who restored the ancient despotism. All his efforts, in peace as well as war, seemed to be in opposition to the policy of Sparta, which was narrow and exclusive in its tendency. He encouraged foreign trade, used coined money, which was a Lydian invention, and introduced the system of weights and measures which the Phœnicians had spread from Babylon over Western Asia. He organized an army strong enough to contend with the warlike Spartans, defeated them, and drove them from the banks of the River Alpheus, where he celebrated the twenty-eighth Olympiad in company with the Pisitans, whose city of Pisa was near Olympia. In the height of his prosperity, Pheidon marched upon Corinth, and fell in a hand-to-hand conflict with the enemy. After his death Argos declined, and lost her prominence.

" Sparta next became the leading power in the Peloponnesus. The Spartans, or Lacedæmonians, owe their great name in history almost entirely to the institutions of Lycurgus. We do not know, it is true, how great a change was made in the laws by that legislator, and so we give him the benefit of the doubt. Sparta was inhabited by three classes, the leading one being composed, with few exceptions, of Dorians. Among these the best of the land was divided, and they lived without manual labor, giving their whole attention to military affairs. The second class were the Periœci, the free inhabitants of towns and villages without political rights, who cultivated their own lands. These were the old Achaian population, found on the soil when the Dorians arrived. The third class were the Helots, who were captives taken in war, and subjugated rebels. These cultivated the lands of their Spartan masters, and paid a fixed rent therefor. There were two kings, each acting as a check upon the other, and a senate of thirty members, including the two kings. The senators were elected from among the Spartans who were more than sixty years old. There were also two officers called ' ephors,' whose duty it was to watch over the constitution, and punish those who infringed it.

"At seven years of age every boy was taken by the state to educate. He was taught the Greek language, music, and gymnastics, with especial emphasis on the last, and his time was chiefly employed in athletic exercises, hunting, and drills. He took his meals at the public tables, and slept in the public dormitories. When he grew up, he had very little more liberty. He was not allowed to have either gold or silver. No money was permitted to circulate, except a heavy iron coinage. With institutions like these, we cannot wonder that Sparta became a military camp, and the people a nation of warriors. We have not time to follow the conquests of the Spartans in Peloponnesus, but must turn to Sparta's great rival, Athens.

"In the Trojan war, according to Homer, 'those who possessed Athens, the well-built city,' were commanded by Menestheus. With him fifty dark ships followed.' Attica — which is the only part of Greece you have yet visited — contained many independent towns, we are told, till Theseus — whose life I hope you will read in Plutarch — united them under the rule of Athens. At first this city was ruled by kings; then by archons for life, then for ten years, and finally for one year. During all this time — the period from 1050 to 752 B. C. — the offices were in the hands of the aristocracy, or oligarchy, who were the interpreters of the unwritten laws. At last the people demanded written laws, and the code of Draco was given to them. Though these laws made death the penalty for almost every crime, they were probably not more severe than those to which the Athenians had so long been subject; but the severity of the Draconian code came to be proverbial. Thirty years later came the laws of Solon, which were a blessing to the people.

"I can only give you a brief outline of the Persian wars; and I recommend you to read Herodotus and other historians for yourselves. The Greeks in Asia Minor were under Darius, King of Persia. They revolted, and the Athenians sent them some assistance; but they were subdued, and the Persian monarch determined to conquer Greece, and sent a fleet under Mardonius, his son-in-law. After some success among the islands, he landed on the main shore, and established himself at Marathon, twenty-five miles from Athens, where the Athenians, under Miltiades, attacked and routed the Persians, who escaped in their ships. Darius was furious at the failure of his army, and determined to renew the attack; but he died before he was ready to do so. Mardonius, who was anxious to redeem his reputation, persuaded Xerxes, the son of Darius, to carry out his father's intentions.

" His army, with its camp followers, is said to have contained five millions of persons. Doubtless the number is a fiction, but it was a large army. It marched on the bridge of boats across the Hellespont, and finally reached Thermopylæ, which is a mountain pass near the sea-shore, eighty miles or more from here. Athens and Sparta were the leading powers, but some of the Greeks in the north-east were too timid to defend themselves. Leonidas, the Spartan king, defended the pass; but the enemy, led through another pass, fell upon his rear, and killed him and all his force (B. C. 481). The Athenian fleet, after meeting the enemy in two engagements, returned and anchored in the Strait of Salamis — in sight from the masthead of the ship. Xerxes marched on the city, and the people, with the aid of the fleet, removed to the Island of Salamis. The Persians moored their ships in a line on the shore of the main land, where the Greeks attacked them, and, though the enemy were three to their one, utterly routed them (B. C. 480). Xerxes went home then, leaving Mardonius with the army. He attempted to win the Athenians over to his cause; but failing in this, he occupied their city a second time, the people fleeing to Salamis again. The

Greeks now raised a large force in the south, and Mardonius retired to Platæa, where his army was utterly defeated (B. C. 479), and he was killed. On the same day the Persian fleet was routed at Mycale. These events ended the second Persian invasion.

" The patriotic exertions of Athens during these wars, and the great increase of her navy, placed the city at the head of affairs in Greece. It now became the most splendid of the Greek cities, and was the resort of all who excelled in philosophy, literature, and the arts. But the golden age was of short duration. In the year B. C. 431 began the struggle known as the ' Peloponnesian war.' The Spartans with their allies were on one side, and the Athenians with their allies on the other. This war lasted twenty-seven years (B. C. 404), and nearly all the states of Greece were engaged in it. The Spartans were finally triumphant; and their supremacy continued for more than thirty years. Many a Grecian state found Sparta a hard master; but at length the day of reckoning came. When the Spartans thought themselves prepared to crush Bœotia, the last of their enemies, they marched into this country, but met with a terrible defeat at Leuctra (B. C. 371) from the Thebans under Epaminondas. Then they fell forever from their high pinnacle. While her great general lived, Thebes maintained her ascendency.

" Up to this time Macedonia was one of the weakest states that bordered on Greece, and just before Philip, the famous Macedonian monarch, had lived three years at Thebes as a hostage for the faithful observance of a treaty between that city and his own country. There he studied the art of war, when the Theban state was at the height of its glory, under Pelopidas and Epaminondas. When he became king, he bent his entire energies to the conquest of Greece. Philip, after much diplomacy and many minor victories, met the united forces of Thebes and Athens at Chæronea (B. C. 338), where young Alexander, Philip's son, turned the fortunes of the day by a brilliant charge. It was a decisive victory, and Greece became a province of Macedonia.

" Two centuries later (B. C. 146) Greece became a Roman province, and during the empire it was the home of philosophy. The Eastern Empire, of which Greece was a part, continued under various names till 1453, when the capital — which was about all there was left of it — was taken by the Turks.

" As early as the middle of the third century the Goths began to appear on the northern frontier of Greece. A few years later they descended upon the coast, and Athens was subjected to the ravages of these barbarians. In the first half of the fifth century came the Huns ; and the country suffered the extreme of spoliation under these swarming hordes. In the eighth century came the Sclavonians, and occupied nearly the whole of Peloponnesus. The Normans overran and plundered the country three centuries later. During the crusades (1095–1299) the Greeks had to suffer again. In 1203 the crusaders took Constantinople, and the Eastern Empire was ruled by western or Latin princes for fifty-eight years. Under their rule, Greece was entirely remodelled ; it was divided into provinces, the last of which, the Dukedom of the Archipelago, or Naxos, lasted till 1566. Another, still more celebrated, the Dukedom of Athens, continued till 1456. In those times the Dukes of Athens were among the greatest princes of the empire; and Athens was the resort of the gayest knights. French was spoken as well there as in Paris. In a few years after the fall of Constantinople, all the main land and most of the neighboring islands of Greece were in the hands of the Ottomans.

"During the next three and a half centuries, several partial movements towards revolution were made; but the only general one was near the close of the seventeenth century, when the Venetians, with the aid of the Greeks, reorganized the whole of Peloponnesus, and even held Athens for a few months. Under the Turks the Greeks had to submit to many forms of taxation. There was a tax on every head in the family; a tax of one tenth of all the crops; a tax of children to keep the ranks of the Janizaries full; and, finally, a tax known as 'tooth money,' which was a compensation to the pacha for the wear and tear of the teeth in eating the food furnished to him and his suite by the Greeks while he was collecting the revenues."

"I wish some landlords in hotels I know of, had to pay that tax on the beef they furnish," said Scott. "I have no doubt the Turks were right on the tooth money, and I hope the idea will be revived."

"Sharp knives make tender beef," laughed the professor.

"To Greece we give our shining blades, as Scott said this morning, when he took some butter," added Wainwright.

"Before the revolution," continued Mr. Mapps, "a better day began to dawn upon the Greeks. They were so much superior to the Turks in mental capacity, that the direction of affairs had to be intrusted to native leaders in various parts of the country, and towards the end of the last century, many Greeks at Constantinople had risen to eminent positions as interpreters, physicians, and even as hospodars in the Moldavian and Wallachian provinces. Others had become wealthy merchants and bankers in the principal cities of the empire.

"In 1821 the Greeks resolved to be free, and to drive the Turks from the soil of Hellas. This was in the days of the Holy Alliance, and the Great Powers gave them no encouragement for a long time. After eight years of war, and when the Greek cause looked hopeless, England, France, and Russia interfered, and, in the great battle of Navarino, the combined fleets of these powers annihilated the Turkish and Egyptian squadrons. The Porte was compelled to yield, and Greece was once more independent. Count Capo d'Istria, a Greek statesman in the service of Russia, became president; but he was unpopular with the Greeks, and was assassinated in 1831. The Great Powers then concluded to organize Greece into a kingdom. The throne was offered to Prince Leopold of Saxe Coburg, late King of Belgium, who finally declined it, and it was given to Otho, second son of the King of Bavaria, then seventeen years of age, who accepted it, and assumed the government under a regency in 1833.

"In 1853 the Ionian Islands, which had before

been, under the protection of Great Britain, were annexed to the Kingdom of Greece. Otho reigned for nearly thirty years; but both he and his queen were tyrants and oppressors, and in 1862 a revolt broke out, which was suppressed, though the troubles were not removed. The king, finding his power and influence gone, abdicated the throne, and left the country. A provisional government was organized, and the Bavarian dynasty deposed. The crown was offered to several, among them Prince Alfred of England, by the vote of the Assembly, but he declined it, and finally Prince George, second son of the present King of Denmark, was elected, and accepted the throne. He is now the King of the Hellenes, under the title of Georgios I. In 1863, at the age of eighteen, he ascended the throne, and four years later was married to Olga, niece of the Emperor of Russia.

"Hellas, as an independent nation, has not made the progress that was hoped for by its too ardent friends; still it is steadily gaining ground now, under its new king. Traces of the Goth, Hun, Sclavonian, Norman, Crusader, and Turk, have almost entirely disappeared from the land, and the modern Greek seems to have most of the characteristics of his ancestors of two thousand years ago. The Greek still has dark hair, brown complexion, and sparkling eyes; is still lively, quick to understand, adroit, eloquent, curious, and eager for novelty.

"The population of Greece is about the same as the State of Massachusetts, — nearly a million and a half, — while it has two and a half times as much territory. One seventh of the land is under cultivation, though agriculture is the principal industry of the people, manufactures being few and unimportant. Grain is not produced in sufficient quantities to supply the home consumption. The favorite crop is the currant, which is the principal article of export, amounting in one year to four and a half millions of dollars sent to England alone. The Greeks are still sailors; and the mercantile marine has a tonnage of two hundred and ninety thousand, manned by twenty-five thousand seamen.

"The money of Greece has the *drachma*, of one hundred *lepta*, for its unit, equal to about seventeen cents of our currency.

"Greece is a mountainous country, and has many peaks over seven thousand feet high. Parnassus, sacred in mythology to Apollo and the Muses, is eight thousand.

"Now, young gentlemen, I have given you a very meagre outline of the history and present condition of Greece; but I hope you will read for yourselves, and be able to appreciate the ancient glories of this classic nation."

The professor retired, and the students began to ask him scores of questions about events to which he had not alluded; some of which existed only in mythology. He referred them to the books, as we are compelled to refer our readers.

CHAPTER XX.

• ATHENS AND ITS SURROUNDINGS.

IMMEDIATELY on the arrival of the squadron at the Piræus, the vessels had been boarded by a health officer, though not until the bill of health which each of them brought from Constantinople had been examined. There was no sickness of any kind on board, and the squadron had been five days at sea ; but no one was allowed to land for twenty-four hours, which was the period of " observation." The yellow fever was raging in Spain, and the small-pox in Genoa and some other ports of the Mediterranean, which increased the precautions of the medical department. Formerly persons who arrived at this port from the East were subjected to a quarantine of forty days, which was the full term, though it was sometimes reduced to ten days, the time depending upon the general health of the country from which they last came. This period was spent in a lazzaretto, an establishment isolated from the outer world, where the traveller was compelled to eat and sleep, and take the plague, cholera, or small-pox, if it happened to be there. But these regulations have been greatly modified, and the detention, if any, is generally very brief.

The twenty-four hours' observation of the squadron did not expire till the middle of the afternoon, on the day of the lecture, and it was too late to make a trip to Athens. Sunday kept them on board the next day; but on Monday morning, after breakfast, the boats were lowered, and all hands landed at the town, which is a place of six thousand inhabitants. Mr. Stevens, whose pleasant books of travel were much used by the students, visited Greece in 1836. He puts an exclamation point after the announcement that an omnibus ran between the Piræus and Athens, and publishes in full the advertisement of this startling innovation. He blesses his fortune that *he* never rode in this omnibus, for it would have destroyed all the glorious illusions of the past. Now there is a railroad from the Piræus to Athens, on which cars run nearly every hour; and doubtless the dust of Themistocles, Pericles, and Aristides is shaken by the thundering train. The students were not at all troubled by reflections of this kind, however it may have been with the professors, who were more deeply imbued with classic lore, and had a greater veneration for the storied past of Greece; and they took their seats in the cars without a single repulsive emotion.

"How much Greece are we to have?" asked Murray, who, as usual, was seated with Dr. Winstock, the captain, and the first lietenant.

"Not enough to make you slippery, I hope," replied Sheridan.

"Not much," added the surgeon. "Probably the instructors will enjoy this country more than the students. Those who are not antiquarians and deeply versed in the classics soon tire of wandering among ruins which have no meaning to them."

"That's my case," laughed Murray. "I had more Greece rubbed into .me yesterday than I ever knew before."

"Most tourists who come to Greece are satisfied with a day or two in Athens. Indeed, our guide in Constantinople said that a few hours were all we needed to see the city. This is true of ordinary travellers, while archæologists, the lovers of Greek art, and the student of Greek history, spend months, and even years, in exploring the country and studying its ruins. Professor Paradyme is one of this class, and he has been in a sort of rapture ever since we sailed into the Archipelago. There he is, talking with the Greek conductor in the language of Demosthenes and Plato."

"They don't get along very well," laughed Cantwell.

"Tolerably well, for the professor has had some experience with modern Greek, which does not differ so much from the ancient as the Italian does from Latin. The difference is .mostly in the pronunciation."

"But are we not to see Thermopylæ, Marathon, Platæa, and such places?" asked Sheridan.

"We are only to see Athens and its vicinity, except as we view it from the sea. Mr. Lowington does not deem it prudent to travel about the country, even if there were any facilities for transporting such a large company."

"Can't he get omnibuses or carts?" asked Murray.

"Even if he could, there are very few roads in Greece. Journeys are made on horseback, or by sea. But travelling through the country is not safe, on account of the brigands."

"I read about the murder of some English people in the paper not long since," added the captain.

"That was Lord Muncaster's party, consisting of eight persons, including two ladies and a child. They went out to Marathon, and on their return were captured by the brigands, who shot down two soldiers, the rest of their escort being in the rear. The captives were hurried up the sides of Mount Pentelicus, and the next day Lord Muncaster was permitted to visit Athens in order to obtain a ransom of twenty-five thousand pounds, which the robbers demanded. The government imprudently sent troops to hunt down the brigands, instead of forwarding the ransom which the captives were willing to pay. The band of miscreants were closely pressed in the mountains, and, either from revenge or for their own safety, cruelly murdered all their prisoners. This was last April (1870). The foreign powers interposed, and great was the indignation of the whole civilized world. Five hundred soldiers were sent in pursuit of the brigands, who were all killed or captured. Eight were decapitated, and their heads exposed in Athens, where possibly you may see them. The remains of the murdered tourists were recovered, and the king, the diplomatic corps, and multitudes of people joined the funeral procession. Probably it is safer now to travel in Greece than before this event, but the principal will not incur any risk. However, I think you will see all you wish of the country and its ruins."

The train moved off, and the students gazed out the windows at the scenery and the houses. In twenty minutes they were in Athens, and walked to the Hotel d'Orient in Eolus Street, where they found Paul Kendall and Shuffles, with their ladies. They had just arrived by the way of Trieste and the Ionian Islands, in the Austrian steamer, having changed their plan at Vienna, and spent the summer in Switzerland. The yachts were at Lutraki, on the Gulf of Corinth, whither they had been ordered by telegraph from Constantinople, for the party desired to sail around the peninsula and among the islands. Guides and carriages were procured at the hotel, and the tourists hastened to the Acropolis, which is a rocky hill flat upon the top. It is about a thousand feet long by four hundred wide. It is oblong in shape, and three of its sides are sheer precipices, while the fourth is only less precipitous. The summit is three hundred feet above the town, and is surrounded by walls, for it was the citadel of Athens as well as its holy place.

The entrance is through the Propylæa, a central edifice with a wing on each side. It is reached by a double flight of stairs, in which is an inclined plane of marble, grooved cross-ways for horses, admitting the ascent of chariots. On the right of the steps is the beautiful little " Temple of Victory without wings," whose disjointed stones, long buried in the ruins, have been gathered up, and the structure restored to its original symmetry and beauty. One wing of the Propylæa was called the *Pinacotheca*, because it contained paintings, while the other was only a gallery. The students passed through the ruins of this structure, and beheld the glories of the Acropolis, the Parthenon, and the Erechtheum. This hill is usually the first place to be visited by the traveller, because it affords a fine, general view of Athens, and gives a correct idea of the topography of the ancient city. Before going to the ruins, Dr. Winstock took his little party to a convenient point near the western end, and explained to them the various objects in view.

"There is the sea," said the doctor. "That is Phalerum Bay, and on the other side of the hills is the Piræus. These were the ports of Athens. Two walls, not more than thirty rods apart, the traces of which can still be seen, extended to the Piræus, enabling the Athenians, when besieged on the land side, to obtain supplies and communicate with their allies by sea. Another wall was built to the Bay of Phalerum for the same purpose. The belt of olive trees which you see extending north and south are on the banks of the Cephissus, a mere brook, nearly dry in summer, whose waters, when there are any, are used to irrigate the land. The other stream, the Ilissus, on the other side of the city, is generally dry. Through this grove passes the Via Sacra, or sacred way, by which the religious procession represented by the celebrated frieze of the Parthenon passed between Athens and Eleusis by the Defile of Daphne, in the hills west of us.

"Now look across the city. The hill you see is Mount Lycabettus, seven hundred feet high. The large building near it is the king's palace. East of us is Mount Hymettus, still famous for its honey, as it was in the days of Pericles. The elevation north-east of us, some ten miles distant, is Mount Pentelicus, from whose quarries the marble for all these structures was brought. Near it, twenty-five miles from Athens by the road, is Marathon.

" Directly in front, and below us, are two hills, one of which is the Pnyx, where the people used to assemble to hear their orators, and in this place Demosthenes spoke to the multitude. At the right of it, higher than the other, is Mars' Hill, or the Areopagus, which was the seat of justice, where Mars was tried for murder. It is more noted, however, among Christians, for the bold address of Paul to the people. The higher hill to the south is the Museum, so called from Musæus, a poet who sang here. On it is the monument of Philopappus, a distinguished citizen."

The students looked down upon modern Athens, and the doctor compared it with the ancient city, pointing out some of its celebrated localities. The party then walked to the Parthenon, " the finest edifice on the finest site in the world, hallowed by the noblest recollections that can stimulate the human heart," as Christopher Wordsworth says of it. It is a magnificent ruin, and enough of it remains to give a correct idea of the original structure. It was built under the administration of Pericles, and is called the Temple of the Virgin, for it was dedicated to Minerva, the virgin goddess. It was two hundred and twenty-eight feet long and one hundred and one feet wide. The height of the columns was thirty-five feet. The perfect symmetry of the edifice is its distinguishing feature. The Madelaine in Paris is a faithful copy of it. Inside of the columns, which extended entirely around the building, was a solid wall, within which was the *cella*, or body of the temple. On the outside of this wall was the celebrated frieze representing the Panathenaic Festival. The subject is a procession, in bass relief, on marble slabs, the figures of which are models of Greek art to the present day. A few of the slabs remain, but a considerable portion of them, with other valuable sculptures, was conveyed to England by Lord Elgin; were purchased by the government, and placed in the British Museum. Many plaster copies of the frieze have been made, one of which adorns the walls of the Girls' High School in Boston.

The general supervision of the building of the Parthenon was given to Phidias, the sculptor, whose colossal statue of Minerva in the Temple was one of the greatest works of art. It was nearly forty feet high. The face and other exposed parts were of ivory, and the drapery and ornaments of solid gold, valued at fifty thousand dollars, which could be removed when the state needed it. It was plundered by one of the tyrants of Athens, three hundred years before Christ. The Parthenon was badly injured by the explosion of a quantity of powder, placed there by the Turks while defending the city from the Venetians, one of whose shells exploded the powder. It has been a heathen temple, a Christian church, and a Mohammedan mosque, in turn, and still remains to be the wonder of the world, and a model in art for all the civilized nations of the earth.

The Erechtheum, the most revered of all the sacred places of Athens, was in honor of Erechtheus, one of the protecting deities of the city. It differs from any other Grecian temple, and is a splendid illustration of ancient art.   In the rear is a portico, the roof of which is supported by six Caryatides, or columns composed of statues of maidens in long draperies.   The structures described are the principal ones on the Acropolis; and the excursionists next visited the Pnyx, the Areopagus, the Museum, and finally came to the Theseum, which is the best preserved of all the ancient structures of Athens.   It is similar to the Parthenon, but less than half its size, and of about the same age.   It is used as a museum of curious relics, and is still nearly in its original condition.

But the party had seen enough for one day; and intemperance in sight-seeing brings on disgust as certainly as any other dissipation.   Mr. Lowington walked to the hotel with Paul Kendall and his wife.   On the way, the principal mentioned the escape of De Forrest and Beckwith.

"I saw two young men at the Hôtel de la Ville in Trieste, whose conduct seemed strange to me," replied Paul Kendall.   "They were Americans, and avoided our party very carefully.   They came into the restaurant when we were there, but as soon as they saw us, they retreated.   I spoke to my wife about it at the time."

"I remember them very distinctly," added Mrs. Kendall.

After comparing notes together, Mr. Lowington was satisfied that the runaways, instead of going home, had come on the French steamer to the Piræus, and taken the Austrian line for Trieste.   But he gave them up for the present, satisfied that their money would soon be exhausted, when they would be glad to return to the ship.

The tourists went back to the port by the train, and the next morning made another visit to Athens. Some of them declared they did not care to see any more ruins — they had seen " rocks " enough for one cruise ; but the majority desired to visit other classic localities in and around the city. All of them were interested in the modern city, which contains forty-six thousand inhabitants. They wanted to see the ladies, who have the reputation of being very beautiful ; but here again their disappointment was not less than when they saw the Turkish houris, some of whom weighed over two hundred pounds. They were on the lookout for strange costumes, but the Greeks are rapidly laying aside the national dress, and adopting that of Western Europe. Some of the ladies, however, have the little red cap on the top of the head, and the lower classes of men wear the great bagging trousers. Except these there was little that was very strange in the streets of Athens.

The party visited the old cathedral and the Church of St. Theodore, which are Byzantine, like the mosques of Constantinople, over which the Crescent is the emblem, while these bore the Cross. The religion of the people generally is the Orthodox Greek, like that of Russia. It has its own sacred Synod and metropolitan, or patriarch. As in Russia, the people have not a very high estimate of the clergy. Education is carefully fostered in Greece, and the university sends forth many fine scholars. The female schools established by Mr. and Mrs. Hill, missionaries of the Episcopal churches of the United States, have exercised a vast influence upon the people, and even upon the institutions of the country. It is rare to find a Greek who cannot read and write.

Among the ancient ruins visited were the octagonal tower near the Acropolis, which contained a water-clock, operated by the fountain of Clepsydra; the gate of Hadrian; the monument of Lysicrates, sometimes called the Lantern of Demosthenes, because the orator is said to have had a study in it, — which is impossible, for the structure is only six feet in diameter, and has no door; the monument of Philopappus, on the Museum Hill; the street of the Tripods, from the number of them seen there; the Odæum of Herodes, a theatre; and the temple of Olympian Jove, a cluster of beautiful columns. Professor Paradyme waxed eloquent over these wonders of ancient art, and the other instructors shared his enthusiasm; but the students, with only a few exceptions, were cold and indifferent. They did not scruple to say they had seen enough of Athens, much to the disgust of the professors.

The next day a boat expedition to Salamis was organized, and successfully carried through. The weather was rather warm, but the air was perfectly clear, and the sky as blue as the dream of a poet. It was a long pull, but frequent stops were made, and the number in the boats afforded each seaman half an hour's rest for every hour he worked. The country was rugged, bare, and desolate, abounding in cliffs and defiles; and the shores of the islands on the left were sometimes headlong steeps. The peaks of the distant mountains were sharp, and except in the low, wet places, there was hardly any foliage to be seen. The party landed on the main shore, and climbed to the top of a hill, after pulling about three miles.

"This is the Throne of Xerxes," said Mr. Mapps, who had stationed himself on the highest point of the hill, where the students gathered around him. "The water upon which our boats float is the Bay of Salamis, in which the great naval battle between the Greeks and the Persians was fought, in the month of September, B. C. 480. This spot is called the Throne of Xerxes, because he sat here to witness the conflict. You have read the story of the battle. The Athenian fleet was ranged along the shores of the Island of Salamis, and the Persian along the main land, reaching down to the entrance of the Piræus, for they had over a thousand vessels, while the Greeks had less than a third of that number. The Persians were defeated, and Xerxes soon withdrew his hosts from the country."

The professor gave the details of the battle, which need not be repeated, for they are contained in the school histories. The boats then passed through the straits, and the party landed on the eastern shore of the Bay of Eleusis. A tramp of two miles brought them to the Defile of Daphne, where there are ruins of the Temples of Venus and of Apollo. The road by which they went was the same as the Via Sacra. There was some fine scenery on the way, but the professors' only object seemed to be to impress upon the minds of the students the fact that they were on the road travelled by the great religious processions of Athens.

Returning to the boats, the expedition pulled to Eleusis, the holy city of the Greeks, because it was the chief seat of the worship of Ceres and Proserpine, in whose honor the Eleusinian mysteries were celebrated. The ancient port, where the party landed, was enclosed by a semicircular pier of stone, the ruins of which still remain. The site of the city is covered with broken stones, pillars, and other wrecks of time. The Temple of Ceres, in which the mysteries were celebrated, is the most important ruin, and near it the pavement of the Via Sacra is visible, furrowed by the chariot wheels of gods and "godlike men." The city had an Acropolis, like Athens and other Greek towns. The arches of an aqueduct were visible, but these had already become a familiar ruin, for the students had seen them in Constantinople and in Athens, and were still to see them in Sicily, Italy, France, and Spain.

"I have had broken columns enough," said Sheridan, as the squads of students walked back to the port.

"And I have had Greece enough," added Murray.

"I can stand more Greece, but I want to see the people and the country, rather than the tumbled-down temples."

"We have an idea of the whole thing, and I am reading up the history of Greece with a new relish," said Cantwell. "We are to go to Austria and Italy next, but the principal does not wish to be there till late in October, for it isn't healthy in Naples and Rome till that time. I suppose we stay on the coast of Greece for two or three weeks more."

A three hours' pull brought the boat squadron to the Piræus again, and the boys were very tired. The next day the recitations were resumed with the port routine, which was a school session from eight till two, for all hands. After the study hours were over, a party went on shore to see the tomb of Themistocles, near the water on the peninsula at the entrance to the port; another party pulled over to the Island of Psyttaleia; and a third went round into Phalerum Bay.

The next morning the squadron sailed for Syra, the ancient Syros, an island in the Archipelago. Greek pilots had been employed to take the vessels through the channels among the islands, for the voyage was made in order to afford the students an opportunity to see more of the scenery of this interesting region, rather than to visit particular places. It was declamation day, and the exercise took place on deck. About one half of those who were to "speak" declaimed " The Isles of Greece," by Byron, which was certainly very appropriate, though it was rather monotonous to hear it after the second or third time.

Before sunset, the vessels anchored in the port of Hermopolis, the site of the ancient city. This place is the centre of steam navigation in the Levant, and the harbor was full of steamships, which are continually arriving from and departing to almost all the ports on the Mediterranean. The next afternoon the students went on shore. The town has a population of twenty-five thousand. In the streets were sailors of all nations — Greeks, Turks, Egyptians, Syrians, and all the European nations on the Mediterranean. The vessels remained for two weeks among these islands, and then sailed for Trieste, in Austria. From Syra the squadron had gone to the southward, and then, by another course, to the northward, so that the departure was from Cape Colonna. The next day it was off Cape Malea, the south-eastern point of the Morea.

"When I passed here in a steamer, several years ago, it was said that a hermit lived on those rocks," observed Dr. Winstock to the officers on the quarter-deck, as he pointed to the rugged side of the hill on shore. "The story is, that he was wrecked on these rocks forty years before, and had lived there ever since. There is his house."

The surgeon indicated what looked like a pile of rocks heaped together.

"What did he live on?" asked Sheridan.

"Fish, I suppose; possibly he went to the town some. miles in the interior to sell his fish and obtain food and clothes.. The steward of the steamer said he always came out when vessels passed; but that trip he did not appear, and it was surmised that he was dead. It seemed to me a little like a fish story."

The same night the squadron was off the high, rocky point that forms Cape Matapan. The watch was set, and nothing but a couple of lights were seen. The boys off duty went to sleep dreaming of the orange groves of Sicily, the palaces of Venice, and the beauties of the Bay of Naples, which they were soon to see. It was the last day of the month, and some were feverishly anxious about the positions they would hold in October. Morley felt lonely in the ship, and though he had studied hard, he felt that he had not accomplished much. Things did not go well with him. He was surly and ill at ease. He thought too much of the position he had lost by his own folly to be successful in working for the future. He was absent-minded, and often failed from inattention.

After breakfast on the following day, all hands were piped to muster, and the merit-roll read. Cantwell was entitled to the position of commodore, now restored; Sheridan was captain, and Murray first lieutenant. Clyde Blacklock had done well enough to make himself fourth lieutenant.

On board of the Tritonia, Wainwright retained his position; but Scott, who was only a fair scholar, made a bad fall from first lieutenant to first midshipman. The joker had expected it from the day it was announced that the old order of things would be restored; and he took it all in good part, and promised to have the work of the third degree of the "Most Respectable Order of Bangwhangers" ready in a few days.

"I am sorry you have lost your rank, Scott," said Captain Wainwright.

"So am I, but I don't cry-baby over it," laughed Scott. "Do you know how I happened to make this slip?"

"No; how was it?"

"The fact is, I have been in Greece so long that I am as slippery as an eel; that's what made me slip."

"I hope you will wipe the grease off, and get up next month."

"No, Wainwright; I haven't brains enough to get ahead of those fellows. A fellow can't have both brains and beauty, and I have to be content with my beauty."

Greenwood was his fortunate successor as executive officer of the Tritonia, while Morley in the ship won no position at all in the cabin, and he was discontented enough to run away. He actually thought of doing this, — the last resort of disappointed ambition in the squadron, — especially as De Forrest and Beckwith had succeeded so well, though the sequel of their adventures was not yet reached.

Mr. Tompion did not join the squadron again, but Mr. Lowington had a letter from him dated at London, in which he expressed deep contrition for his conduct. Though he did not ask to be restored to his situation, this was doubtless what he desired. The principal would not take the hint, and only sent him a draft for the payment of his salary, which enabled him to return to the United States, if he wished to do so.

Mr. Primback continued to act as vice-principal of the Tritonia, though, as he was not a nautical man, he was anxious to be relieved from duty in this capacity. Mr. Lowington had a plan in his mind, upon which he had already consulted Paul Kendall. He desired to appoint Augustus Pelham, a graduate of the Academy Ship, as vice-principal, in place of Mr. Tompion. Pelham was now the sailing master of Paul Kendall's yacht; but her owner consented to the transfer, for Bennington, another graduate, was his first officer, and could be promoted to the command. The change was to be made as soon as the yachts joined the squadron, after their visit to Constantinople.

The squadron was headed to the north-west, with

the shores of Messina in sight. It sailed between the Ionian Islands and the main land, and the students looked into the Gulf of Corinth, which, however, they did not care to enter, having seen enough of the white towns of Greece, and of its ancient ruins. Day after day the vessels continued on their course up the Adriatic Sea, with light and contrary winds, so that one day the students looked upon the sunny shores of Italy, and the next upon those of Austria. What they saw and what they did in those countries will be related in SUNNY SHORES; OR, YOUNG AMERICA IN ITALY AND AUSTRIA.

NEW AND ATTRACTIVE PUBLICATIONS

OF

LEE AND SHEPARD, Publishers,

BOSTON,

LEE, SHEPARD, AND DILLINGHAM, New York.

OLIVER OPTIC'S NEW BOOKS.

MONEY-MAKER; OR, THE VICTORY OF THE BASILISK. 16mo. Illustrated. $1.50.

THE YACHT CLUB; OR, THE YOUNG BOAT-BUILDER. 16mo. Illustrated. $1.50.

LITTLE BOBTAIL; OR, THE WRECK OF THE PENOBSCOT. 16mo. Illustrated. $1.50.

THE COMING WAVE; OR, THE HIDDEN TREASURE OF HIGH ROCK. 16mo. Illustrated. $1.50.

THE YACHT CLUB SERIES. 4 vols. In neat box. Per vol., $1.50.

> 1. LITTLE BOBTAIL.
> 2. THE YACHT CLUB.
> 3. MONEY-MAKER.
> 4. THE COMING WAVE.

In this series each book contains an entirely independent story, with a hero or heroine of its own, and having no necessary connection with any other volume. Each volume contains thirteen full-page engravings, expressly designed for it by the well-known American artist, C. G. Bush.

RUNNING TO WASTE. The Story of a Tomboy. By GEO. M. BAKER. 16mo. Illustrated. $1.50. This is the second volume of the Maidenhood Series.

"A Perfect Little Gem."

NEW SONGS FOR LITTLE PEOPLE. By MRS. MARY E. ANDERSON. Small 4to. Cloth. Illustrated. $1.25.

"An Instructive and Interesting Book."

STORIES OF A GRANDFATHER ABOUT AMERICAN HISTORY. By N. S. DODGE. 16mo. Illustrated. $1.25.

"An Example of Honor and Fidelity."

THE YOUNG ENGINEER. A Memoir of Frank Russell Firth. With an Introduction by Rev. E. E. HALE, and a Sketch of the Life of OTIS EVERETT ALLEN. 16mo. With Portrait. $1.50.

A Prize Volume.

HOW MARJORY HELPED. By M. CARROLL. 16mo. Illustrated. $1.50.

A New Compilation.

THE COLUMBIAN SPEAKER. Consisting of Choice and Animated Pieces for Declamation and Reading. Selected and adapted by LOOMIS J. CAMPBELL and OREN ROOT, JR. 16mo. Cloth. 75 cents.

To be followed by other books, each complete in itself, graduated to the capacities of the various classes of pupils and students.

By the Author of "Amateur Dramas."

THE READING-CLUB AND HANDY SPEAKER. Being Selections in Prose and Poetry, Serious, Humorous, Pathetic, Patriotic, and Dramatic, for Readings and Recitations. Edited by GEORGE M. BAKER. No. 1. 16mo. 50 cents.

PAUL COBDEN'S NEW BOOKS.

TAKE A PEEP. 16mo. Illustrated. $1.25.

THE BECKONING SERIES. 4 vols. Illustrated. 16mo. Per vol., $1.25.

1. WHO WILL WIN?
2. GOING ON A MISSION.
3. THE TURNING WHEEL.
4. GOOD LUCK.
5. TAKE A PEEP.

BY POPULAR AUTHORS.

LOTTIE EAMES; OR, DO YOUR BEST AND LEAVE THE REST. 16mo. Illustrated. $1.50.

"A successful picture of New-England life." —*J. G. Whittier.*

RHODA THORNTON'S GIRLHOOD. By MRS. MARY E. PRATT. With eleven full-page Illustrations. 16mo. $1.50.

GIRLHOOD SERIES. Complete in 6 vols. Illustrated. Comprising:—

1. AN AMERICAN GIRL ABROAD. By MISS ADELINE TRAFTON.
2. ONLY GIRLS. By MISS VIRGINIA F. TOWNSEND.
3. THE DOCTOR'S DAUGHTER. By SOPHIE MAY.
4. THE MOUNTAIN GIRL. By MRS. E. D. CHENEY.
5. LOTTIE EAMES. By a favorite author.
6. RHODA THORNTON'S GIRLHOOD. By MRS. MARY E. PRATT.

"A Charming Romance of Girlhood."

THE SEVEN DAUGHTERS. By MISS A. M. DOUGLAS. 16mo. Illustrated. $1.50. Being the initial volume of the Maidenhood Series.

PROF. J. DeMILLE'S NEW BOOKS.

THE WINGED LION. 16mo. Illustrated. (In press.)

THE SEVEN HILLS. 16mo. Illustrated. $1.50.

AMONG THE BRIGANDS. 16mo. Illustrated. $1.50.
Completing THE YOUNG DODGE CLUB SERIES. 3 vols.
Illustrated. Per vol., $1.50.

      1. AMONG THE BRIGANDS.
      2. THE SEVEN HILLS.
      3. THE WINGED LION.

Prof. DeMille's books are noted for their abundant humor as well as for stirring adventures and useful information.

SOPHIE MAY'S NEW BOOKS.

MISS THISTLEDOWN. 18mo. Illustrated. $0.75.

LITTLE GRANDFATHER. 18mo. Illustrated. $0.75.

LITTLE PRUDY'S FLYAWAY SERIES. 6 vols. Illustrated. Per vol., $0.75.

      1. LITTLE FOLKS ASTRAY.
      2. PRUDY KEEPING HOUSE.
      3. AUNT MADGE'S STORY.
      4. LITTLE GRANDMOTHER.
      5. LITTLE GRANDFATHER.
      6. MISS THISTLEDOWN.

"Life and Nature are as charming in small editions, and sometimes more so than in large ones; and, if Dotty and Prudy were not the pictures of infantile good humor and kitten wit, we hardly know where to look for such things." — *Boston Post.*

www.ingramcontent.com/pod-product-compliance
Lightning Source LLC
Chambersburg PA
CBHW021747110726

47902CB00006B/1435